"See? I didn't need that shoulder to lean on after all,"

Sara told Nik.

Directly behind her, in the window of the shop, was a white negligee. Nik couldn't help wondering what Sara would look like in it.

He forced his mind back on the conversation. "That's not how I see it."

Her mouth curved. "You're a typical man, you know."

Had she seen him looking at the negligee and guessed what had passed through his mind? He lifted a brow. "How's that?"

She smiled then, guilelessly. "You always think you're right."

"Oh, and you don't?" Amusement highlighted Nik's expression.

His question struck her as a little ambiguous. "Think you're right? No. Think *I'm* right? Yes."

Nik shook his head. He wouldn't have expected anything else from her.

Dear Reader,

The holiday season is here, and as our gift to you, we've got an especially wonderful lineup of books. Just look at our American Hero title, another "Conard County" book from Rachel Lee. *Lost Warriors* is the story of a heart that returns from the brink of oblivion and learns to love again. That heart belongs to rugged Billy Joe Yuma, and the saving hand belongs to nurse Wendy Tate. To learn more, you'll just have to read the book. Believe me, you won't regret it.

And here's another special treat: Judith Duncan is back with *Beyond All Reason,* the first of a special new miniseries called "Wide Open Spaces." It's set in the ranch country of Alberta, Canada, and will introduce you to the McCall family, a set of siblings you won't soon forget. More miniseries news: Marie Ferrarella completes her trilogy about the Sinclair family with *Christmas Every Day,* Nik's story. And the month is rounded out with books by Christine Flynn, a bestseller for Special Edition, Alexandra Sellers, and a second book from Julia Quinn called *Birthright.*

So from all of us to all of you, Happy Holidays—and Happy Reading!

Yours,

Leslie Wainger
Senior Editor and Editorial Coordinator

CHRISTMAS EVERY DAY

Marie Ferrarella

Silhouette®
INTIMATE MOMENTS®
Published by Silhouette Books
America's Publisher of Contemporary Romance

SILHOUETTE BOOKS

ISBN 0-373-07538-3

CHRISTMAS EVERY DAY

MARIE FERRARELLA

was born in Europe, raised in New York City and now lives in Southern California. She describes herself as the tired mother of two overenergetic children and the contented wife of one wonderful man. She is thrilled to be following her dream of writing full-time.

To Mary Ann Johnston,
a one of a kind lady

Chapter 1

What Sara Santangelo liked about life was that if you looked hard enough, there were usually choices. She had one now as she deplaned at John Wayne Airport. She could either drive up to Eagle Rock, a development within Newport Beach, and see her father, or she could go to meet the man who was going to be her employer during her temporary stay in Southern California. It never even occurred to Sara that the man might not give her the position. To her it was a foregone conclusion.

As was her choice. She'd face her father later.

Depositing her suitcases in the car she had just rented, Sara decided to drive to Sinclair's, the restaurant co-owned by her new cousin-in-law, Julia.

By nature Sara was not a coward. But it was just that, almost fifteen years after her parents' breakup, there was still too much emotional baggage for her to unpack. This close to seeing her father for the first time in over a decade, and suddenly the tips of her fingers felt icy and the pit of her stomach had contracted into a tight, angry knot.

Perhaps after she managed to get things in gear at Sinclair's, Sara reasoned, she'd feel more like facing the man who had broken her heart and walked away from her and her mother when they had needed him most.

After all this time, it still hurt.

Raymond Santangelo hadn't just divorced his wife, he had divorced his daughter, as well. There had been a handful of visits in the first year and perhaps a dozen cards and notes. And then nothing. A stark, empty nothing.

It was hard for Sara to feel charitable toward him after that.

With the address memorized, Sara easily found her way to Sinclair's. Pacific Coast Highway's serpentine route hadn't changed all that much in the past fourteen years, and she was blessed with a photographic memory that absorbed everything around her, cataloging it all away for future use.

It was a nice-looking restaurant, Sara decided as she pulled up in the parking lot. She would have expected nothing less from something that Brom was involved with. Her cousin had begun by wanting to remodel the restaurant at his Tahoe casino and had wound up remodeling his life by marrying Julia Sinclair, the woman who had taken on the task of bringing a touch of class to a heretofore drab restaurant.

Sara had been duly impressed with both Casino Camelot and Sinclair's/Tahoe when Brom and Julia had shown her around yesterday afternoon. Impulsively stopping at Brom's house en route to staying with her father, she had left as emotionally fortified as she could for the long-delayed meeting ahead.

Her father had called a week ago, having tracked her down through relatives who kept tabs on the nomadic life she led. Sara spent six months in one place, a year with another firm, nine months with a third. She left when things threatened to turn stale. Or serious. She always stayed clear of anything serious. It was a war wound, left over from her parents' divorce. That was the way she had thought of her parents' divorce. As a war.

The conversation between them on the telephone had been painfully awkward. Raymond Santangelo had been diagnosed as having a clogged left artery. He faced the possibility of intensive heart surgery. And he was facing it alone. He'd asked that Sara come to stay with him until he recuperated. She had wanted to say no, but the word that had come out of her mouth had been yes.

So here she was, dealing with ghosts after all these years.

Sara sat for a moment in the rented tan Mazda, thinking. Beyond the building the ocean peacefully communed with the shore less than a half mile away. She could see Catalina in the distance, its form distinct against the horizon like that of a proud whale sunning itself beneath the golden rays. It was one of those perfect days that Californians liked to brag about.

But Sara wasn't really thinking about Californians or the weather. She was thinking about her life. And her cousin's.

Brom had it all. A tiny spark of envy flickered within her soul before it went out again. A home, a family and a lucrative business. Sara laughed softly to herself as she thought of it. She'd never have guessed that he would turn out this way. Out of the assorted collection of cousins who huddled beneath the giant family umbrella, Brom had always been thought of as the black sheep. But his roots went deep.

Why shouldn't they? A touch of uncharacteristic bitterness framed the question in her mind. His parents had never divorced. He had been one of the lucky ones. His world hadn't dissolved right before his eyes.

Sara took a deep, cleansing breath, then consciously shrugged off her mood as if it was a physical thing, like a heavy sweater being shed as the day warmed. There was no reason to feel this way. She liked her life. She had toured the country in the past six years.

Hell, she'd toured the world and enjoyed it all to the hilt. She spoke two foreign languages and could order dinner in three more. For some people, roots were good. For others, herself included, they just tended to tangle things up. She liked living out of a suitcase. That way, nothing owned her and she was free to come and go whenever she pleased.

Freedom meant a lot. Freedom to do. Freedom not to be hurt.

She tried not to think about what had brought her to Southern California in the first place.

Time to meet the man who was going to be her boss for as long as she let him. Sara got out of the car and absorbed her idyllic surroundings for a long moment. Composed, she crossed the parking lot and pulled open the heavy oak door that led into Sinclair's.

There seemed to be almost a hush as the door drifted back into its frame. Sara felt as if she had entered a church.

No, a dwelling out of the pages of time was more like it, she decided, looking around. Crossing the threshold of Sinclair's/Tahoe had instantly catapulted her into Arthurian England. This restaurant didn't go back quite that far.

The journey stopped at the brink of Queen Victoria's time. The ambience was pleasantly old-fashioned, but not stiflingly so.

"How many in your party?" the woman at the reception podium asked.

Sara turned, startled. For a moment she had been so lost in her reverie, she hadn't noticed that there was someone else here. She felt no embarrassment at having been caught daydreaming.

"Just one," she said with a smile.

And it's been that way for a long, long time.

She had no idea why that made her feel momentarily sad. She decided that her father's call had set everything temporarily on its ear. It was going to take some effort on her part to get everything back on line again.

But she had done it before, she thought cryptically. No reason to suppose she couldn't do it again. Practice made perfect.

Jennifer Sinclair Madigan picked up a tall, dark green menu. For a change there were no catering arrangements to see to. Which was fortunate, because Ginger had called in sick this morning, leaving the hostess podium unattended. Once this had been Julia's position, until her sister married Brom and moved away. Now Jennifer manned it when she wasn't busy trying to juggle several other responsibilities, as well.

She glanced down at her small waist. There was no sign yet. But with the new baby coming, Nik was definitely going to have to hire someone to help out around here.

Jennifer offered the dark-haired woman a genial smile and turned. "This way, please."

Sara laid her hand on Jennifer's arm before she could go any farther. "Oh, I'm not here to eat."

Jennifer looked at the attractive woman quizzically. "Excuse me?"

Sara scanned the dim room as her eyes acclimated. She could discern more details now, and tried to decide which restaurant she liked better, the one in Tahoe or this one. It was a hard choice.

"I'm here to work," she replied, preoccupied. "Maybe." She tossed in the qualifying word as an afterthought. Better not to sound too confident. Employers hated an overconfident employee. She didn't mind playing a part in the beginning.

Jennifer studied the petite woman more closely. She had short black hair and animated dark eyes. She looked like a cross between a dark-haired Tinker Bell and a gypsy.

The description immediately struck a chord. Those had been Julia's exact words on the telephone yesterday when she was describing Brom's cousin. Which had been just after Nik had accidentally destroyed the accounting disc and it had flat-lined on them. A single, eerie white line lying horizontally across a blue field had announced the death of five months' worth of accounting information. In desperation, Jennifer had called Julia to ask if the accounting firm they used had a branch office in California. Brom had promptly volunteered Sara.

Jennifer felt like embracing the woman. "You're Sara."

A mouth that was wider than her delicate oval face dictated split into an even wider grin. Somehow it looked appealing, Jennifer thought.

"How did you know?" Sara asked, surprised.

Jennifer shifted the menu to her other hand and took the smaller woman's hand in hers. "I'm Jennifer," she said warmly. "Julia's sister. Brom's sister-in-law," she added for good measure.

This was the surrogate mother, Sara thought with a touch of wonder. Brom and Julia had been quick to set Sara straight about the baby when she had commented on how much the little girl looked like a combination of Julia and Brom.

"And A.J.'s—"

"Aunt." Jennifer finished the sentence tactfully, but firmly.

She had carried Aurora Jennifer under her heart for nine months, had given her sister the supreme gift of a tiny life as only one woman could do for another. But now the ties had to be put in their proper place. The baby had Brom's blood running through her veins. Brom's blood and Julia's love. It had begun that way. There was no need to alter anything else with biological details just because Julia was unable to conceive. A.J. was their daughter, not hers.

Sara looked at Jennifer for a long moment through eyes that were filled with genuine amazement. She couldn't quite comprehend that sort of a sacrifice, that degree of selflessness which the situation required. She had never known anyone capable of that before. It took her breath away.

"They told me all about it. Julia and Brom," she added quickly. "The baby's beautiful."

"This way." Jennifer gestured for Sara to follow her through the dining room into the kitchen. She stopped one of the waitresses at the threshold between the two rooms and asked the young woman to take over the desk for a few moments.

That done, Jennifer allowed herself a moment to bask in Sara's compliment. "The Sinclairs make beautiful girl children. Boy children, however," she said as they entered the kitchen, "tend to turn out just a little surly around the edges."

The kitchen, as always, was a beehive of activity. A rather warm beehive, since the air conditioning was being temperamental again and the repairman was over an hour late.

Nik looked up just as Jennifer concluded her pronouncement. He allotted one curious glance in Sara's direction, decided she was some new friend of his sister's and continued with his work without missing a beat. The knife flew over the carrot on the chopping block. Tiny pieces emerged, popping out like a well-rehearsed marine drill team.

"Jennifer, I'm busy."

He was going to have that chiseled into his tombstone—and soon—if he didn't start slacking off. Jennifer shook her head. "So what else is new?"

He spared one dark look in Jennifer's direction. He didn't have time for intrusions, or to act polite. Maybe he'd even forgotten how. But they were shorthanded today and he had a party of thirty coming in at noon above and beyond the usual large crowd of diners that the restaurant enjoyed. Polite would only get trampled to death in the rush.

Jennifer nudged Sara forward. Sara's eyes were glued to the flying knife as it reduced a stalk of celery into confetti before her eyes. "This is the lady who might change some of that for you."

Nik had no idea what Jennifer was talking about. His mind was on half a dozen different pots and ovens at once. Blotting the sweat from his forehead with the back of his wrist, he looked at Sara. He didn't remember calling the temporary agency. Had Jennifer?

"Do you cook?" he asked Sara as he moved to one of the myriad of pots on the seven stoves in the kitchen.

As a rule, Sara frequented take-out places, not supermarkets. "No, but I burn pretty well." Intrigued, drawn by the aroma, Sara peered into the huge pot that Nik was attending. The aroma was almost seductive. Her salivary glands stood at attention. "I don't know tomato paste from poster paste."

Nik replaced the lid on the pot firmly and looked at Sara as if she had just declared a preference for drinking furniture polish over aged wine. "Then why—?"

Jennifer was quick to jump in. Nik became more irritable when things became obscure. "She's here about our accounting mess. You remember, Nik. This is Brom's cousin, Sara."

No, he didn't remember. Not really. Life was becoming more muddled for him than mulligan stew. He remembered a disc dying and Jennifer saying something about calling Brom for a recommendation. Then he vaguely remembered Jennifer talking to him while he had been supervising the pastry chef's newest creation. But as to the exact words, they eluded him. He wondered if he had agreed to something he was going to regret.

His sister and Sara remained standing there, waiting for him to make some sort of acknowledgment. Nik sighed. He didn't have time to leave the kitchen, but he couldn't just hire the woman on the spot, either, even if Brom *had* vouched for her.

He waved toward the door. "Yes, I remember," he lied. "I'm a little busy right now." Now *there* was an understatement, he thought. Nik looked over toward where the new apprentice chef, Chris, was slowly filleting a tray of halibut. "Why don't you have something to eat in the dining room and I'll come out when I can?"

Sara knew when she was being dismissed. Turning, she glanced toward Jennifer as they walked out through the white swinging doors.

"Is he always that friendly?" She'd met corporate heads filing chapter eleven papers at court who were more cheerful than the broad-shouldered man in the apron.

Jennifer led Sara over to a cozy booth close enough to the kitchen for Nik to easily find Sara. "He used to be a lot more easygoing," Jennifer confided. "But after Julia got married and moved away, things went from bad to worse."

Sara looked around the dining room. It was deceptively arranged so that even when it was filled to capacity, it didn't appear crowded.

"Doesn't look all that bad to me," Sara assessed. In her estimation it looked about as busy as its sister restaurant in Tahoe.

Jennifer was tempted to sit and talk for a few minutes, but there just wasn't any time. If she had any to spare, she had to pop into the back office to see how Katie was doing. There was always someone on break, minding her daughter when Jennifer was busy, but nothing took the place of looking in for herself.

"No, the business end is fine," Jennifer agreed. "But Nik's swamped and he's trying to do everything himself." She smiled fondly as she looked over her shoulder toward the double doors that led to the kitchen. "He has trouble delegating." That had been true of him since childhood. Everyone always relied on Nik to get things done. It had only intensified after their parents' death, when Nik had taken over being father, mother and sole provider for them.

Sara had gotten a good sample of the man's disposition in the kitchen. The man had been chopping, directing and mixing all at the same time. She supposed she could relate to not wanting anyone else's finger in the pie to mess things up. She felt the same way about some things herself. "So I gathered."

Jennifer resisted saying anything further. If she pleaded Nik's case too much, Sara might be put off. Or Nik might become offended if he found out. "Well, I have to be getting back to the front desk." Jennifer began to back away reluctantly.

Sara wondered if Jennifer felt obligated to entertain her for some reason. She waved the other girl's words away. "Oh, please, don't stay on my account. I don't need anyone to hold my hand while I wait for your brother." She looked around again. She was going to like working here. It had a nice feel to it. She set great store by her initial reactions. "I like my own company."

Jennifer studied Sara for a moment longer. *Yes, I think you do.* She placed the menu she was still holding on the table before Sara. "Order anything you like. It's on the house. Lisa'll be here in a few minutes to take your order."

"What was that terrific thing Nik was making?" Sara asked suddenly as Jennifer turned away. "That big pot he didn't want me looking into?"

Jennifer stopped, smiling. "Nik gets possessive about his work. That was beef Stroganoff." One of the specialties of the house.

"Beef Stroganoff," Sara repeated, as if memorizing the words as she attached them to an image.

After Jennifer left, Sara perused the long, slender menu. It was an impressive selection, she thought, with an equally impressive price range. She scanned the large dining room. Something, apparently, to appeal to everyone. She closed the menu, her order already decided upon. She'd have the Stroganoff.

Sara had finished her meal, consumed three glasses of mineral water and had found several different ways to fold her napkin before Nik finally emerged out of the kitchen, worn around the edges, with a streak of flour on his cheek.

Without any empty chatter to pave the way, Nik sank into the booth next to Sara as if he was collapsing beside an old friend who didn't require any niceties. He sighed and stretched his feet out before him. The last time he'd sat down, he mused, was the day before Halloween. Nineteen ninety. Or, at least, it felt that way.

He closed his eyes for a moment, absorbing the sensation of not being on his feet and moving. When he opened them again Sara was looking at him quizzically.

"Sorry," he muttered, straightening. With very little encouragement he could probably fall asleep right there, sitting up.

Sara held her glass between her hands, rotating it slowly on the table. She had all but given up on him. "I should hope so."

Her reply had him narrowing his eyes. "What?"

Maybe the pending trip to her father's had her unduly antsy and short-tempered. Whatever the reason, she didn't feel very forgiving at the moment.

"I don't like to be kept waiting more than an entire season. When I first sat down, this was a tall candle." She pointed to the stubby yellow waxed candle flickering in the bowl in the center of the table.

Glancing at his watch had become second nature to him, as involuntary and unconscious as breathing. As he did so now, he realized that Sara had been sitting here over an hour. He'd still be in the kitchen, working, if Jennifer hadn't come in and all but pushed him out.

Nik dragged a hand through his light brown hair. He really didn't have the time to conduct an interview. The irony of it struck him. It was like being given a time-saving device and not having the time to read the manual in order to make the device work.

"Listen," he began, "today's rather hectic—"

Sara leaned closer and looked at him knowingly. "Do you really think tomorrow will be any better?"

"No." He didn't even have to think about it. It had been like this for the past six months. And while he blessed his patron saints for watching out for his business, this pace was going to burn him out soon. "I don't."

She rested her case. "I didn't think so. Jennifer told me how well business was going," she added when he raised a brow. She laced her hands together, her eyes on his face. It was a nice face, she thought, strong and broad and sincere. "I'll make it easy for you. Tell me the salary you're thinking of, point me toward the work and I'll give you my answer." She smiled. "That shouldn't take us too long."

Rather than be pleased at her solution, Nik held it suspect. He was always suspicious of things that were too easy. "Are you always this slipshod?"

Her eyes held his for a long, pregnant moment. Hers were the color of hot chocolate on a cold, toe-freezing winter's morning. Or maybe caramel, warm, melting caramel, sliding slowly downward along a mountain of ice cream.

Nik roused himself. He had definitely been slaving over a hot stove too long.

Sara's smile tightened just a smidgen around the edges. "Never. The word, Mr. Sinclair, is fast. I have always been fast." At times she resented having to defend that gift. "Fast does not mean sloppy, or careless, it just means being blessed with quick reflexes and a quick mind."

And obviously, Nik thought, a large ego. There was no room in his operation for something like that. It was just asking for trouble. His doubts multiplied.

"You seem to think a lot of yourself, Ms.—?" He didn't even know her last name, he realized.

"Santangelo," she supplied.

She moved her napkin aside, deciding to dig in and take this man down a little. She didn't know why she felt challenged, but she did.

"A positive image always helps," she told him. "If I don't think well of myself, why should you?"

Nik supposed it made sense in a simple sort of way. He rose and gestured toward the back. "You have a point, I guess." He began to lead the way to the back office, then stopped abruptly. Maybe Brom hadn't filled her in completely. "Listen, this isn't going to be a permanent position."

Nothing ever was, which was just the way she liked it. Sara shrugged carelessly in response. "Good. I'm not looking for anything permanent."

Anticipating an argument, Nik continued quickly, walking her through the kitchen. Force of habit had him scanning the area to ascertain if everything was proceeding as usual.

"This is just until I get everything back on the disc that was blown up and in general get things under control again." Her words replayed themselves in his mind. "Why aren't you looking for anything permanent?" Nik held the back door open for her.

Sara stepped out into the narrow corridor, brushing against him as she passed. She felt a shimmer of something warm and pleasurable ripple through her. She looked up in surprise and saw by his expression that he had experienced the same unsettling reaction. Just random chemistry, she told herself. Her eyes held his. Or maybe not so random. She wasn't altogether certain she wanted to find out.

After a beat she realized she hadn't answered his question. "I'm here on family business. When that business ends, so will my time here."

That was an odd way to put it, he thought. He was already aware that he wasn't dealing with an average woman, no matter how vague his memory of the gender—outside of his sisters—was as a whole. "You make it sound like you're serving a jail sentence."

The knot in her stomach twisted a little tighter as she thought of what lay ahead of her this afternoon. She wasn't very good at confrontations.

"Close, but not quite." It was bad enough she had to go through it; she didn't want to talk about it, as well. She changed the subject. "So what is it that you want me to work on? Your books, or your program, or what?"

"I think it's in the realm of 'or what,'" Nik answered in a moment of weakness as he opened the office door.

Candy, a college freshman who worked at Sinclair's part-time, was on the floor, playing with Katie. She looked up, startled and then pleased. She got up slowly, like smoke rising in the air, her eyes on Nik. Candy ran a hand over her picture-perfect hair, gave Nik a sensuous look that drifted right over his head and smiled. The invitation was so blatant it would have knocked over a more receptive man. Nik appeared completely oblivious to it.

"I guess I'd better be getting back to work," she said in the best imitation of Marilyn Monroe that Sara had heard in a long time. "My break's over."

Sara was tickled that Nik was apparently unaware of the come-on. She decided right then and there that she was going to like working for him.

"You run a nursery on the side?" She nodded toward Katie.

The little girl was clutching a fat crayon and seriously decorating a huge sheet of paper in front of her. With a sigh befitting an artist, she lay the crayon down and appeared to survey her work.

Sara had been an only child, but there had always been cousins galore of every size and shape while she was growing up. Instinct took over. She crossed to the little girl and picked her up. She smelled of apple juice and baby shampoo.

Katie's cornflower blue eyes opened wide as she studied Sara's face. A smile broke through as she obviously decided that Sara was to be trusted.

The little girl was going to break a lot of hearts when she got older, Sara thought. She turned toward Nik, who was watching her quietly. She couldn't tell if he approved or disapproved of her holding the child. "Everywhere I turn, there seem to be babies associated with you people."

"That's because we're so family oriented," Jennifer told Sara as she looked in the doorway. She had seen Candy leaving and had come to check on her little girl. Jennifer looked from Nik to Sara. "Everything okay here?"

Sara jiggled Katie on her hip and the little girl laughed. "Couldn't be better," Sara answered.

Nik, Jennifer could see by the expression on his face, wasn't completely sure about that yet. She wondered if his disquietude had to do with Sara's qualifications, or just surrendering a piece of the control in general.

With the front desk at a lull, Jennifer took the opportunity to steal a few minutes with her daughter. She crossed to Sara. "I see you've met Katie."

Katie stretched her arms out to her mother. "Yours?" Sara asked as she handed the child over. Jennifer nodded, brushing her cheek against the tinier one. Sara turned toward Nik. "Where are yours?"

Right now the only way he could have children, he thought, was to send away for them through a mail-order house.

"I don't have any." He nodded toward his sister. "Raising Jennifer and Julia was enough for me, thanks."

Which wasn't completely accurate. Lately, seeing Julia with her family and Jennifer with hers, a longing had risen within him, a longing in the form of a faint voice that echoed, *Where are mine?*

But it was usually blotted out by the sound of pots and pans. When it wasn't, he tried not to pay attention to it. Someday he would do something about it, but not now. He was far too busy.

Raising them? Sara looked at Nik dubiously. "You don't look old enough."

"He wasn't," Jennifer confirmed.

She set her squirming daughter back amid her colorful chaos. Nik had had the room transformed into a giant play area for his niece. He had left only a few bare essentials to identify the fact that this was also an office where all the business transactions were conducted.

"But he managed, anyway," she added fondly. She looked at Sara. "So, are you taking the job?"

Nik noticed with annoyance that Jennifer had completely bypassed his input in this scenario.

Sara always went with instincts. Instinct told her to take the job. Prudence told her to go more slowly than she was normally accustomed to. Nik didn't look as if he was up to her normal pace.

"I don't really know what it is yet." Blocks crashed in an orchestrated avalanche as Katie clapped her hands together. "Is she going to be my junior helper?"

Jennifer laughed as she got down on her knees to clear away the debris. "Not if you're lucky. You're going to have enough trouble as it is."

Sara wasn't quite certain whether or not Jennifer was joking. "Trouble?"

Jennifer nodded toward her brother. "Because of Nik."

Now she thought of bringing him into it. To be insulted. "It's not my fault," he protested darkly. "It was the damn computer."

Sara moved toward the desk that was pushed against one wall to maximize space for Katie. She looked at the dormant computer. "Uh-huh, famous last words."

Jennifer joined her. She switched on the computer and it hummed to life. Within a few moments the single, lonely white line appeared. It lay rigidly stretched out across the screen. Jennifer pointed toward it. "He did that yesterday."

"Any backup discs?" Sara had a feeling she already knew the answer to that.

Nik hated admitting that he had made a mistake. He wasn't used to making them. Despite all the responsibilities that were laid across his shoulders he had always made the right choices, done the right thing. In short, he had always handled everything well. The fact that they now needed an outsider to handle something he considered to be a key part of the restaurant really grated on him.

He scowled at the machine. "No."

"I see." A challenge. Sara nodded thoughtfully. Because Jennifer was more receptive, Sara turned to her with the next question. "Any paper files?"

Jennifer nodded at the towering file cabinet. "Lots. In there. We keep the drawers locked so that Katie isn't tempted to create her own version of a ticker-tape parade in here."

"Very wise. Also a tremendous relief." Sara circled the file cabinet like a magician contemplating the best method of making a tiger appear before an audience in place of a lady. This was the kind of thing best tackled early in the morning, when she was fresh. Right now there was something weighing too heavily on her mind for her to concentrate. "I can start tomorrow morning at about nine or so."

Just like that? Was she desperate, or careless? Nik couldn't make up his mind. "I haven't quoted you a salary," Nik reminded Sara. The woman was going faster than Julia ever had. His head began to hurt again.

Sara looked at him, surprised that he would think of that as a deterrent. "I'm Brom's cousin. I don't figure you'll insult him or me by paying me minimum wage. Besides—" she shrugged her shoulders in a gesture that was beginning to make Nik feel oddly itchy "—I'm not taking it because I need to make a living at this moment." She had more than enough saved to see her through this episode, had never needed much to begin with.

"Oh?" Nik asked skeptically.

"No." Her wide mouth turned up in a broad smile. "I'm doing it as a favor."

Nik crossed his arms in front of his chest and pinned her with a look. He'd be damned if he was going to be pitied. "For whom?"

"Brom," she answered easily. "And Julia. She said that you were desperate."

Julia always exaggerated even the simplest of things. "I'm never desperate," Nik informed Sara before she began laboring under the wrong impression.

Jennifer weighed the matter quickly and thought that this was a safe time to override Nik. Sara was going to find out, anyway. She nudged him out of the way and moved closer to the other woman. "We're desperate."

Nik knew when he was outnumbered. What did it matter? It was only temporary. They were both in agreement on that part.

Sara began to carefully pick her way through the scattered blocks. "Fine. I'll be here tomorrow, then." She stopped at the threshold. "Oh, one more thing. I need the day after tomorrow off."

Nik stared at her. She was nervy, he'd give her that. "Already?"

"Already," she answered cheerfully. "Those are my terms." She waited to see if he'd turn them down. If he did, he was a fool.

"We'll take them," Jennifer answered for both of them, afraid to let Nik say anything.

But it wasn't good enough. Sara looked at Nik. "Okay with you?"

As much as Nik hated to admit it, he really had no other choice. Sinclair's couldn't go on indefinitely without some sort of up-to-date accounting system. With business being what it was, he had no time to feed the damned information into the miserable computer again, and neither did Jennifer.

That left him with only one viable alternative.

He sighed, Lee surrendering his sword to Grant at Appomattox with whispers of "The South shall rise again," echoing in the background.

"Okay by me." The words sounded as if they were being forcibly dragged out of his mouth.

Sara laughed as she exited. "It's going to be great working for one of the less popular seven dwarfs," she mused aloud, closing the door behind her.

Nik scowled at the door. He gave the arrangement one week, tops.

Chapter 2

The smile on Sara's lips slowly faded as she slid behind the wheel of her car. There were no other stops she needed to make. It was time to see her father.

A hollow feeling seeped through her like seawater into the hull of a ship that wasn't quite airtight.

"No more excuses, Saratoga, you're a big girl now. You can do this."

Sara jabbed her key into the ignition and turned it. Anger and anxiety faced off within her like pro tennis players at a Wimbledon play-off. Gripping the wheel, she gunned the engine and peeled out of the parking lot, hugging the road as if the car was part of it.

Nik winced when he heard the noise, certain that it was Sara driving away. Just what he needed, an Indianapolis 500 trainee.

He eyed Jennifer as she prepared to leave for a consultation with a catering client. "Brom say what Sara does in her spare time? Stunt driving for movies?"

Jennifer slipped her purse strap onto her arm. Affectionately she patted her brother's cheek. Her fingers touched a tiny bit of stubble Nik had missed shaving this morning.

And that wasn't all he was missing lately, she thought. Life was whizzing by him. "She's probably just in a hurry to see her father. You grumble too much, Nik. You're getting too stodgy and cranky in your old age."

Old age. The phrase rankled him a little more than it should have, perhaps because he felt it was merited. He resisted it all the more for that. Nik gave Jennifer a black look. He was only thirty-five. Why did it feel as if he had already lived an entire lifetime?

And why, at the same time, did it feel, with all this responsibility he had to shoulder, with all the work he had to do, with all the family around him, as if life was mysteriously passing him by?

"Watch it, Jenny, I'm only five years older than you. If I'm old, what does that make you?"

"Still young and happy." Her expression softened slightly as concern edged its way in. She wanted him to have the same things she did. If anyone deserved happiness, he did. "Maybe you should take the time to enjoy life before it's too late."

Nik frowned. Not that again. He wasn't in the mood to listen to another verse of "Poor Overworked Nik" being sung in the key of Jennifer. He knew all the words by heart. "I'll see if I can schedule it in by the end of the month," he quipped, turning away.

Maybe Jennifer was right, he mused reluctantly as he opened the door to the kitchen. Maybe he *was* working too hard. The problem was, he didn't know how else to approach life anymore except at full throttle. The little engine that could—did. And would undoubtedly continue to do so until it blew itself up.

Now there was a heartening prospect.

Nik sighed. Now his sisters had him doing it, making him feel that he was overdoing everything. He didn't feel overworked. Not *exactly*. Just a little harried, as if he was missing something by being here all the time. But for more than the past decade, in order to first make a living for them and then keep the restaurant going according to his high standards, this was all he had had time *to* do. Hard work had begat success, which begat more hard work. It was like being on a merry-go-round that had lost its Stop button.

He wondered if a vacation was the answer.

A noise in the kitchen caught his attention and thoughts of vacations dissolved like greasy dishwater before an emulsifier.

Nik strode into the large room and crossed directly to the new apprentice chef. He eyed the portion of halibut beneath Chris's knife critically. The fish looked as if it had been tortured to death.

"Unless you're trying to get a confession out of that halibut, you're going about filleting all wrong. Watch."

With a shake of his head Nik took hold of the long knife and went to work on the next piece of fish.

It had been almost fourteen years since she'd ridden down this path. Fourteen years bracketed by painful, lonely memories. Yet she remembered the way as if the route was forever painted onto the pages of her mind. The car moved as if it was on automatic pilot. There was no hesitation at corners, no fumbling with written directions, indecisions on whether to turn left or right. Sara never forgot anything.

She set her mouth hard. No, she never forgot anything. Not the good times, or the bad.

She was almost there already, she realized. The trip from Sinclair's to her father's house had gone by much too fast to suit her. She had secretly hoped for a blowout or a traffic snarl to delay her, to give her just a little more stalling time.

"Coward," she muttered under her breath. "What are you afraid of?" Her voice rose over the sound of the music on the radio. "He can't hurt you anymore." She was clutching the steering wheel so hard that her knuckles were literally turning white. She eased her hold, though the tension refused to go. "You're past that, remember? He has his life and you have yours. You're just doing a good deed because you happen to be kinder than he ever was.''

If that's all there was, why was her throat constricting like wet leather left out in the sun as she approached her father's development, for God's sake?

Annoyance bubbled within her like unattended boiling water on the stove, threatening to overflow. She needed to be strong, to be self-confident now of all times, not suddenly fighting with shadows from her past.

Needing to distract herself, she started flipping to different radio stations, searching for heavy metal music that would fill the car and take up the space in her brain. Sara desperately wanted to be anesthetized by the time she reached her father's door.

She wasn't.

Sara parked across the street from the familiar address and shut off the engine. Instead of opening the car door and getting out, she remained where she was, waiting for the feeling to return to her suddenly numb legs. She sat for a long while, just staring at the tidy-looking house. Her father lived in a single-story stucco house. The walls were dove gray, with white paint accenting the wood trim. It appeared to be freshly painted.

It was just the same as when she'd seen it last. Fourteen years and he hadn't changed the color scheme, she thought. At least her father was steadfast about some things.

Bitterness rose in her throat, bringing with it a sickly taste. Sara forced it down. No recriminations, she had promised herself before boarding the plane. Recriminations would only serve to rip open tender skin that covered wounds that had never properly healed. She didn't want to hear his excuses, because they weren't any good.

There *were* no acceptable excuses as far as she was concerned, no reason in the world for a man to turn his back on the daughter who worshiped him.

Sara closed her eyes and searched for inner strength. She'd come this far; she couldn't fall apart now. "C'mon, Sara, remember Drama One. You can carry this off. At least your conscience will always be clear.''

She knew that if she'd turned a deaf ear to her father's plea, justified or not, she would carry the burden of that guilt with her no matter what the outcome of the operation. It wasn't in Sara to walk away from a plea for help no matter how much she might want to.

Woodenly Sara emerged from the car and slammed the door behind her. The three suitcases she always traveled with were butted up against each other in the trunk, but for the time being she left them there. It was almost as if, subconsciously, she was denying the fact that she had agreed to stay with her father for the duration of his surgery and recovery period. If her suitcases remained in her car she might still feel as if she was just passing through. She wanted to hang on to that feeling a little while longer. It might make the first few hours here that much easier to handle.

She glanced around for traffic on the street and then crossed to number five Avalone.

That was all she was doing, Sara assured herself. Just passing through, the way she had through all those dozens of other places that had floated by in the past six years.

"Just another adventure, Saratoga. No more, no less." She pressed the doorbell.

As she stood there, waiting for a response, it was as if there were two completely different projectors in her mind, vying for the same screening space. One reel was filled with scenes from her childhood, happy scenes with her parents, with her father, taking trips, going on family outings together. All her happy memories.

The other held only a single vivid scene. It was the moment her father had, for the last time, walked out of the house he and her mother had once shared. He had promised Sara that he'd return the following weekend. He hadn't. Week after week she had waited, hoping, praying. But he had never come.

She felt the ache inside her chest building again. Damn it, she wasn't that young girl anymore. *She wasn't.* Sara blinked back the tears that had begun to coat her lashes. She had grown light-years away from the girl who'd cried, who had felt so abandoned.

The door opened.

Sara sucked in her breath as the tall man in the doorway moved forward. The eyes were the same. A soft brown. But where they had once resembled those of a small boy, twinkling with secrets and mischief, her father's eyes now belonged to a man who had been beaten down by something or someone. Apart from his eyes it was difficult for Sara to recognize Raymond Santangelo. He was thinner now and years older. The years were all there, etched on his face in lines of sorrow. His once-thick brown hair had thinned and his hairline was receding. Though physically tall, he somehow seemed smaller to her than he had fourteen years ago.

This was her father?

Sara wanted to deny it and run, to hold on to her last memories and close the door firmly behind her.

She remained where she was.

"Saratoga?" He whispered her name in hopeful disbelief the way a prisoner did upon receiving a long-awaited parole from the review board. Nervously he moved to take her hand, then stopped, running bony fingers through his gray-flecked brown hair.

Because her father was nervous, Sara found the resolve to be strong. "Hello, Dad." She forced a distant smile she didn't feel to her lips. "Funny running into you like this."

Raymond Santangelo was a policeman with eighteen years of service behind him. In his time he had faced down more than one criminal. And in all that time his hands had never felt this clammy. He brushed them against the back of his jeans and then found the courage to clasp his daughter's hand in his.

"Saratoga, you're beautiful."

She frowned. She referred to herself by that name at times, but no one else did any more. Most people didn't even know it was her legal name. "I'd rather you didn't call me that. It's Sara now."

She had suffered years of teasing because of that name. She had endured it without complaint because her father had named her after the town he had met her mother in.

Sara had once thought it was the height of romance. After he left there hadn't seemed to be much point in Sara being reminded of it.

"Saratoga sounds too much like the racetrack."

Raymond nodded, uncomfortable at the reminder. Did she know, after all? Or just suspect? He'd tried so hard to hide it from her.

"Sure. Sara." His head bobbed again. "Sounds fine. Fine." Feeling awkward, needing somewhere else to direct his gaze, Raymond looked down at the doorstep. "Where's your luggage?"

"In the car." She nodded over her shoulder. The idea of going to a hotel was beginning to appeal to her. "I thought that I'd—"

But Raymond was already striding past his daughter, intent on reaching the car before Sara. At least he could carry her bags for her.

"I'll get them." He walked with a sense of determination as he crossed the street. "And you can park the car in my garage." He gestured behind him without looking. He was all right as long as he didn't see the accusing hurt in her eyes. Raymond spoke quickly. "It'll be a tight fit, but it's supposed to be a two-car garage and—" He reached the car and suddenly swung around, carried away by the emotions swelling within him. He'd missed her so much. "God, Saratoga—Sara, I'm glad you're here. I know this wasn't easy for you."

Sara reached the other side of the car and opened the trunk. "Easiest thing in the world." She purposely kept her voice as distant as the physical space she maintained between them. She saw her father raise his brow. "I buy airplane tickets all the time. This gives me an excuse to see Southern California again. It's been fourteen years."

She wasn't unaware of the wince her words evoked from her father.

Guilty? Good, you should be. But the thought brought her no satisfaction.

"Yes, it has been a long time...." His voice trailed off with nowhere to go.

As her father reached into the trunk for the first suitcase Sara quickly stopped him like a no-nonsense nurse walking in on a patient about to light up a forbidden cigarette.

"I'll get them." She ignored the frustrated look on her father's face. "I'm not the one having heart surgery," she reminded him crisply. "You are. You're not supposed to be carrying anything heavy."

"Sure. Anything you say."

Sara didn't bother to comment. She took out the first suitcase and then the second. The third was a small case with a shoulder strap. Slipping it over her shoulder, she managed to pick up all three bags.

Raymond watched her helplessly. He licked his lips, wanting desperately to find the right words to break down the barriers that had grown between them. He knew that he deserved every bitter nuance that she tossed his way, but for far different reasons than she was aware of. He ached for the love he had been forced to turn away from so many years ago.

Sara walked back to the house. Raymond hurried so that he could hold open the door for her.

"You'll be staying in your old room." He pushed the door back and the doorknob bumped against the wall with a thud.

Sara crossed the threshold, valiantly shutting herself off from a fresh onslaught of memories. The familiarity clawed at her and she knew she shouldn't have come. But she was here and had to work with that.

"I don't remember staying in it often enough for it to be thought of as my room." She set down one suitcase to get a better grip on the handle.

"Are you sure I can't help...?"

She wanted to throw her arms around him, to cry, to beat her fist against him and demand to know why he hadn't said those words years ago, when he *could* have helped.

Her grip tightened on the suitcase handle as she straightened. "I can manage. I've been doing it for a long time."

Raymond faltered slightly before turning and leading the way toward the rear of the house. "I'm sure you have."

Sara looked around as she followed him. There was hardly any furniture in the living room and the dining room was completely empty. The faded wall outlined bright rectangles of color where once paintings and framed photographs had hung.

Raymond turned to see the surprised look on her face. "It looks pretty Spartan," she commented.

Her father nodded. His second divorce had been bitter and painful. "Joyce decided to take more than her share." He shrugged helplessly. "I thought she'd earned it."

And what about us, Dad, Mom and me? Didn't we deserve more than we got?

Sara moved around her father as she entered the small bedroom, careful not to allow the slightest physical contact between them. "Very sporting of you."

Raymond heard the hurt in her voice, the brittleness, and wished he had the words with which he could cut down the brambles that had grown between them. Now more than ever he regretted what had happened.

But he was an optimist at heart. Even in the face of darkness he always believed that there would be light. Maybe soon.

Sara tried not to look around as she placed the suitcases down next to the bed. Memories ricocheted from the walls despite her efforts, threatening a fresh assault. She had known this was going to be hard, possibly the most difficult thing she'd ever done. But she hadn't fully realized that it was going to rip through her this badly.

She'd never forgive herself if she cried in front of him. She braced her shoulders as she turned to face him. Searching for something to say, she wrinkled her nose. "It's dusty."

Raymond leapt on the neutral topic like a starving dog onto a bone. He ran his hand along the footboard and wiggled his fingers at the layer of dust that coated them.

"I never was much on cleaning." Self consciously he wiped his hand on his jeans and then shoved both hands into his back pockets. "I kept meaning to get a woman to come in to clean after Joyce left, but you know how it is." He shrugged as if to punctuate his statement.

Sara picked up a suitcase, placed it on the light blue bedspread and snapped open the locks. "No." Her voice was low. "I don't know how it is. And I probably never will." She shook out a sweater and crossed to the narrow closet. It was empty inside.

"I'll get you some hangers," Raymond volunteered quickly, anxious to avoid any emotional confrontation.

Sara laid the sweater over the back of the chair that was next to the white, lacquered desk. The furniture was intended for a young girl. A young girl, she thought, who had barely gotten to use it.

Raymond stopped in the doorway. His voice grew even more uncertain. "How's your mother?"

Sara tried to hold on to her anger. Her father had put her up in the same room she had occupied as a child and now he was asking about her mother. Didn't he realize how difficult he was making this for her? It was all she could do not to give in to the need to hurl accusations at him. If this was going to work she needed to keep everything, all her emotions, under wraps. Maybe he was doing this intentionally. Maybe he needed forgiveness, but she couldn't find it in her heart to give it to him.

"Fine." The word shot out as if it was a bullet. "She and Larry moved to Arizona three years ago."

Or maybe it was four. Sara had lost track after her mother had distanced herself from her daughter. It arose from the fact that each time she looked into Sara's face, her mother saw traces of her failed dreams there.

"He raises cattle. She frequents the artsy-crafty places. It works out." Sara felt as if she was reciting a human interest story about two people who were strangers to her.

Selectively, Raymond remembered soft laughter and better times. "I'm glad she's finally happy."

A blouse held tightly in her hands, Sara raised her eyes to her father's face, but said nothing.

The silence vibrated like an oppressive dirge within the room. Raymond wished he was on a stakeout, or somewhere where he had a clue as to what he was doing, what was expected of him. He had no clues here. He had no idea what to do or what to say next. The road between then and now was littered with so many mistakes he was at a loss as to how to begin to clear a path to his daughter.

Frustrated, helpless, angry, he gestured toward the kitchen. "Have you eaten? I could whip up a macaroni and cheese casserole. Remember how you—"

She didn't want to remember. Anything. "Yes, as a matter of fact, I have eaten. I had lunch at a place called Sinclair's on Coast Highway. Know it?" Raymond shook his head. His experience ran to fast-food places. Both his line of work and his finances dictated it.

Sara continued removing things from her suitcase. She hardly knew what she was handling. She just knew she had to keep her hands busy. She had a feeling that when she finished she'd have no idea where anything was.

She placed her nightgown in the bottom drawer of the bureau. "I'll be working there."

"Working?" Raymond's face brightened. It was as if the sun had come out after forty days of rain. "Then you're going to—"

"Stay?" She second-guessed him.

The word turned as if it were a knife in his gut. Raymond could tell by the way she said the word that she wasn't.

"No." She slammed the bottom drawer with finality. "But I don't like vegetating, either." Returning to the bed, she realized that there wasn't anything left inside the suitcase to remove. She closed it and lifted the second one onto the bed. "I looked in on Brom before flying down here. He's married again."

She wondered if her father even knew that Brom had been married before. Or that his first wife had died suddenly. Probably not. He was too busy with his own life to know. Or care.

On automatic pilot, she began to unpack the second case. "And his new wife's part owner of Sinclair's." She lined up a few tubes of makeup on top of the bureau. "Seems they need a temporary accountant. And that's me."

Her eyes met her father's in the mirror above the bureau. "Temporary." Her tongue wrapped around the word carefully, as if it was jagged. Her father looked away. "Just passing through. I don't like to stay anywhere for very long." A briskness underscored her manner as she emptied the rest of the suitcase on top of the bed. "There are too many places to see and too many things to do in life to let myself stagnate in one place too long."

It was his fault. All his fault. He'd known it for years. But for reasons other than she thought. Raymond reached out to touch her arm.

"Sara, I—"

Sara's head jerked up and she pinned him with a look that had her father dropping his hand impotently to his side. "Yes?"

Raymond Santangelo backed down from the slight, dark-haired woman the way he never would from a confrontation with any hood on the streets.

He shook his head. "Nothing. I'll leave you to your unpacking." He hesitated as his tongue nervously outlined the border of his dry mouth. "Maybe later you'd like to just sit and talk?"

Sara's immediate reaction was to refuse, to say no, they couldn't sit and talk now. Talking was something they should have done years ago when it still could have done some good. But she let her temper cool, and nodded.

"Sure. You can fill me in on your doctors' names and the rest of the details about your tests and diagnosis." It was the accountant in her speaking. She knew she was on safe ground if she just stuck to cut-and-dried details. Things she could maintain at an antiseptic distance.

Sara already had her back to him. She tried to sort out the clothes on the bed that were swimming before her as her eyes grew moist. Pressing her lips together, she curled her fingers into her palms, digging in with her nails. The moisture abated.

"Sara?"

Under control, she still refused to turn toward him. "Yes?"

He stood, looking at her back, remembering. And was grateful. "It's nice to have you here, even under these conditions."

Without realizing it he ran his hand over his chest. The small, nagging pain was with him almost constantly now. An irritant to a vital, active man who had once thought himself on the edge of immortality.

She turned and caught the unconscious movement. She refused to let it penetrate her wall. "These were the only conditions under which you could have me here," she answered quietly, her voice a single, steely note. Turning her back on him again, she returned to her sorting. "I'm a Culhane. And Culhanes don't ignore their responsibilities."

Raymond opened his mouth to say something, then shut it again. There was no point in it right now. "I'll see you after you've settled in."

Sara knew she would have slept better if she had slept on a bed of nails. Spending the night in her father's house had her tossing and turning for endless hours, haunted by thoughts, by memories. And by guilt. Guilt she felt she didn't deserve. But it gnawed at her anyway, like a hungry mouse at a huge ring of cheese.

She rose at first light, more dead than alive. Forcing herself to move quickly, she showered and dressed, hoping to leave the house before her father was up.

She succeeded.

Maybe it was the coward's way out, she thought as she made her way down to Coast Highway. But she just couldn't bring herself to sit across from her father over breakfast. Dinner had been hard enough with the ghost of years past sitting right there between them. She was good at small talk when the need arose, but last night she had had to dig deep to keep the stillness at bay.

The stillness and the hurt.

After a sleepless night she was in no mood to wage another war. Especially not when she had a full day of work before her.

Her stomach grumbled a protest. Sara was used to eating first thing in the morning. The beauty of working at a restaurant, she told herself, was that she could get her breakfast there.

Provided Mr. Personality didn't have some rule against employees eating on the premises. She thought of Nik, and her mood shifted from tension to amusement. He reminded her of the type who was accustomed to exercising complete control over things. She could relate to that. And enjoy sparring with him.

Anything to get her mind off the house on Avalone Drive.

When she pulled in to the gray, graveled parking lot, there was only one other car there. It was a battered old car, vintage unknown. Its color depended on the side she was standing on. It had a red hood and beige right side and rear. The left side was black. The rickety car was a composite of accidents.

She wondered if it was Nik's. It was rather early to be here, but Nik struck her as the type to open up the place on his own. If it was his car, the man was definitely eccentric.

Her stomach grumbled again as she got out of her car. She rubbed it, as if that would stave off the pangs that were growing.

Sara knocked twice on the back door. There was no answer. With a sigh she knocked once more. Nothing. Time to find a fast-food take-out place, she decided.

She had crossed to her car and was just taking out her key when the back door of the restaurant opened.

A snowy head peered out. The man squinted at her from behind his glasses. "We're closed," the man announced, his spidery fingers splayed on the door.

Sara was back before him in a minimum of steps. "Yes, I know. But Mr. Sinclair wanted me to get an early start on the accounts." Before the man could say a word in protest, Sara had slipped her hand into his and was shaking it heartily. "I'm Sara Santangelo. I'll be working here for the next few weeks."

The old man blinked as he pushed his wire-rimmed glasses up his short, wide nose. His expression was still rather

doubtful. "Mr. Sinclair didn't tell me nothing about anyone coming in here before him."

Easing her way in, Sara nodded as if this was to be expected. "He must have forgotten, Mr.—" She looked at the
maintenance man. "I'm sorry, I missed catching your
name."

He ran a coarse thumb beneath the suspender of his
bibbed overall. "I didn't throw it." He paused, eyeing her.
Sara outwaited him. "Sam," he mumbled. "My name's
Sam."

"Sam," she repeated, her generous mouth spreading into
a wide smile.

A beat later Sam closed the door behind them and followed her into the restaurant.

Chapter 3

The two aspirin he had taken just before leaving his house definitely weren't doing the trick, Nik thought, disgruntled. More than that, they were making things worse. Instead of taking the edge off the pain that was pulsating in his neck like the rhythm section of a rock band, they were slowly, methodically, burning their way through his esophagus, creating a hole in his stomach.

At least, it felt that way.

The pain didn't put Nik in the best of moods as he pulled his '78 Mustang into the parking lot in front of Sinclair's. His disposition would have been judged surly in comparison to a wounded bear's.

Served him right for trying to stay up while his whole body begged him to go to bed. He'd fallen asleep in his recliner again last night, poring over his notes for the new recipe he was working on. A meal had to be choreographed just so, both for taste and appearance. Nik spent hours choosing and discarding different arrangements, searching for the perfect marriage of ingredients with the right visual complement of main course with side dishes.

There was a time he'd stayed up all hours trying to trim pennies from budgets that were already cleaved to the bone, in order to keep the restaurant running a little longer, until it turned a profit. Now budget worries were essentially a thing of the past, yet there always seemed to be something that kept him up at night.

Both Jennifer and Julia had been pleading with him to stop doing the actual cooking and just concern himself with the creative end of running the restaurant, but it was hard for him to let go. Hard to let go of any of it. He knew he had a very real need to feel in control of it all. It was difficult to break old patterns, even in the face of prosperity.

Nik shut off the engine. Massaging the back of his neck, he rotated it slowly, desperately attempting to alleviate the stiffness. It clung like a suction cup to a smooth glass surface.

He sighed, getting out of the car. Eventually the pain would taper off. What he needed right now, he decided as he walked toward the restaurant, was something in his stomach to coat it. The aspirin felt as if they were well on their way to burning a hole straight down to his toes.

It was tantamount to the old, closing-of-the-barn-door-after-the-horse-had-run-off theory, he thought sarcastically. But eating something certainly couldn't hurt any more right now than this miserable burning sensation going through him, and maybe it would help.

Slipping his key into the lock, Nik opened the large oak front door. Once inside he closed the door softly behind him. He felt the peace embrace him immediately.

The dim lighting cast shadows all around him, reinforcing the hushed silence. He could hear himself breathe here. Even the hum of the refrigerator wasn't audible. It was almost like a cathedral, he mused. In a way, maybe it was, to him. He'd done a lot of praying here, a lot of invoking of heavenly intervention to keep the.bill collectors at bay and to spread the word through satisfied restaurant critics.

His prayers had worked.

Time to get the cathedral up and running, Nik thought, pocketing his key.

He didn't bother turning on any more lights. He could easily maneuver his way around in the dark. Every inch of Sinclair's was familiar to him. With long, sure strides he made his way to the kitchen. If he didn't eat something soon to quell this fiery stomach he didn't know if he could concentrate on his work.

It was dim in the kitchen, as well.

Nik stopped when he heard a noise coming from the walk-in refrigerator. Frowning, he flipped on the switch. There wasn't supposed to be anyone here except Sam. It wasn't like the maintenance man to just help himself to anything. It wasn't that Nik minded if the man fixed a meal when he came in early. It was just that he knew that Sam was a stickler about not taking what wasn't his. That meant that someone else was in the kitchen.

The door to the walk-in hung open like the mouth of a steely cave. From his vantage point, the first thing Nik saw as he approached was a very well-rounded, jean-clad posterior. The owner of said anatomy was bending over, examining the contents of one of the large metal pots that were kept stored there.

Nik glanced at his watch. It was too early for her to be here. He winced as the movement sent another arrow of pain shooting through his shoulder blades. "Change your schedule, Harri?"

Sara dropped the huge flat lid onto the pot and swung around. She'd been so engrossed in her explorations that she hadn't heard Nik approaching. Quick to recover, she gave Nik an intrigued smile.

"Harry? I look like Harry to you?" She glanced around at her posterior. "I must need more exercise than I thought."

It was her. The accountant. Sara. Nik was reminded of the pain in his stomach and neck simultaneously.

"From this angle you look just like Harri." He saw the dubious look rise in Sara's eyes as she followed him out of the refrigerator. "Harriet Sugarman," he clarified. "The woman who comes here to collect the restaurant's leftovers every morning."

Stopping at the pantry, he bent and opened the lower drawer. He dragged out an unopened two-foot-long loaf of white bread, laid it on the counter and expertly cracked it in half as if it was a mere egg. The white wrapper on both sides tore easily. Nik extracted two slices from the middle, then moved the loaf aside.

Sara stared, fascinated by the size of the loaf. She nodded toward the refrigerator. By her own cursory inventory, she had seen that there were a great many leftovers stored there. "Isn't that an awful lot of food for just one woman?"

Nik took a bite out of the bread before answering, feeling as if he was making an offering before a fire god. He managed a smile, thinking of Harriet and the work she did.

"Harriet has a large family." That was the way she regarded anyone in need, as her brother or sister, Nik thought. There was a lot to be said for that sort of generosity. He did his own small part by throwing open his kitchen to her. He hated seeing food wasted.

Sara opened her mouth, but Nik wasn't in the mood to answer more questions. "Actually, she collects food from local restaurants and supermarkets to take up to the homeless mission in Orange. She's usually here at nine." He took another bite of the bread for good measure and debated making a sandwich. "I should have realized you weren't her."

For one thing, from that angle Harriet didn't look nearly as firm as Sara appeared to be, but he decided against making the comparison out loud.

Nik glanced at his watch. It was only a few minutes past eight. "What are you doing here so early, anyway? You don't have to be here before ten."

He sounded as if he was annoyed with her, she thought. He was acting like someone who'd caught a poacher on his land. She wondered if he actually regarded this as his little kingdom.

Nik had surprised her before she'd had a chance to fix anything. Now Sara helped herself to a slice of bread, then proceeded to tear little holes out of the middle as she ate.

"I thought I'd get an early start. Okay with you?" She raised large brown eyes to his face, waiting.

He shrugged. "Fine with me." Nik watched as Sara wadded up the small pieces and popped them into her mouth. It was almost sacrilegious. He resisted the temptation to take the bread out of her hand. "Who taught you how to eat? A sparrow?"

She popped another piece into her mouth before answering, then raised her chin, as if daring him to take a swipe. Her eyes laughed at his seriousness. "Big Bird, why?"

He moved the loaf back onto the butcher-block top. It hit the row of toasters, rattling them. "You can't savor it if you eat like that."

Sara stared at the slice in her hand. By now it was only a crusty frame surrounding a white-rimmed hole. "This is white bread, not escargot." As if to reinforce her point she held the bread up, dangling it before him.

This time Nik *did* take it from her, and then tossed the crust into the garbage. "Doesn't matter. All food should be enjoyed, or what's the point?"

Her slender shoulders rose and then fell in a careless shrug. She wondered if Brom had neglected to tell her that his brother-in-law was some sort of a fanatic.

"I don't know." She'd never been much for frequenting fancy restaurants and stuffing herself on rich, overpriced food. Sandwiches and Twinkies were fine with her, washed down with soda pop. "Fuel? Survival?"

Nik didn't care for either of the two choices she offered. The sigh he emitted hissed through his teeth as his hand clamped down on her wrist when she reached for another slice of bread. Their eyes held for a minute, hers defiant and amused as she waited.

"Have you had breakfast yet?"

"No, that's what I thought I was doing now." Her eyes indicated the imprisoned hand. When he followed her gaze, she wiggled the slice of bread she was still holding. "You can take it out of my pay."

Nik released her wrist. It was going to be a challenge working with this woman and not wrapping his hands around her long, slender neck. He looked at it now, letting the image play across his mind.

"Sit down." Nik motioned toward one of the stools that were tucked under a long counter on the side of the room. When work was hectic, some of the employees took their meals here. "I'll cook it for you."

Before Sara could say anything, Nik walked into the refrigerator. A moment later he emerged with a large bowl filled to the brim with eggs. He placed it near the closest stove.

Sara remained standing where she was. She didn't much care for being motioned off anywhere like a lowly servant. "Don't bother." Sara reached around Nik's side toward the pile of eggs in the bowl. "I can—"

For the second time in five minutes Nik caught her wrist. This time his grasp was firmer. He felt her pulse jump under his thumb. It made him wonder why. Maybe she was girding up for a battle. "You told me yesterday that you don't cook."

It figured he'd remember that. Sara shrugged, annoyed. She could certainly manage beating up two eggs, for heaven's sake. "I don't, but—"

Nik caught up the last word. "*But* I'd rather not see this kitchen in a mess before I even start."

Amusement was the best way to handle this bear, she decided. As if in surrender, she raised her hands in the air, away from any utensils or ingredients. "Wanna make your own mess, huh?"

He didn't particularly like being laughed at, not when he felt as if his neck was going to snap off and his stomach was the scene of an intense inferno. "Santangelo, go chew on an abacus until I'm finished."

Exasperated, he banged down the metal pan that was shiny despite years of use and pulled open a drawer beneath the butcher-block table.

"Are you always this charming first thing in the morning?" Sara watched him almost snap off the top of the antacid bottle and shake out two tablets. They bounced from his hand and landed on the table.

He reached for the tablets. Sara beat him to it. He raised a warning brow. "No, usually I'm worse. Just ask Jennifer."

Smiling sweetly, Sara offered up the prize, pouring the two tablets from the palm of her hand into his. "Don't tell me I'm giving you heartburn."

"No." He threw the two tablets into his mouth and chewed with a vengeance, wishing they could act instantly. Or, at the very least, make *her* disappear. "The two aspirin I took this morning beat you to that." *This time.*

"Aspirin? You have a fever?" Sara placed her palm to his forehead.

Nik moved his head aside. He didn't quite like the fact that her hand felt soothing. The rest of her certainly wasn't.

"No, a pain in my neck." He saw the slight flash of annoyance in her eye. "Literally." Without meaning to, he ran his hand along the back of his neck and winced slightly. "All the aspirin did was give me a burning sensation in my stomach." He turned back to the pan. "Now, if you're finished taking inventory—"

Sara had stopped listening. Instead, she circled behind him. Nik felt as if he was being stalked. Before he could ask her what she thought she was doing, Sara was standing on her toes, placing her long fingers on either side of his neck.

She probed, her fingers surprisingly sturdy. "Here? Does it hurt here?"

He tried to move aside, but he couldn't. Sara was holding him in place. "I'm paying you to be an accountant, not a masseuse."

The man was a mule. She took a deep breath and discovered that his cologne created a very pleasing sensation, conjuring up all sorts of warm, sensual images within her. Probably essence of paprika mixed with equal parts onion powder, she mused.

Her hands remained firmly in place despite his attempt to shrug her off. "You're not getting a masseuse. This is something I learned from a chiropractor in New York."

Nik opened his mouth to protest being a guinea pig for her experiments when suddenly there was a sickening, crunching noise. It came from his neck. "Oh, God."

Miraculously, his pain was gone.

Nik took a slow, tentative breath, as if to test whether his head was still connected to the rest of him or had fallen off somewhere. He turned to look at her, his expression incredulous.

"The pain's gone."

Sara tried not to appear too smug, but lost the fight. She slipped back onto the stool. "Yes, I know. Works every time. *Now* I feel like I've earned my breakfast."

He stood a moment, flexing his muscles uncertainly, as if he expected something to pop off. What, he wasn't sure. "You do this often?"

She shook her head. "Not that many people I know get pains in their neck."

He eyed her for a moment. "I find that hard to believe." He had a few more choice things to add, but he swallowed them. He was best at just cooking, and decided to concentrate on that exclusively for the time being.

Sara watched, fascinated despite herself, as Nik created an omelet for her. His fingers seemed to fly from dicing ingredients on the chopping block to the frying pan and back again. Bits of ham, green pepper and what appeared to be three kinds of cheese, not to mention things that flew out in an array of interesting colors from containers on the spice rack, all met and melded on the sizzling pan in an edible rainbow.

Sara crossed her arms in front of her. It was a little like watching an artist create a masterpiece. Or, more appropriately like a magician conjuring something out of nothing.

Holding a corner of the plate through a towel he had picked up, Nik placed the dish before her. "There. Breakfast." He took silverware from the same drawer where he kept his antacids. He handed the knife and fork to her.

The omelet was huge. There was no way she could ever manage to finish it on her own.

"Aren't you going to join me?" She cocked her head as she looked at him. "This is way too big for me."

Getting off the stool, she opened the drawer he had just shut and took out another set of utensils. She offered them up to Nik.

He regarded the knife and fork uncertainly. He had a dozen details to see to before the restaurant was open for business. Details he liked attending to himself. He didn't have time to share a meal with a woman he found as annoying as he found attractive.

"I, um . . ."

The utensils remained aloft. A smile curved her mouth. "Or did you manage to poison this somehow when I wasn't watching?"

He took the knife and fork from her and sat down, even though he'd had no intentions of doing either. "Of course it isn't poisoned."

She smiled wider, wondering if he even knew that he was sitting down. "Then there's no reason not to join me, is there?" She bent closer, her body suddenly very much in his space. "Unless you don't like the company."

Hot chocolate. Her eyes definitely reminded him of hot chocolate. That hot chocolate had been his favorite drink as a child seemed oddly disconcerting to him right now. "I'm not sure exactly *how* I feel about the company."

The answer pleased her. "Good. I've never liked being thought of as predictable." She tossed her head. The large hoops at her ears swung back and forth. "It's far too stifling." She scanned the length of the spice rack. "Have any hot sauce handy?"

He did, but he wasn't about to let her commit the ultimate sin by splashing his creation with a fiery red wave. "My omelet doesn't need any hot sauce."

No ego problem here. Resigned, Sara took a bite. It was like a warm surprise on her tongue, tangy and flavorful and light. She looked at Nik and saw that he was watching her reaction. She decided to play it straight. "This is good."

He relaxed a little. No matter how long he went on cooking, Nik knew that people's opinions would always matter to him. And one unfavorable critique canceled out a dozen praises the way a single swipe of a hatchet could cut down a year's worth of growth for a sapling.

He cut himself a piece of the omelet. "Of course it is."

She grinned as Nik swallowed. "No one's ever going to accuse you of allowing a rampant case of modesty to get in your way."

Nik was about to put her in her place when Sam looked in. The old man pursed his lips as he regarded the two of them at the counter. "I see you found her."

There would have been absolutely no way to have missed her, Nik thought. "Yes, I did."

Sam pulled on his chin. Day-old white bristles poked out all along the bottom half of his face, pointy and sharp like the spines of a bristled porcupine.

"It was okay, my letting her in, then?" Sam yanked a little more on his chin as he looked uncertainly at Nik from beneath shaggy brows.

Nik was suddenly reluctant to give his tacit approval. He didn't want Sara's early-morning appearance to become a habit. He had no intentions of sharing breakfast with her every day. This was the time of day when tranquillity was supposed to reign supreme and he was allowed to enjoy his domain in peace and quiet. Still, he didn't want to make Sam feel as if he'd done something wrong, either. Sam tended to be on the sensitive side.

"Frankly, Sam, I don't quite see how you could have stopped her."

Sam took that to be a yes. He nodded his head toward the rear of the building. "I just come to tell you that Ms. Harriet's here."

Nik placed his fork next to the plate and rose. "All right, tell her that I set the breads aside for her in the back office. Everything else is in the walk-in. I'll help her out to the van with it when she's ready."

Given the choice of the omelet or following Nik, Sara opted to satisfy her curiosity. She was off her stool and had caught up to Nik in a few quick strides.

"Do you do this every day?" He looked at her, confused. Was she talking about breakfast? "Give away food?" she clarified.

Nik opened the walk-in and left it that way. He moved to the rear and felt the temperature drop. "Yes."

Sara nodded her approval. "Good thinking. It's a hell of a write-off."

Was that what she thought? That he was doing it for tax reasons? Was she the type of person who only did something if it benefited her? Nik had never cared for self-serving people. And he definitely didn't care for being thought of in that light.

"I don't do this for a write-off."

The annoyance in his voice didn't stop her. Sara didn't know exactly why, but somehow she'd known he was going to say that. And she was glad he had. "Charitable impulses?"

He pulled out a large cardboard box filled with yesterday's pastries. Let them eat cake, he thought cryptically. But there were more substantial items to accompany the pastries, and everyone should be allowed to indulge a sweet tooth once in a while.

"I don't like anyone to go hungry, even if they can't leave a sizable tip at the end of the meal." He fairly growled out the words, not enjoying having his motives examined under a microscope. He gestured toward the counter. "Don't you have an omelet to finish?"

There was a distinct edge to his voice. Maybe she'd satisfy her curiosity about Harri and the mission food another day. Giving Nik a smart salute, she retreated. "Yes, I certainly do."

The pain in his neck was gone, Nik thought as he turned his back on Sara, but the one in another region of his body was obviously just beginning.

"You look like you've been dumped right in the middle of a blizzard."

With a page in each hand, Sara looked up to see who was addressing her. There were columns and scribbled entries dancing in her head.

Jennifer was on the other side of the room with Katie. They looked as if they had been there for a while. Sara hadn't even heard them come in or walk by her.

She dropped the papers on the desk. "How long have you been here?"

Jennifer grinned as she finished fixing Katie's braid, which had come undone. "Oh, long enough to hear you mumbling to yourself about the messes some people got themselves into."

Sara flushed, wondering if Jennifer had taken offense. "That long, huh? I didn't mean that the way it sounded." She looked down at the multicolored folders spread out all over her desk. There were many more housed within the top two drawers of the file cabinet. "It's just that this has got to be the most creative accounting system I've ever seen outside of a courtroom."

Jennifer picked up a file. She knew exactly how Sara felt. "Most of this is Nik's own way of keeping track. Once a month Julia used to sit down and try to make heads or tails of his system. After she left, I got the wonderful task."

She flipped open the file and took a deep breath. It wasn't fair to have Sara tackling this all on her own right from the start. It would take hours to unscramble Nik's notations. "I could sit down and—"

Ginger popped her head into the office, glancing at Sara curiously. "Jennifer, Mrs. Lorenzo's on line one about tomorrow's dinner party." She grinned at Sara. "Hi, I'm Ginger. You're new."

"Yes, I know." Sara laughed.

Jennifer glanced toward the telephone. She couldn't wait until the Lorenzo catering job was behind her. Mrs. Lorenzo called on a daily basis to change her mind about every detail. "Sara's here to reconstruct everything on those discs Nik blew up."

Ginger looked at Sara sympathetically. "Lots of luck." Ginger pointed toward the telephone. "Line one," she reminded Jennifer, then ducked out again.

Katie reached for the telephone. Jennifer just managed to place her hand on the receiver first. Jennifer looked at Sara apologetically.

"That's all right," Sara assured her. She'd been at this for over three hours now and was actually making some headway. "I think I can probably work my way backward from some of the older files and data discs."

As Jennifer picked up the receiver, Sara dug in again.

Twenty minutes later Jennifer hung up. Before her was a rather extensive list of last-minute changes that Mrs. Lorenzo had requested for her fiftieth wedding anniversary party. Jennifer's ear felt flattened. Mrs. Lorenzo had changed her mind about the main course. Again. And there were more waitresses to recruit now. Mrs. Lorenzo had informed her that twenty more people were being invited. She had calls to make and people to see. Still, Jennifer felt guilty about leaving Sara to cope with this paper storm all on her own.

Torn, Jennifer glanced toward the doorway and saw Nik standing there with a tray. Silently Jennifer moved toward her daughter and watched the scene unfold.

It was obvious to Jennifer that Sara was oblivious to Nik's presence as she sat, making notes on a large yellow pad. The woman appeared to be valiantly attempting to arrange the different files into piles that could be cross-referenced between inventory and accounting.

And it was just as obvious that Nik felt awkward about what he was doing. He had a determined set to his jaw that made him look as if he was about to enter a boxing ring.

Nik slid the tray onto the desk, nudging aside several folders. One opened and fell to the floor, a flurry of papers hitting the beige carpet.

Sara looked up, surprised. "You trying to make this job impossible?" With a sigh she bent to pick up the papers.

Nik joined her on the floor. With a swipe of his hands he collected all the sheets in a single, jumbled mess. "Don't get smart. That was an accident." He deposited the papers on the desk. Sara debated throwing them into the trash, then calmed down.

"I just brought you something to eat," he muttered needlessly.

There was a salad, a cup of coffee and, as she lifted the lid on the center dish, a succulent offering of sliced lamb with baby carrots and baby peas. She replaced the lid. "What, no dessert?"

He lifted a brow. "Sugar tends to make you sluggish in the long run."

"Never happen," she assured him. She nodded at the tray, curious. "Isn't this service a little above and beyond the call of duty?"

He didn't want her making more out of it than it was. If he was being honest with himself he wasn't sure what had prompted him to throw together a tray for Sara when he'd realized that she hadn't come in for anything to eat. It certainly wasn't because she looked as if she needed someone to take care of her.

Nik was already edging his way out of the room. "Just eat. You haven't taken a break or eaten anything since you sat down here after breakfast."

Jennifer hurried after her brother, catching his arm just as he moved beyond the door. "And since when do you notice when someone takes a break, unless they happen to be standing right next to you? Or in one of your pots? You're oblivious to everything that isn't on a spice rack."

He shrugged off her hand. "I notice a lot more than you think."

Jennifer leaned against the wall as she crossed her arms in front of her. Well, well, well. Maybe she'd better call Julia and get a little more information about their new employee. It had been a long time since Nik had shown an interest in a woman.

"Apparently," she murmured.

Nik saw the look that rose in Jennifer's eyes. He didn't have to stay and take this. He turned and headed toward the kitchen. His soufflé was almost ready. "I've got work to do, Jennifer."

"It's about time, Nik," she called after him.

He heard the grin in her voice. Nik turned just as he reached the kitchen, his hand on the swinging door. He knew he was going to regret asking. "About time for what?"

Jennifer laughed as she relished the scene. She anticipated Kane's expression tonight when she told him that the immovable object was finally being moved.

"Now that part's up to you, brother, dear. Just remember—" she eyed the office door behind her "—don't drag your feet."

Nik scowled. "Try to do something nice for someone and it gets blown out of proportion."

"If you say so." Jennifer's expression told Nik that she wasn't buying his protest.

He waved at his younger sister, dismissing her. "Go to work, Jennifer."

Jennifer laughed as she turned to reenter the office. At the last moment she looked over her shoulder. "You, too, Nik. You, too."

She heard Nik muttering under his breath as he walked into the kitchen.

Chapter 4

The noise level in the kitchen had decreased a while ago as activity wound down. Most of the staff had already gone home. Nik looked over toward the large clock that hung on the wall near the rear exit. Ten-thirty. He had put in a four-teen-and-a-half-hour day. He was bone tired. It was time to call it a night.

He looked around for Antonio. Nik saw the silver-gray mane bent forward as the older man sat on a stool, entertaining one of the waitresses with a story. He was like an old fox, Nik thought, amused, always eyeing the young chickens wistfully. Antonio had been with him at Sinclair's almost from the beginning and everyone knew he was harmless.

Nik crossed over to him as he untied his apron. "Want to lock up for me tonight?"

He dropped the apron into the side bin, where all the day's laundry was collected. The waitress flashed an inviting smile at Nik, then sensibly departed, leaving the two men to talk.

Antonio remained seated on his stool. He regarded his former protégé with keen interest. "Getting old, eh, Nikolas?"

Antonio laughed, his booming voice rattling around the kitchen. He leaned around Nik's body to get a better view of the departing waitress before the door swung shut on her. Then, looking up at Nik, he patted the stool next to him.

Antonio Rossi was well into his sixties. He had started out as a busboy in an exclusive hotel in Naples at the age of ten. There he had worked diligently under the tutelage of his maternal uncle. Eventually he was running the kitchen at the same hotel. At thirty, his talents took him to America. He was the best backup chef Nik could have wished for.

Nik glanced at the empty stool, then decided that if he sat down now, he'd never have the strength to get up again. "I'll never be as young as you, Tony."

Nik turned to leave, but Antonio held up one finger, stopping Nik as he dug into his back pocket with the other hand.

"Wait." Rising, he pulled out his wallet. The cracked brown leather case was thick with photographs. "Did I show you the new picture of my granddaughter?"

Nik laughed and shook his head. Antonio had five children and twice as many grandchildren. And everyone at Sinclair's knew them by sight, thanks to Antonio's ever-present wad of photographs.

"No," Nik answered. Antonio began riffling through his wallet. "Not in the last fifteen minutes."

The broad shoulders, which appeared far too wide for his frame, shrugged as Antonio stuffed the wallet back into the recesses of his pocket. "When are you going to get pictures of your own, eh?"

Nik ran his hand over the back of his neck. He felt the knots that had been building up all day. "I've got pictures."

"Nieces." Antonio waved a dismissive hand in the air like a chess player pushing the pieces off a board. "They do not count."

Nik shook his head, amused. "You'd better not let Jennifer or Julia hear you saying that."

Too short to reach Nik's shoulders, Antonio wrapped a surprisingly strong arm around Nik's back.

"No offense to your lovely sisters or your charming nieces, but there is nothing like bouncing your own baby on your knee, Nik." A wide grin split the tanned face, spreading the well-groomed silver mustache. Tiny fringes of hair hung over teeth that were whiter than new-fallen snow as Antonio winked slyly. "Unless, of course, it is bouncing a pretty lady on your knee instead."

Antonio had enough energy for both of them. "You're a dirty old man, Tony."

Antonio looked pleased by the assessment. "Yes." He nodded his head as he hit his chest with one powerful fist. "But that is how I stay young."

His expression grew serious as he regarded Nik. "You work too hard, my friend, and do not let me work as much as I should." Antonio pushed the younger man toward the outer door, which led into the hallway. "Go, I take care of the kitchen for the last hour. Get some rest."

Rest. It sounded almost seductively alluring at this point. Nik nodded. He remembered muttering good-night as he left.

As the kitchen door closed behind him Nik looked down the darkened hall. He was surprised to see a beam of light pooling on the floor. It was coming from the small office. Jennifer and Katie had long since left the restaurant. Kane had come by on his way home from the precinct to pick up his wife and daughter. As for Sara, as far as he knew she had left at six. Or so he surmised. That meant the office was empty.

Curious, Nik walked down the hall and looked in. Sara was sitting hunched over the desk. Her shoes had been kicked off to the side and her bare feet were curled up against one another like two woodland creatures huddling for warmth. She was moving the toe of one against the sole of the other as she concentrated on the screen. It constituted the only movement going on in the room. Sara had her head propped up on one fisted hand and she seemed totally engrossed in the spreadsheet she had typed in on the computer.

Nik knew he should just walk away. It was late and he was asking for trouble. But he leaned his shoulder against the doorjamb and just watched her for a moment, fascinated by what he saw. Only a single lamp illuminated the room. The beam gently played across her features, dusting them with shadows and lights, making them seem soft. Sara looked totally unanimated and utterly docile. And almost sweet. Nik felt something stir, something very basic and strong.

It took him completely unaware.

He straightened, squared his shoulders as if a battle cry had silently sounded, then walked into the room. "Don't you have a home to go to?"

Sara turned to look in Nik's direction. She seemed so unfazed by his entrance it was as if she had been expecting him all along.

She thought of the house on Avalone Drive. And of her father. "Not really."

Nik's brows drew together as he plucked a fragment of a conversation from his memory. Had he misheard? "I thought you said you were staying with your father."

Sara sat up in her chair. Lacing her fingers together over her head, she stretched, flexing her body like a graceful cat trying to warm herself on all sides by the fire. Nik tried not to notice that her breasts were straining invitingly against the thin fabric of her sweater. Maybe he wasn't as dead tired as he'd thought.

She let her hands drop bonelessly to the desk. "I am."

Had he lost the thread of the conversation somehow? Didn't that mean she had a home to go to? "Then...?" He let his voice trail off as he waited for her to explain.

A quirky smile lifted her lips. "Doesn't necessarily make it a home, does it?"

Nik detected the defensive note in her voice and saw a similar look in her eyes before her expression melded into an amused look.

"I could ask you the same question, you know. It's what?" She twisted her wrist to get a better look at her watch. "Ten-forty. You've been here a long time."

She probably enjoyed arguing more than she enjoyed breathing, he thought. Nik decided to oblige her. He rested a hip against the corner of her desk. "I own the place. What's your excuse?"

"I won't be here tomorrow, remember? I thought I'd do as much as I could. Besides—" She pushed away from the desk. Suddenly he seemed to be crowding into her space, and she needed air. "I found your creative bookkeeping utterly fascinating."

He crossed his arms in front of his chest and tried to get at the gist of her meaning. "Creative bookkeeping is a term usually reserved for people serving five to seven in Folsom."

The sound of her laughter drifted to his ears like snowflakes from the sky. "I didn't mean to make it sound as if I suspected you of having two sets of books." She tapped the closest file. "One set like this would be hard enough to come up with."

She looked at the sea of folders on the floor that she'd already gone through. A myriad of others fanned out across the desk. More waited within the metal cabinet drawers. She repressed a shudder. "Does the word organization mean anything to you?"

Nik had never reacted well to criticism. Now was no exception. He lifted a brow. "The restaurant is organized. It's just the paperwork that isn't."

"Now there's an understatement." She sighed, stretching again. She *was* tired. Lifting her head, Sara saw the way his eyes were gliding over her, and felt a warm shiver weave through. She was flattered. And just the tiniest bit on guard. "You're watching me."

"Sorry." Caught, he made no effort to look away. "You're the only thing in the room that's moving."

She let out another sigh and leaned over the keyboard. Pressing a combination of keys, she stored the material she had spent hours inputting. When she returned, she was going to have to look into getting all this set up differently. What Nik had, working from the old disks that remained and an old copy of the software program, was far too cumbersome.

Hitting the last key with a flourish, she leaned back. "I guess I've slaved enough for one day." She switched off the machine, then looked up at Nik. "You've gotten your pound of flesh."

He didn't care for the insinuation. "I didn't ask for a pound of flesh," he reminded her. "I just asked for competence."

Saying thank-you probably would have killed him, she thought. Sara shrugged nonchalantly. "Consider it a bonus."

He still had no idea why she had come in so early or why she had stayed so late. As he'd said, it wasn't her restaurant. And the pay was good, but she wasn't working to impress him so that he would give her a raise. They both knew this arrangement was temporary.

The woman was a complete enigma.

Sara had told him the truth, but only in part. She'd stayed longer because his way of keeping records had been unorthodox and haphazard at best and it was a challenge to get things organized. She enjoyed challenges. But that wasn't the only reason she'd stayed here hours longer than she should have. She wanted something to occupy her mind. Something to keep her busy and to keep all thoughts of her father and tomorrow at bay. She didn't want to think about tomorrow. Not tomorrow or all the yesterdays that had been missed. She really didn't want to think about her father at all.

She suddenly realized that he wasn't wearing his apron. "You going home?" He nodded. She moved aside several files on the floor and opened the bottom drawer, where she'd tossed in her purse. It was time for her to go, too. She couldn't very well sleep here. "I guess I've made enough headway for one day."

Nik crossed to the doorway. He was about to leave, but something was holding him back. He looked over his shoulder at her and heard himself saying something he'd no idea he was going to say until the words came out. "Buy you a cup of coffee?"

White teeth flashed in a grin that was just the slightest bit off center. "Seeing as how you own the restaurant, that's mighty big of you."

He wondered if there was someone special in her life and if there was, how the man put up with her. "Do you ever give it a rest?"

Sara grinned even more broadly in response. Maybe he was right. She was sparring just a wee bit too much, even for her.

She ran her fingers through her cropped hair and laughed. "Sometimes." She turned her face up to his, amusement highlighted there at his expense. "Yes, I'd love a cup of coffee." Her eyes fluttered shut for a second as she envisioned the hot liquid winding down her throat and the heat pouring through her veins. "Warm and creamy and rich."

She made drinking a cup of coffee sound erotic. For a second, just for a second, he was tempted to touch her face, to let his fingers slide down her cheek and vicariously share the experience with her.

Nik fell back on the only thing he knew well. "I thought you didn't care for food."

Sara opened her eyes. "Coffee's not food, it's a religion. I couldn't live without it." Grabbing the straps of her purse, she lifted it from the drawer and followed him out the door. "Got any cappuccino?"

Because it was late and she was new, he decided not to be insulted by the question. "Yes, we have cappuccino. Since you're such a coffee aficionado, I'll give you a choice. Sinclair's has ten different kinds of coffee to choose from."

Without thinking she linked her arm through his and laughed, her hair brushing lightly against his chest. The skin underneath his shirt tingled. He thought maybe it was the fabric softener he'd used with the last wash. "Ten? I think I may be in love with you."

The word echoed and vibrated inside him, startling Nik into silence. He began to wonder who this woman was and what she really thought. He had a feeling that there were layers here that needed to be peeled back before he had his answer.

When Nik and Sara walked into the kitchen Antonio looked up, surprised. He set the large pot he was holding down on the table as his eyes narrowed. "I thought I told you to go home."

Nik nodded at Sara. He saw the way Antonio's eyes slid appreciatively up and down Sara's well-rounded, diminutive frame. Lucky thing Antonio was a family man, he thought.

"Our newest employee wants some coffee," Nik explained.

"Temporary employee," she interjected. Dropping her hand away from Nik, she moved toward Antonio. She shook his hand warmly, both her small hands covering his. "Hi, I'm Sara Santangelo."

Antonio's face lit up. He knew it. "Ah, Italian."

And so was he, she guessed, by the look of him. "Half," she corrected.

Antonio was unabashedly prejudiced. He kissed his fingers, then spread them wide, as if the kiss had suddenly taken wing and sprung up away from them. "Always the best half."

Nik turned to Sara just then and saw that her cheeks were flushed, not in embarrassment—he didn't think her capable of that—but in fleeting annoyance. Why? He found himself wanting to unravel the riddle that she was beginning to represent.

Rather than recite the different types of coffee he had available, Nik picked up a menu that was lying on the side. One of the waitresses had brought it in. There was a small rip on one of the pages, which meant it was to be discarded. Nik liked things to be as perfect as humanly possible.

He handed the menu to Sara and pointed to the last page. He heard her anticipatory sigh.

"Mocha mint with whipped cream sounds heavenly."

"Mocha mint it is." Nik turned to where the well-polished row of coffee machines stood in the rear of the room like a vanguard of gleaming knights. They could produce five hundred cups of coffee at will.

Antonio grabbed Nik's sleeve. "You go outside with the pretty lady. I fix the coffee. Go." He was all but shooing Nik out of the room the way a farmer's wife shooed away an aggressive chicken in the barnyard.

Nik could see exactly what was on Antonio's mind, but this was no time to get in a discussion over it. Instead, he took Sara's arm and urged her toward the inner door that led back into the dining room.

She looked at the old man as he began to prepare two cups. "Does he order you around like that often?"

Nik smiled. "When I first started out, Antonio was working for an exclusive restaurant in Beverly Hills. I was his apprentice chef. All thumbs and eager to learn, with two kid sisters to provide for."

Sara heard the affection in his voice and it warmed her without her realizing it.

"He showed me the ropes. Stayed after hours to teach me things you don't pick up in cookbooks. He didn't have to do that. When I got Sinclair's going, I asked him to come work for me." Nik's mouth curved fondly as he looked over his shoulder at the other man's back. "He still thinks of me as that kid he took under his wing. No harm in that. The way I figure it, I owe him."

Nik led Sara to a secluded booth in the main dining room. There were only a handful of couples left, all lingering over their desserts or after-dinner drinks, moved by the company and the atmosphere.

It all seemed suddenly and uncomfortably intimate to Sara. She wasn't used to feeling vulnerable anymore. It was probably just because she was tired, she thought. Just tired.

She slid into the booth and waited until Nik sat across from her.

Now what? she wondered, nerves jumping through her like beads of water on a hot skillet.

She looked toward the door that separated the dining room from the kitchen, hoping that Antonio would come out with the coffee soon. When she turned back toward Nik she saw that he was studying her. The beads of water jumped higher on the skillet. This wasn't a good idea.

Sara started to rise. "Maybe I should just—"

For the third time that day Nik caught her wrist in his hand. It was getting to be a habit, he thought. And not a totally unpleasant one as far as habits went. Her skin was silky soft and her hand felt almost frail in his. Deceptive packaging. He found himself wanting her to stay, although God only knew why.

"What's your hurry?"

"Nothing." She pulled her hand away, not wanting the contact because it was too easy to let it happen. "It's just that I—"

She thought of the house, of her father possibly waiting up for her. By some standards it was still early. She hoped he'd given up and gone to bed. She was less in the mood to talk tonight than she had been this morning.

Sara shrugged and forced herself to settle back in the booth. "No, no hurry at all." She saw the kitchen door open and almost sighed with relief. "Ah, Antonio. You're a lifesaver."

Nik had the feeling she was a lot more serious than her smile let on. What was she afraid of? He certainly had no designs on her and even if he had, what could he do in a public place?

The older man beamed as he set down the two cups of coffee and bowed with a flourish. He moved the small cup filled with pitch-black liquid in front of Nik and a masterpiece of froth and sculpted foam before Sara.

"Your mocha mint, *signorina*."

"Sara," she prompted with what Antonio thought was a beatific smile. "Thank you."

She took a sip and sighed. It *was* heavenly.

Antonio took his leave, looking well pleased with himself. He winked conspiratorially at Nik as he passed him. Nik pretended not to see.

Toying with his espresso, Nik watched Sara. She appeared enraptured by the drink. He enjoyed seeing someone savor something so much. He wondered if she took the same delight in a really good meal. And if she brought her gusto to bed with her, as well.

Sara raised her eyes to his. "You're watching me again, and I'm not moving this time."

Nik leaned back, his hands bracketing the small cup of espresso between them on the table. Who was she? "You always throw that term around so easily?"

He'd completely and effectively lost her. She cocked her head and stared at him. "What term?"

He was thinking back to her declaration when he told her of the number of coffees the restaurant habitually carried. "Love." He sat, waiting.

The word, when he said it, brought a small chill to her as it danced along her shoulder blades and down her spine. She shrugged, taking another slow, appreciative sip before answering. "Sure. It's the easiest word in the world to say."

Sara leaned over the table and looked up into Nik's eyes. In the dim light it was hard to discern the color. But not the power. She could feel his strength even now. Anticipation hummed through her like the plucked strings of a harp. She ignored it.

"I love you," she whispered. The words spilled out into the darkness like a velvety liqueur amorously coating the sides of a glass. And then she shrugged carelessly, settling back. "See? Easy. Nobody means it."

He'd felt something tighten within him like a wound-up coil when she'd looked into his eyes and whispered the phrase. He knew it was utterly ridiculous, but for the space of that one moment it was as if he was gazing into a crystal ball and looking into the future. He didn't believe in premonitions.

And yet—

Nik mentally shook himself free of the mood.

He didn't like the fact that she seemed to take such a dim view of love. He'd never really been in love himself. There'd never been time. But he had hopes that, someday, love would find him. Everyone needed love.

"What makes you so sure?"

She was letting the atmosphere get to her, she thought. She was feeling oddly unarmed right about now.

"What? That no one means it?" She thought of her parents, of what her mother had told her. *Don't trust anyone, Sara. Men lie just to get their way.* "Maybe they do, when they say it, for about three and a half seconds. After that—" Sara snapped her fingers "—it's gone, and with it, any obligations that might have been created by that declaration of love." *Like a father abandoning a child.*

It was too harsh a philosophy for someone as young as she was. "How old are you, Sara?"

Why was he playing twenty questions at this hour? "It's on that employee form you had me fill out." She paused. She could see he was waiting for her to answer.

Maybe he hadn't looked at the form. "Twenty-eight."

At twenty-eight he had buried two parents and had the world on his shoulders. Even so, he had never felt this cynical. "That seems awfully young to take such a dark view of life."

She didn't like being analyzed. Sara raised her head defensively. "You'd be surprised." She looked down into her cup. It was almost empty. "Besides, I don't take a dark view of life. I just see it as it is. That's why I try to enjoy myself when I can." She tilted the cup and watched the few remaining drops coat the bottom. Her mouth curved in a half smile. "This is a cup of coffee, not a dry martini, Sinclair. Why are you playing bartender and looking for confessions?"

"I wasn't aware that I was." He moved back slightly, giving her room. "I thought I was making conversation."

Who had hurt her? he wondered. Had there been some man in her life who had made her so cynical? Had someone walked out on her? Or worse, stayed long enough to trample all her dreams?

The quirky smile was back. "You were asking questions. That's usually called prying."

The more she resisted, the more he felt he wanted to know. That in itself was unusual. Nik always gave people more than their share of space. "Only if you don't want to answer them."

Their eyes met and held. Sara knew that she didn't want him inside of her head. She gestured airily. "I rest my case."

At this point, he thought of just calling it a night. The conversation definitely wasn't going well. Yet, tired as he was, he was reluctant to relinquish her company. There was something about her that made him feel she needed someone to talk to, and he was the likeliest candidate around.

Nik decided a change in topic was in order. He stretched his legs out in front of him, still studying her. "So, you're going to be out tomorrow."

"Yes," she said slowly, wondering where this new line was going to lead.

"It's pretty unusual taking the second day at a job off." He watched the way the yellow flame from the candle on the table seemed to make love to her skin. The faint ache within him grew. Maybe he shouldn't have had the espresso after all. "What's so special about tomorrow?"

"Nothing. You're being a bartender again," she admonished, but this time she was smiling. Sara wished the topic didn't bother her so much. "My father's going in for surgery. He needs me to take him in, that's all."

Nik wasn't fooled by the indifferent tone of her voice. She was hiding emotions behind it. The tension was there in her shoulders. "Serious?"

Her father had told her what the doctor had said. That there was always the possibility of a heart attack while on the operating table. She distanced herself from the feelings that were pounding on the closed door of her heart with both fists. She didn't need this.

"Maybe. It's an angioplasty. He has a blocked artery." She looked away as her voice drifted off.

She was trying to appear nonchalant, but she wouldn't have dropped everything and flown here if she didn't think it was serious. Nik's heart went out to her. He remembered what it was like, walking down those long hospital corridors not once but twice, having to deal with the fact that one of his parents was slipping away from him. He remembered the impotent frustration raging within him because there was nothing he could do.

He stifled the urge to take her hand in his. "What time is the surgery?"

She shrugged, as if the detail was too inconsequential for her to remember clearly. Nik waited. "Ten," she mumbled, looking away.

At ten o'clock her father would be stripped of all defenses, facing a surgeon's scalpel. What if—

No, she didn't care. She didn't. What happened in his life was his business, not hers. He'd forfeited her caring about him when he walked out on her.

Nik watched in fascination as emotions played over her face like neon lights going off and on along a marquee. "Want some company while you're waiting?"

His question took her by surprise, cracking the tight shell of her thoughts. She swallowed. The last thing in the world she wanted was someone there with her, offering her pity.

She took a deep, fortifying breath. "Are you planning on burning down the restaurant tomorrow?"

Talk about something coming from left field. Nik looked at Sara as if she'd just lost her mind. "No."

"Then you'll be busy, won't you?" she pointed out briskly. "But thanks for the offer." Fidgeting inwardly, she began folding her napkin into fours. "I won't be hanging around the hospital, either, actually. I'm just going to drop him off and then go shopping or something."

Sara sounded as if she was talking about boarding a dog at a kennel, Nik thought. For a moment he was annoyed at her flippant attitude. But then he realized that it was all only a facade. She was having a great deal of trouble dealing with this. He could see it in her eyes.

Sara looked down and saw that she was wadding the napkin into a ball. Carefully she laid it on the table and smoothed it out with the palm of her hand.

"California has some of the best malls in the country." If her tone was stretched any further to sound cheerful, it was going to crack right down the middle. Her eyes shifted to his, daring him to take exception. "Maybe I'll even drop by here later and work on the mess you left."

Before he could say anything, Sara rose abruptly. "Thanks for the coffee, boss. I'll see you the day after to-morrow."

And with that she quickly walked away from the table and toward the front door.

Nik sat, silently watching her as she left. Was she as brash as she let on? He shook his head. He knew the answer to that before the question had even posed itself to him. Nik knew hurt when he saw it. He'd lived through it more than once himself. Sometimes building up walls around yourself was the only way to deal with it.

But walls, he knew, kept you in as well as kept every-thing else out. He didn't think she was the type who wanted to remain in prison indefinitely.

Chapter 5

The second night was even worse than the first had been. Sara woke up every half hour as if there was some sort of inner alarm clock ticking off the minutes within her. Each time her eyes opened, thoughts of the pending surgery would explode on her brain, haunting her. She tried to ignore it, reminding herself that she didn't care about her father anymore. He was just another human being on this planet. It didn't help.

At five she gave up all attempts at getting any additional restful sleep. Her father had to be at the hospital in less than two hours, so she might as well get up.

More dead than alive, Sara dragged herself to the bathroom, hoping that a shower might help restore some of her depleted energy. The blast of cold water that came out of the shower head when she turned the faucet toward *H* gave her an instant headache. It reinforced the tension that was throbbing in her temples like a bugle corps practicing for a recital.

The edginess within her was building. Sara tried to busy herself with the mechanics of getting ready, struggling to hold a tight rein on her thoughts. As she hurried, she found that she seemed to be all thumbs this morning. Sara shook her head disparagingly. It figured.

She was desperate for a cup of coffee and wanted to get into the kitchen to make one before her father was up. The doctor had forbidden him to have any food or liquids after midnight. Though she couldn't make herself forgive her father, it would be cruel to sit there drinking coffee in front of him when he had to abstain.

The hair dryer she was wielding with the kind of grace that a magician employed with his wand began to emit a tiny wisp of smoke. She saw it trail into the air as she glanced in the mirror. At the same time, an acrid smell assaulted her nostrils. The motor was burning out.

Muttering, Sara shut it off. She ran her fingers through her hair. It was still damp in places, but it would have to do. She sincerely doubted that her father owned a hair dryer.

She grabbed her purse from where she had hung it on the bedroom doorknob and, carrying her shoes in one hand, made her way into the kitchen, confident that she had time enough to make the coffee.

She was wrong.

Raymond Santangelo was in the kitchen, his back to the doorway. It brought back memories from Sara's childhood, when she would tiptoe downstairs early on a Saturday morning to find her father in the kitchen making breakfast for all of them. Her mother always liked to sleep in on the weekends.

Sara hesitated, fighting against giving in to the sentiments the memory created. She debated going back to her room. Her father turned around before she could make up her mind.

His wan face brightened immeasurably when he saw her. "You're up. Good morning, Sara."

He sounded so chipper, she thought, anyone would have thought that he was on his way to a picnic instead of a hospital operating room. Sara crossed stiffly over the threshold and walked into the kitchen. The room was too small and crammed to accommodate more than two people adequately. Sara felt almost claustrophobic being here with her father.

She nodded in response to his greeting. "Morning."

There was still a hundred miles between them, Raymond thought sadly, though his expression never hinted at the sorrow he felt. He gestured toward the coffeemaker. It was making spasmodic sounds as it used the last of the water to produce coffee. The pot was only one-quarter full. Just enough for one.

"I made you some coffee."

She remembered how much he always loved drinking coffee in the morning. It was he who had introduced her to her first cup during one of those early Saturday mornings they'd shared, sneaking it to her behind her mother's back. She'd been eight at the time.

Sara eyed the glass pot suspiciously. "You didn't have any—?"

He second-guessed her question. "Myself? No, some rules I can follow." He maintained a smile, though the edges appeared strained to her. "I'll just sit here and smell yours if you don't mind."

Raymond poured a mug full for her and placed it on the small kitchen table. Pulling out one of the two chairs, he sat down and waited for Sara to take the other seat.

Feeling awkward again, Sara lowered herself onto the chair slowly, as if she was trying to find the best way to sit on a keg of dynamite.

Raymond pushed the matching sugar bowl and creamer toward her on the table. Sara shook her head as she moved the mug closer.

It wasn't getting any easier facing him, she thought. She cupped her hands around the mug as if she was attempting to anchor herself to something real. If anything, it was getting harder each time she was alone with him. Her nerves were becoming more frayed.

In actuality, they were never really alone. There were always ghosts in the room with them. Ghosts and a myriad of jumbled emotions swirling within her, trying to storm through.

Her fingers tightened around the mug. There was anger—no, more than that. It was rage fibrillating through her, rage at having all her old feelings awakened. Time had numbed her a little. The years had worn away all the sharp edges. Seeing him, being here like this, honed those edges to razor-sharp points all over again. And they were pricking her.

If she'd realized it was going to be this bad, she wouldn't have come. Maybe she should leave now. Sara thought of the job she'd just undertaken. Unlike her father, she never left anything undone. She prided herself on always finishing what she started. She couldn't leave.

And what about Nik?

The unexpected question exploded within her brain, startling her. Where had that come from? Slightly unnerved, she pushed his image from her mind. Nik had no place in any of this, other than the fact that he owned the restaurant where she worked. It was just being here with her father that had thrown her so off balance, making her mind wander.

She looked down into the mug and watched the light from the fluorescent fixture overhead shimmer along the black liquid. There were so many things to say and no way to say them. So she sipped her coffee instead, and said nothing.

The liquid seeped through her and she pretended that it was helping to fortify her.

Raymond watched her expression, his own almost sadly hopeful. "Good?"

She set the mug down, but didn't release it. "Good."

He nodded toward the creamer and sugar bowl she had ignored. When he'd made that first cup of coffee for her all those years ago, it had been three quarters milk. "You take it black now."

She ran a fingertip over the mug's handle and realized that it had been glued together. There was a tiny crack where it had broken. Some things, even when fixed, were never like new again. "I don't like having my caffeine diluted."

She took another long sip and felt his eyes on her. It was as if he was trying to absorb her, as if by doing so, he could somehow make up for all those years he had let slip by.

Too late. You can't do that, Dad, she thought.

"I like mine the texture of motor oil in the morning."

His laugh bore only a faint resemblance to the loud, booming sound she recalled, the sound that used to make her feel so warm and secure.

"Then you're not disappointed." He didn't wait for her to say anything, as if afraid that if she did, it would negate the tenuous strands he was trying to work with, the ones he was desperately attempting to weave into a bridge that would span the chasm between them. "I always made the coffee at the precinct when I got in. Santangelo's sludge they called it." He smiled, remembering. "Among other things. But the pot was always empty by the time we went out on patrol."

He'd been a police officer when they lived in Tahoe. She remembered the time he had taken her for a ride in a squad car. She'd been so proud of him, so proud to be his daughter. Being a policeman was all he had ever known. Was he still a policeman? She realized that she didn't know. There was a whole segment of his life that was missing, that she had no idea about.

She looked at him through the warm mist hovering over her mug. "Are you retired now?"

"No." He leaned forward, eager to be engaged in any sort of a conversation with his daughter. "I'm on disability. But they're going to put me behind a desk when I finally get back."

He frowned. Behind a desk. It meant he was growing old, and he hated that. Part of his life had finally fallen into place, even after his second divorce, and then this had happened. He had tried to shrug off the weakness, the strange, nondescript numbness in his left shoulder. But he had made the mistake of mentioning it to one of the detectives. The next day he'd been forced to take a physical. The blockage in his left artery had been discovered then.

A desk job. Sara nodded, remembering how much her mother used to worry about her father returning home safely, even though Tahoe was a relatively peaceful place. "It's safer that way."

Sara saw something flicker in her father's eyes. An impotent anger. Passion filled his voice. Sara set down her mug and listened, compassion nudging at her though she tried to deny it.

"I didn't become a policeman to be safe, Sara, or to sit home and collect a pension after twenty years. I did it to make a difference. Punching keys isn't going to make a difference."

Instincts had her attempting to soothe him before she could stop herself. "Lots of ways to fight crime, Dad. Not everyone is Clint Eastwood." She realized what she was doing and emotionally backed away. "Even Eastwood's slowed down some."

The stillness returned and discomfort stirred again, like flies buzzing over fruit on a sticky July night. She searched for something more to say. "What precinct are you with?"

"Newport Beach."

His answer struck a chord. Jennifer had mentioned something about her husband being assigned to the Newport Beach precinct when she'd introduced him yesterday. "Do you know Detective Kane Madigan?"

Raymond looked at her in surprise. Madigan had been the detective who had recommended that he go in for his physical. But there was no reason to bring that up, especially if he was a friend of Sara's.

He looked longingly at the coffeepot, then forced himself to look away. Coffee wasn't what he needed now. A little luck was in order. Or maybe a lot of it.

"Yeah, I know him. Sharp guy." Raymond thought back to his impression of Kane when the detective first transferred to the precinct. "He was a real loner until about a couple of years ago."

Sara moved forward in her chair, interested. "What happened?"

"He got married." There was a framed photograph of the man's wife and daughter sitting on his desk these days. Madigan, who had never shown any emotions before. It had stirred a lot of comments. "I guess marriage changes some people."

Sara remembered what her mother had told her about her marriage. How life had gone from happiness to sorrow. Sara's eyes met her father's. "Yes, it does."

The mood was back, closing the temporary opening between them as if it hadn't, for a glimmer of a moment, been there at all.

Sara took a breath, then set aside her mug. It was empty. She pushed herself away from the table. She wanted to get this over with. More than that, she wanted to be somewhere else, away from here.

"Well, if you're ready, maybe we'd better get going." She started to rise, but something in her father's eyes stopped her. A wariness she wasn't prepared for. Whatever else her father had become, he had always been an unshakable rock. The man before her was far too mortal for her liking. "What?"

A strange, nervous smile played across his thin lips. He shrugged without being conscious of doing so.

"I don't know. Maybe I'm scared." He raised his eyes to hers. "Kind of funny, huh? I've been in some pretty hairy situations, been assigned to some precincts where every minute on patrol could have been my last and I never really turned a hair. I loved it." His tongue caressed the very words as he thought of his professional life, of living on the edge where he had to depend on his own instincts to help him survive. "The excitement, the uncertainty. The thrill of beating the odds and making it through another day. I loved it all."

On the streets he felt as if his fate was in his own hands. Now it was in the hands of some strange surgeon he'd met twice. He looked down at his hands, not really seeing them.

"And now I'm scared." He whispered the words.

For a fleeting moment the urge to comfort him was almost overwhelming. Sara wanted to put her arms around him and say it was going to be all right.

But she couldn't.

It was as if she was paralyzed, as if her emotions were immobilizing her, turning her to stone as surely as if hot lead had been poured all over her.

"Think of it as another challenge." Her voice sounded so brittle it made her cringe inside. And yet she couldn't help herself. "From what you've told me, the odds are in your favor this time. You'll make it through this, too."

It was the best she could do, but she couldn't shake the guilt, even though she told herself he didn't deserve more.

Raymond rose and nodded as he smiled at her. He hadn't wanted to fall apart like that. It was just that fear was gnawing holes in his resolve. "Thanks."

She lifted her shoulder and let it fall, blocking his simple gratitude. "C'mon, you don't want to be late." She forced what passed for a smile to her lips, though it felt pasted into place.

She desperately wanted to hate him, to cocoon herself in that overpowering emotion and be invulnerable to any and all feelings that were attempting to break through her ramparts. But hatred wouldn't come, wouldn't rise up no matter how much she attempted to summon it.

She couldn't hate, couldn't love. She felt lost and confused.

With ambivalent feelings slamming into each other like children piloting bumper cars within her, Sara just shut down emotionally. She walked into the living room, then turned to look at him. "Where's your suitcase?"

"By the door." He indicated the small valise. "I've been ready for hours." He picked it up. Sara moved to take the suitcase from him, then at the last moment decided to give him his dignity.

Raymond looked at his daughter for a long moment, saying things with his eyes he couldn't find the courage to say with his tongue. "Let's get this over with."

She nodded, then opened the front door. Stepping aside, she waited for him to pass first. A tiny bit of his cologne wafted by her. He still used the same brand. Old Spice. The name popped into her mind automatically and she thought of the old tuneful commercial. The smile she forced this time came a little more easily.

"It'll be all right," she promised softly, shutting the door behind her.

He seemed to brighten at her words, even though there was no way that she could guarantee anything. Neither of them could.

"Are you expecting a phone call?"

Antonio's voice penetrated the thick fog of thought that seemed to be clogging his brain this morning. Pinching the bridge of his nose as if that helped to gather his thoughts together, Nik looked at the man. "No, why?"

Antonio pointed toward the clock with the cleaver he was using on the row of guinea hens that were lined up before him on the worktable.

"You have been looking at the clock every five minutes. It is not like you." A thought struck Antonio and he suddenly smiled knowingly. "Did she call in?"

The back doors opened. Two large, wiry men walked in, each carrying a large crate of fresh fish. There were four more crates coming to complete the order. Nik nodded at one of the men. "Who?" he asked Antonio absently.

Antonio waited until Nik turned his attention to him again before continuing. He saw the line of impatience creasing Nik's brow, but it wasn't the first time Nik had been annoyed with him and it wouldn't be the last. With a snap of his wrist he cleaved another hen in half.

"That pretty girl you had coffee with last night. The Italian one." He said it with such gusto that there was no missing Antonio's stamp of approval.

Nik crossed to the men who were bringing in the crates. The taller one handed him a receipt mounted on a clipboard to sign. Nik opened the first crate and gave it a cursory look. He'd been dealing with the same market for ten years and was confident of their product. Nodding, he scribbled his name on the form.

"See you Friday," he murmured as the man took back his clipboard.

When Nik turned around, Antonio was standing at his elbow, waiting for an answer. "No." He fairly huffed out the word at the older man.

That only meant one thing. "You made her quit already?" Antonio shook his head, distressed. "Where have I gone wrong with you, Nikolas?"

Nik waved over two of the busboys and indicated the crates. "Take these into the walk-in and unpack them." He looked over his shoulder at Antonio. The man was following him around, conducting an interview for "The Dating Game" while there were chickens waiting to be boned and orders to be filled. He knew Antonio well enough to know that the man wasn't going to go back to work until he had his answer.

"She didn't quit. She's taking her father in to the hospital for surgery today."

Antonio nodded gravely as he took the information in. Returning to his worktable, he resumed cleaving chickens. "Maybe she needs someone to hold her hand."

Aware that the conversation was attracting attention, Nik moved closer to Antonio. "I offered. She said she didn't."

Antonio looked at Nik as if the man had just announced that he had bought a controlling share in the Golden Gate Bridge from a street peddler. "And you believed her?" He shook his head and laughed.

"Why shouldn't I?" Annoyance began to infiltrate Nik's voice, partially because he was carrying on the same debate silently in his head that Antonio was insisting on dragging out into the open.

"Because all women need to have a man to lean on no matter what they say." Antonio smiled, thinking of his wife and the years they had shared, both turbulent and calm. He would have been lost without her. "And all men like to have a woman in their lives to turn to." He looked at Nik meaningfully.

He could just hear what Sara would have to say about the first part of Antonio's comment. "She's not exactly like other women."

Finished, Antonio set his cleaver down and picked up a boning knife. "That is exactly my whole point, my friend. You deserve someone who is extraordinary."

Nik raised his voice as someone switched on the mashed-potato machine and the low hum pulsated through the area. "I have you, Antonio. I figure that's about all the extraordinary that I can handle."

A loud gasp brought both men's attention around to the stove in the rear of the kitchen. A high yellow-blue flame had suddenly leapt up, surrounding both sides of a pan that Chris was handling.

Stifling an oath, Nik hurried over to the stove, with Antonio on his heels. Chris pulled down the fire extinguisher and aimed the nozzle at the flame as Nik quickly removed the pan. Nik switched off the burner. Chris let out a deep sigh and let the nozzle fall limply to the side of the metal canister.

"Not quite so high next time, Chris," Nik instructed evenly. "The customer asked for stir-fried vegetables with lamb, not charcoal chips."

Chris ran a jerky hand through his hair as he nodded. He replaced the extinguisher and offered Nik a rueful smile. "Sorry, Nik," he murmured as he took over again.

"Why don't you go to her?" Antonio coaxed as he followed Nik to the worktable.

"Are you still on that?" When Antonio nodded, Nik sighed. "I'm not sure where she'll be."

It didn't sound like such an insurmountable obstacle to Antonio. "You can have her paged. But she is bound to be in the waiting area."

That was what Nik would have liked to believe, but Sara had made it sound as if she was indifferent to the outcome of the procedure. Nik raised a brow as he looked down at Antonio. "How do you know?"

Antonio spread his hands wide, as if it was obvious to anyone who bothered to look. "I look in her eyes, I know.

Go. Call." He gestured around the kitchen. "There is nothing here I cannot take care of and that I have not taken care of before you knew the difference between a carving knife and a potato peeler."

A protest rose to his lips and faded silently away. Nik debated for a moment, then surrendered to his impulse. The hospital was only five miles away. He was going to see if he could find her.

All morning he'd been vicariously reliving the time his parents had died. The memory brought with it a sharp ache. Both his parents had died more than ten years ago, yet there were times when he missed them so much that he could hardly bear it. From the very beginning, family ties had been important to him.

Maybe Antonio was right. Maybe it was just all talk with her, all bravado. Maybe she did need someone's hand to hold and was just too proud to say anything. Nik remembered how much he had needed to lean on someone. He couldn't because he was the oldest, the "strong one." There had been his sisters to care for and no one to confide in. If he had let on to Julia and Jennifer how unnerved and afraid he had been at times, it would have made them feel insecure. Their world had been shaken up enough without his adding to it. So he had gone on, silently dealing with his fears, feeling alone.

He didn't think anyone should have to go through what he had by themselves.

Nik untied his apron. There was a phone in the kitchen, but he opted for the privacy of the office. Jennifer was out on a catering call and Katie was down for a nap.

As he walked off he thought he heard Antonio utter a triumphant noise behind him. But when he turned, the old man looked inordinately busy boning the chickens.

There were twelve magazines spread out across the shiny black lacquered coffee table in front of her in the lounge. Agitated, Sara had arranged and rearranged them into piles, straightened them until the edges all appeared to be marching down the edge of the table. She couldn't concentrate long enough to even read the names that were written across the front covers.

Damn him, she wasn't supposed to care. After the way he had abandoned her, she had every right in the world just to drop him off at the front door and keep going. She shouldn't even *be* here.

And yet, she was.

She had had every intention in the world of bringing her father to the hospital admissions desk and then just leaving the premises. But at the last moment she couldn't bring herself to do it. It wasn't even that her father had asked her to stay. Not verbally, at least. But the set of his shoulders had.

And her own concerns got in her way.

Why couldn't she just divorce herself from her father the way he had from her?

She slapped a magazine angrily on the table. Tears gathered in her eyes as she knotted her hands helplessly in her lap.

Damn, it wasn't fair. Why did she have to care?

"How is he?"

Sara literally jumped at the sound of the softly spoken question. She had been so engrossed in the internal war she was conducting she hadn't even realized that there was someone standing over her. She looked up and saw the last person in the world she expected to see.

Nik.

She shifted on the oatmeal-colored sofa. The soft vinyl molded to her body, making her feel as if she was sinking in. "What are you doing here?"

If he concentrated, he could actually see her defense mechanism activating. "Offering a shoulder."

She lifted her chin defiantly, a smile playing on her lips. It didn't reach her eyes. "I don't need a shoulder. I have two of my own." She rotated first one, then the other, like a gymnast warming up. "See?"

Yes, he saw. "And a damn stubborn head in between, it seems."

The smile faded. "You're not paying me enough to listen to you talk to me like that."

Under normal circumstances her retort would have been enough to make him turn and walk away. He didn't need to put up with some woman's flippant attitude. But he'd watched Sara for a few moments before he had spoken to her. He'd seen the way she fidgeted with the magazines, the way she twisted her fingers together as if she was trying to braid them. He'd seen the unconscious concern on her face and knew that everything she was saying now was a sham, a facade she was throwing up for the world.

But why, was the question. To protect herself? From what? Curiosity made him want to find out.

"I'm not talking to you as your boss," Nik answered quietly, his eyes intent on hers.

Nerves jangled within her, but she couldn't draw her eyes away. "What other position are you applying for?" she challenged.

"Friend."

The single word made her feel ashamed of herself. Sara lifted a shoulder and let it drop, embarrassed. She offered him an apologetic smile.

"I guess friends snap at friends sometimes. Want to sit down?" Sara indicated the seat next to her with her eyes.

Nik sat beside her. Her nerves, he knew, had to be raw right about now. His had been, he remembered. Except that each time he'd been in this hospital, waiting in this very same lounge, the news, when it arrived, had not been good.

"It would be dull otherwise," he agreed. "And I've a feeling that you're anything but dull."

She laughed a little then, the way he'd hoped. "You've been talking to Brom."

"No, but maybe I will." Maybe Brom had some information that would shed light on this mercurial woman who pretended not to have a care in the world for reasons Nik didn't understand. Yet.

"So." Nik looked down the hall that led to the operating room. "Any news?"

She shook her head. Her hands felt icy as she pressed them into her lap. She tried to think of something else besides what was happening in a room a few feet away from her.

"How did you know that I'd be here?"

Antonio had been right, Nik thought, looking at Sara. There was concern in her eyes. "I called the number on your application form first. There was no answer."

Why was he putting himself out like this? She was nothing to him. Sara resented his very presence here.

And yet—

Now that he *was* here, she realized that she was glad he was. But she still didn't understand why he had come. "I said I'd be shopping."

Nik smiled as he sat back on the sofa. It was new. They'd changed the color scheme in the lounge since he'd been here. And the furniture. But the room still made him tense. He couldn't get away from what being in the room represented.

"Antonio said you'd be here. I've known Antonio a lot longer than I've known you. I went with a sure thing." He glanced at his watch. "The hospital said your father went into surgery over an hour ago." Sara's eyes narrowed as she looked at him in surprise. "I checked first before I came over."

She nodded vaguely at his explanation. Her eyes drifted toward the doorway. Why hadn't the doctor come out to talk to her? Had something gone wrong? The coil within her stomach tightened again. "It's only a forty-five-minute procedure."

Her voice was whispery, as if it was a slender thread that would break if she raised it even a decibel louder. His heart went out to her, even though he knew she'd probably jump all over him if he offered her sympathy. "Sometimes it takes longer than they expected."

Sara nodded. "So I've heard."

It was a stupid thing to say. She hadn't heard. She didn't know why she even said that. Didn't know why her nerves were jumping now like tiny frogs leaping over one another.

A doctor dressed in the green livery habitual to operating rooms stepped into the lounge. Seeing him, Nik placed his hand over Sara's.

Without realizing it, she curled her fingers around it and clutched, hard.

Chapter 6

Untying his green surgical mask, the doctor approached the sofa in slow, measured steps. There was no one else in the small lounge. His eyes were kind but tired as he looked down at Sara.

"Ms. Santangelo?"

Sara shot to her feet. She had to stand. There was this feeling coursing through her that she would be crushed by the weight of any bad news if she was sitting down. Belatedly she realized that her hand was still in Nik's. It tethered her. Sara pulled it free. She was vaguely aware of Nik rising beside her.

Quickly she scanned the doctor's face, trying to discern a glimmer of information from his expression. All she could see was that the man looked exhausted.

"Yes?" Tension pulsed in the single word.

"I'm Dr. Brice." The surgeon shook her hand, then glanced curiously at Nik as he wiped his brow. "You're her husband?"

"No." Sara's quick, emphatic denial left absolutely no room for speculation as to the nature of their relationship. There wasn't any.

Nik shook the doctor's hand, offering an amiable smile. "Family friend." His tone smoothed over the jagged edge that Sara's renouncement had left behind.

The doctor's smile was automatic, if a little worn. "We had a close call halfway through the surgery. The vein we were working on collapsed and I thought we were going to have to do an immediate coronary bypass. We always have an operating team standing by during these procedures," Dr. Brice assured Sara. His smile was warm, genuine. "Luckily they didn't have to step in. I managed to get the vein reopened. Your father's doing fine now."

She had heard a commotion down the hall earlier and seen several green-clad people rushing to the operating room. She'd been afraid to inquire what was going on.

"Fine?" she echoed. Sara scrutinized the man's face to see if there was any hesitation in his pronouncement. She found none.

"Fine," he repeated. "I can't make any promises, of course." The doctor slipped his cap off and wadded it in his hand. This sort of thing never failed to humble him. "The next seventy-two hours will tell us if the surgery took. And I'll want to see him in my office two weeks after that for an EKG. A treadmill test would be better, but he'll be in no condition for that for a while." Dr. Brice leaned over toward Sara. "Don't tell him I said so," he advised. "He's crusty about his pride."

Weren't they all? Nik thought, glancing at Sara.

Sara nodded. The numbness temporarily refused to drain out of her limbs. He'd made it. "So—" she took a deep breath "—what happens now?"

"He'll be taken to recovery, then to the Coronary Care Unit for two of the three days he's to be here. He'll be monitored continuously." The doctor smiled at her again. "I wouldn't worry if I were you."

Sara drew herself up. Now that the worst was over, she could return behind the walls she'd carefully built. "I'm not."

The doctor nodded. "Good. If you have any questions, feel free to call my office." He inclined his head to both of them. "Good day."

Nik waited until the doctor was gone. He'd been studying Sara as she received the news, watching the different emotions play over her eyes. Watching the line in her jaw grow rigid and then slack. For someone who pretended not to care, she was a cauldron of tension. He had no trouble identifying with that. He'd gone through it himself.

Sara didn't trust her voice for a moment. The relief she felt vibrating within her was too overwhelming. She hadn't thought that she would feel like this, but she did. It was as if a wave had dashed over her, washing away all the grit on her body.

She stared down the hallway. At the end was the operating room. "We're not out of the woods yet," she murmured.

True, but the doctor's words had been encouraging. "You don't strike me as a pessimist."

"I'm not a pessimist. I'm a realist." Sara turned away from the hall and looked at Nik. He was analyzing her again. She liked it even less the second time than she had the first. A tall man and a woman entered the lounge. Sara lowered her voice. "And you strike me as a man who doesn't normally abandon ship for no reason at all."

Nik crossed his arms in front of his chest, but made no attempt to answer her.

"Well?" she pressed.

The woman gave a new spin to the word *exasperating*. But somehow, Nik sensed that she needed him to ride out the storm. "I'm waiting for the subtitles to kick in. Right now I haven't the vaguest idea what you're talking about."

"You left the restaurant," she pointed out.

His eyes teased her, but he maintained a straight expression. "Apparently."

She moved, stepping into the hall, glad to be out of the lounge, knowing he was right behind her. "From what Julia told me before I came here, you practically have to be dynamited out of there."

When she turned to look at him, she found that they were standing too close to one another in the small hallway. She took a step back and felt her shoulder touch a wall. "There was really no reason for you to come."

A nurse hurried past them. Nik moved over and brushed up against Sara. Something warm and fluid coursed through his veins. He saw her expression tighten just a little.

"I already told you, I thought you needed a friend." He grew serious. "Look, my parents died within seven months of each other...."

She hadn't known. For a moment empathy flowed between them, unguarded. "I'm sorry."

"Yeah, so am I." They were standing almost directly in front of the gift shop entrance. Nik took her arm and moved her aside as two women emerged from the shop. "But what I'm trying to say is that I had to face that on my own."

She didn't quite understand. "But your sisters—"

"—Were little more than kids themselves." At sixteen and eighteen there was little else he could think of them as. "They needed to have someone to turn to, not someone to dump on them."

He couldn't have been that much older than they were at the time. He surprised her with the depth of his understanding. "No grandparents?"

Nik shook his head. "No anybody." They had been entirely on their own after their parents' deaths. On their own with next to no money to fall back on. Thank God the house had been paid off. "The point I'm trying to make is that I understand what it's like to suddenly find yourself facing the fact that your parents are mortal. I know how frightening that can be."

Sara managed to steel herself against his sympathy. She didn't need it, she told herself. She was doing just fine.

"I'm sure you do, but you don't have to concern yourself about me, or my feelings. They're quite unfazed, thank you." She saw Nik's brows draw together in a question. Maybe she owed him the smallest of explanations for putting himself out, even though she hadn't asked him to. Or maybe she just wanted to say it out loud for once. "My father gave up the title of parent, with all the associated rights that are tied to it, fourteen years ago.''

She believed that, he realized. Or thought she did. "Then why are you here?" he prodded quietly.

Sara squared her shoulders. "I keep asking myself the same question.''

Nik thought he already knew the answer to that. "I think it's because you care, Sara.''

Sara's face grew somber and her eyes became dark. "Don't transfer your own philosophy onto me." Her mouth twisted cynically. "Not everyone is as noble as you are, Nik Sinclair.''

He refused to believe she was devoid of feelings. "Nobility has nothing to do with it. Being human does.''

"Oh, I'm human enough." She gave a short laugh, looking away. "Human enough to remember, even if he doesn't.'' She realized that she was saying too much. "See?'' She turned her eyes toward Nik. "I didn't need that shoulder to lean on, after all.''

Directly behind her, in the window of the gift shop, was a white negligee arranged amid boxes of candy and stuffed baby toys. Nik couldn't help wondering what Sara would look like in it. The vibrations she gave off were laced with passion that was seeking a release.

He forced his mind back on the conversation. "That's not how I see it.''

She didn't want to argue and she knew that, in his own way, Nik was trying to be kind, even if he had no right to put his two cents in. Her mouth curved. "You're a typical man, you know.''

Had she seen him looking at the negligee and guessed what had passed through his mind? He lifted a brow. "How's that?''

She smiled then, guilelessly. It made her seem almost beautiful. "You always think you're right.''

"Oh, and you don't." Amusement highlighted Nik's expression.

His question struck her as a little ambiguous. "Think you're right? No. Think I'm right? Yes.''

Nik shook his head. He shouldn't have expected anything else from her. "Hospital coffee's pretty poor as I remember it, but if you're game, I'll spring for a cup in the cafeteria."

Because there was something about his kindness that made her want to lose herself in it, Sara resisted. She knew where giving her trust to someone led. To a dead-end street. "Your good deed is over, Sinclair."

"The way I see it—" Nik took her hand and led a semi-unwilling Sara down the hallway to the bank of elevators in the rear of the hospital "—it might just be beginning." The elevator door opened and he gently herded her into the elevator. The car was empty.

Sara looked at him defiantly as the doors closed again. "Let's get something straight. I don't like people meddling in my life."

The cafeteria was located in the basement. Nik leaned around Sara to press the button marked *B*. "I'm not meddling," he told her innocently. "I'm buying two cups of coffee."

Sara sighed and leaned against the elevator wall, feeling suddenly very drained. Maybe coffee would help chase away the feeling.

Nik noted the way she seemed to just collapse, like a balloon whose air had just whooshed out. "What's the matter?"

"Nothing." Self-conscious, Sara straightened again just as the doors opened. Arrows pointed the way to the cafeteria. "I'm storing up energy for round two."

He thought about taking her hand again and decided against it. He wasn't about to play tug-of-war with her. She could follow on her own if she chose. "This isn't a fight."

Sara fell into step next to him. "Maybe not, but you're crowding me."

Nik stopped just short of the entrance and looked at her, stifling his annoyance. "Lady, do you always snap at a hand that's being offered to you in friendship?"

Their eyes met and held. The man behind them walked around them in order to enter the the cafeteria. "Until I know what's up their sleeve."

"Hair," he said. "Light brown." He pushed his sleeve up to show her. "Any more questions?"

She laughed then. The light sound dissolved the tension hanging between them. She followed Nik into the food service area. "No, not at the moment."

"Good." He picked up a tray, then indicated the various desserts that were spread out on the ice behind the glass. "Now, do you want anything to eat with your coffee?"

Sara gave the display a cursory glance. She wasn't really hungry. Nerves had sopped up her appetite like bread absorbing the last drops of gravy on a plate. She shrugged. "Surprise me."

"Get us a table," Nik instructed, going toward the coffee urn.

Sara sat at the first empty table she came to. Her legs felt oddly hollow. Maybe she'd been subjected to more tension than she'd initially realized, waiting for the doctor to come and speak to her. Now that this hurdle had been surmounted, things could go back to the way they had been. She and her father would return to their separate camps, their separate lives.

Maybe she'd go to Hawaii next, she mused, her eyes drifting closed. She had always wanted to live in Hawaii. At least for a while.

The sound of a tray being laid on the table had Sara opening her eyes.

Nik was just placing an ice-cream sundae dripping with multicolored sprinkles before her. Sara looked up at him in surprise as he slid into the seat opposite her. "You look like the ice cream type."

The observation brought a smile to her lips. "I am." The appetite that hadn't been there a moment ago suddenly materialized, full grown. She drew the dish closer and picked up the spoon Nik had brought her. He seemed oddly intuitive, especially for a man. "How could you tell?"

He grinned as he watched her dig in. A certain gusto had returned to her face. "It wasn't that hard to deduce. Your eyes took on a sensuous light when you looked at the whipped cream Antonio had put on the mocha mint coffee the other night."

Sara loved all ice cream, high-quality and bargain-priced brands alike. It was her one indulgence. She considered coffee a necessity of life, so that didn't count. "Very observant of you."

She had downed three ice-cream-laden spoonfuls before she noticed that Nik had nothing more than half a cup of coffee before him. And he wasn't drinking it. "Aren't you having anything?"

Nik tasted the coffee. It was weak and tasteless. "Chefs don't sample other people's food."

She'd noticed his physique the first time they'd met. Muscular, he was broad shouldered, with slender hips and an incredibly flat stomach. She was beginning to understand why.

"Jennifer says you don't sample much of your own, either." She let another spoonful slide down. "What *do* you eat?"

He thought for a second. "Vegetables and fruit mostly, usually on the run."

Sara grinned slyly. She had caught him in a contradiction. "I thought you said food was supposed to be savored."

He knew she'd remember that. Sara struck him as the kind of person who would catalog almost everything in order to save it as future ammunition.

"Don't throw my own axioms back at me." He pushed aside the coffee. It was hopeless. "That's for other people, not me."

She nodded knowingly. "Oh, I see. An exceptional man."

He grinned to himself.

She'd unintentionally managed to feed his ego, she thought. "What, you accept the homage?"

"No." He let her in on the private joke. "It's just that Antonio referred to you as an extraordinary woman today."

Actually, he had been the one to make the reference, but Nik didn't think he should mention that to her. In her present frame of mind she might think he was coming on to her. And he didn't want her thinking that, although, he realized, his eyes slowly drifting over her face, he wouldn't mind doing exactly that. There was something about Sara that attracted him, sharp tongue and all. He dragged a hand through his hair. Maybe he'd been spending too much time with his pots and pans, after all.

Sara accepted his remark at face value. "Antonio's a good judge of character."

The sundae was almost gone. Sara concentrated on it, blocking everything else from her mind. It was easier that way. And a great deal simpler.

Nik folded his hands before him on the table and just watched her in silence.

His eyes made her feel fidgety, as if she was swimming in calm waters but anticipating a shark attack. She swam for shore and familiar ground. "I should have your system all caught up within two weeks."

Nik nodded. That was a lot faster than he could have managed the job. Forever was a lot faster than he could have managed it, he admitted ruefully to himself. "Sounds good."

She kept her eyes on the quickly disappearing dessert, wishing there was more, if only to keep her occupied. "And then I want to transfer it."

He looked at her uncertainly. "To what?"

"Another software program." She didn't think that the name of the program she intended to use would mean anything to him. From everything Jennifer had told her, Nik wasn't software oriented by any stretch of the imagination. Even if he had been, this was strictly an accounting program. "I worked with it when I was doing accounting for TruBlu."

"The jewelry company?" The name was familiar, even to him. TruBlu was second in reputation only to Cartier's and Tiffany's. She had been employed by them? Then what was she doing here?

Sara nodded. "They were using this cumbersome accounting method when I came to work for them. I made a few minor suggestions and they let me streamline the program for them."

Nik leaned back, studying her. The more he knew about Sara, the more amazing she became. And the more enigmatic. "Why aren't you still with them?" He imagined that TruBlu paid quite well.

"I got itchy." Her spoon met the bottom of the dish and she sighed, retiring it. Raising her eyes, she saw that Nik was watching her. She realized that he was waiting for more. Sara shifted a little in her seat. "I don't like to stay in any one place too long."

It was something he would have expected a man to say. He supposed that was prejudiced of him, but he'd always pictured women as wanting commitment and roots. He had always believed that to be one of the better qualities of the gender.

"Why?"

She placed the empty dish on the tray. "Because there are so many other places to see, so many other things to do."

She said it so vehemently, and yet somehow it didn't seem to ring true. "Don't you ever think about settling down?"

"No."

The single word left no room for further discussion. Her coffee was cold. Sara drank it, anyway, just to have something to do. When the cup was empty she looked at her watch.

"My father should be out of recovery by now." She rose. "I'll check with the nurse to see if he's there and then we can leave."

Nik quickly bused the tray, laying it on the conveyor belt that snaked its way into the kitchen. He hurried after Sara. "Aren't you going to go see him?"

Why did he have to keep prodding at her? Hadn't she done enough? How much more was she supposed to give? Until it hurt all over again? "Why? I remember what he looks like from this morning."

For reasons that weren't altogether clear to him yet, Nik didn't want her making a mistake. And that was where this was leading. "That's pretty harsh, Sara."

He had no right to chastise her. He didn't know what she'd gone through. He had no idea what it felt like to be fourteen and think your father hated you. He didn't know what it was like to lie in bed at night, trying to understand what it was that you'd done wrong. "Maybe he deserves it."

The misery he saw flicker in Sara's eyes had him reining in his assessment. There were things going on he didn't understand. But it didn't change his basic gut feelings. "Maybe he deserves a second chance, too."

Anger flared. "What are you, his lawyer?"

Nik took hold of her shoulders. She tried to shrug him off, but he wouldn't let her. "Sara, family ties are important, even to someone who likes to flutter from place to place."

Now he was sitting in judgment of her. Who the hell did he think he was? Sara pulled free of his grasp.

"I don't 'flutter' and family ties are fine for people who have families. What I have are broken pieces of what *used* to be a family." She lowered her voice as an orderly walked by them in the hallway. "My mother made it perfectly clear to me that I was in the way when she remarried. We exchange Christmas cards once a year and little else. My father hasn't sent me a Christmas card in fourteen years, and now—" she gestured impotently in the air "—all of a sudden I'm supposed to forgive and forget and be daddy's little girl again?" Her eyes grew hard. "It doesn't work like that, I'm afraid."

Nik didn't know where to begin. He only knew that he had to. She was in too much pain. "Sara, maybe it's not my place—"

Sara seized on his words. "No, it's not your place. Thank you very much for your concern, but it's not your place to butt in to my life and tell me what I'm supposed to feel and how I'm supposed to act.''

Fed up, he surrendered and turned away.

Guilt clawed at her as she watched him go. For a second she remained where she was, then, with an angry huff, she ran after him. ''Where are you going?''

He jabbed at the elevator button without bothering to look at her. Hurt or not, he couldn't fathom her behavior. ''To the Coronary Care Unit.''

The elevator arrived and she stepped into it without thinking, her eyes on Nik. ''Why?'' Her father was a stranger to him. *She* was a stranger to him. Why was he behaving as if he cared about either of them?

''To let you know how he's doing in case you decide that you want to know,'' he said evenly.

She still didn't understand. ''He's my father, not yours.''

Nik looked at her, his expression solemn. ''Exactly.''

She sighed as the elevator doors closed. ''You're not married, are you?''

He wondered what brought that on. ''No.''

''I didn't think so.'' He looked at her quizzically as he pressed for the first floor. ''If you were married, your wife would have probably killed you by now.''

Then he wouldn't be standing here, talking to her. ''Isn't that rather convoluted reasoning?''

Sara let out a breath. Maybe it was. She didn't know. His talking was jumbling up everything inside her. ''I don't care if you *are* here for the best of intentions, I have to say this.'' She looked at him. ''Shut up, Sinclair.''

He merely chuckled to himself. It was amazing that just when he wanted to strangle her she'd say something in the next breath that made him laugh. Life with her would undoubtedly be no bed of roses, but a constant challenge.

Belatedly she realized that he had pressed for the first floor. Had he decided to leave, after all? ''Changed your mind about playing devil's advocate?'' She pointed to the button he had pressed.

''CCU is on the first floor.''

It seemed an odd piece of information for him to have at his fingertips. "How do you know that?"

Nik looked straight ahead at the gunmetal-gray doors. "It's where my father died."

"Oh."

It was all she could say as the elevator doors opened. That he was willing to do this for her after what being here reminded him of left Sara speechless. She silently followed him through doors that sprang open automatically as they approached. Nik led her to a desk where a squadron of nurses sat watching monitors, each tuned to a different patient.

Nik stopped by the first nurse. "Has Mr. Santangelo been brought in yet from recovery?"

The young woman paused only for a moment to read a roster before nodding. "Room twelve." Her face was compassionate as she looked from Nik to Sara. She rose to show them the way. "But you can only stay five minutes."

"That's fine," Nik replied.

When he took her hand again, Sara didn't resist. She welcomed the warmth and silent support, even though she knew she shouldn't.

The rooms were really only glass-partitioned cubicles with a myriad of machines circling a single hospital bed like an army of metal soldiers. And in the midst of the platoon lay her father, asleep and pale, with so many tubes running through his body it was as if a child had scribbled loops upon the drawing of a man.

She wanted to cry.

He looked so frail, this man who had once picked her up and tossed her toward the sky each night when he returned from work.

Nik's hand tightened on hers. Sara realized that he was reliving a memory of his own. Perhaps he had seen his own father in a bed like this. She felt ashamed for having given him such a hard time. If only he hadn't interfered. He didn't know what had transpired in her family. He had no right to impose his own beliefs on her. No right to make her feel guilty.

She was doing a damn fine job of that herself.

Sara blinked hard to keep from crying. She'd promised herself no tears and she meant to keep that promise. Just because he looked like a broken old man was no reason to forget fourteen years of no phone calls, no contact.

She was aware that Nik had retreated, letting her have a moment alone. She couldn't even touch her father, she thought. There were too many tubes in the way.

His hand looked almost translucent where the IV was attached. She reached out and barely brushed her fingertips along his.

"Certainly don't look like Clint Eastwood now, do you?" she whispered.

She could have sworn that she saw her father's eyes flutter ever so slightly and try to open. It was just her imagination, she told herself.

She'd been so sure that after all that had gone before, she had distanced herself sufficiently so that this wasn't going to bother her. She'd been wrong.

Sara pressed her lips together, wishing she hadn't come.

She stepped back, as if to deny what she was seeing. That failing, she desperately attempted to harden her heart to it.

Zero for two.

Turning away before she broke down, Sara saw that Nik had gone back to the nurses' desk. Now what was he doing? As she approached, she heard him talking to the nurse. "Will he be all right?"

The nurse briefly scanned the information available to her on the monitor transmitting from room twelve.

"All his vital signs appear to be A-okay." The young woman gave Nik an encouraging smile. "He should be just fine. Is there a number where we can reach you if a problem does arise?"

Sara opened her mouth to respond, trying to recall the telephone number at her father's house. To her surprise, Nik gave the nurse his number before she could say anything.

Chapter 7

As angry as she was at Nik's presumption, Sara still didn't want to cause a scene in the middle of the hospital. She waited until they were outside the Coronary Care Unit before saying anything to him.

"Boy, you really take this friend role to heart, don't you?"

They were on the cusp of another argument, Nik thought. It fascinated him how Sara's temperament seemed to go in waves, first up, then down, then up again. Nik didn't even bother to try to figure out what it was she was talking about now. He asked.

"What do you mean?"

How could he play dumb? He was interfering in her life, stomping smack in the middle of it with both feet. And no one had invited him in. Nothing she had done could even remotely be construed as encouragement to meddle.

She struggled to keep her voice from rising as they walked through the winding hallway toward the lobby. "What's the idea of giving that nurse your number instead of mine?"

So that's what this was about. Nik shook his head. Sara was being territorial again. "It wasn't mine," he informed her tersely. "It was the restaurant's phone number. You're going to be working there, aren't you?"

She wanted to shout at him that that wasn't the point, but of course it was. She was going to spend the better part of each day at work. It was only logical that they would contact her at the restaurant.

But she still didn't want Nik taking charge like that. He was taking matters out of her hands as if she was some helpless dolt he had to take care of. She'd been on her own too long to feel comfortable about someone else exercising that kind of control over her.

"Yes," Sara ground out the answer between clenched teeth.

Nik stopped abruptly. He felt he needed to have both feet on the floor at the same time in order to deal with her. Ignoring him, Sara continued walking. She was marching ahead like a soldier heading straight into battle. Nik laid a hand heavily on her shoulder to keep her in place. "So what's your problem?"

Did she have to hit him over the head with a two-by-four before he backed off? She shrugged away his hand. "My problem is that you keep butting in where you have no business being."

For two cents—

Nik suppressed the urge to clip her one on that pretty little chin she insisted on sticking up at him. He shoved his hands into his pockets. And to think he'd felt sorry for her, believing that she was going through the same thing he had. Right. That would give her credit for feelings.

His eyes narrowed as he looked at Sara. "You know, you'd be a damn sight more attractive if you stopped looking for a fight every couple of seconds."

This was all his fault, not hers. "I am not looking for a fight."

Typical woman, always twisting things around. The next time Antonio urged him to hold Sara's hand he was going to lock the old man up in the walk-in refrigerator and leave him there until he came to his senses. "Then what do you call it?"

That was easy. "Protecting my own space."

His green eyes darkened and then went flat. "If you're not careful you're not going to *have* a space." With that, he walked out of the building.

Incensed, Sara hurried after him before the electronic doors had a chance to close again. "And what's that supposed to mean?"

He didn't bother turning around as he scanned the sea of cars just beyond the entrance, looking for his Mustang. "Ever hear the old saying about cutting off your nose to spite your face?"

She set her mouth hard. She hated being lectured to. "I despise trivial sayings."

He looked over his shoulder at her. "Then stop proving that they're true."

Sara didn't bother answering him. Instead, she stormed past him down to the circular path that led into the hospital parking lot. When she stopped to look around, he was right behind her.

Enough was enough. "Are you going to follow me all the way home and tuck me into bed, too?"

Her words created a momentary image in his head that surprised him with its intensity. He managed to maintain an unfathomable expression.

"It's too early for that."

The way he said it left a lot of room for interpretation. She studied him for a second. Was he coming on to her in the middle of an argument? She couldn't be sure. She thought of giving him a dressing-down, just in case. Yet, as much as she refused to admit it, there was something about the possibility that stirred her.

"I'm going to my car." He pointed to it. The dark blue vehicle was three lanes over from Sara's. "It's parked right over there."

Sara suddenly felt very stupid. And maybe just a shade unjustified in her waspishness. But he *had* brought it all down on his own head.

"Oh." Sara bit her lip, choosing her words. "Sorry." She took a deep breath as she turned toward him. "Look, Nik, I'm sorry if I came across like a wounded bear."

He had to laugh. *"If?"*

What was the use? The man was hopeless. Sara threw up her hands. "I was going to apologize, but never mind. I'll see you in the morning." She rounded the side of a black van. "Oh, damn."

Nik had already begun walking away, but her oath had him turning back, though he had a feeling he'd probably regret it. "What?"

The black van had pulled in after she had parked her car. The driver had used up more than his own share of space. The van's right side was all but blocking her access to the driver's side. Sara gestured at it impatiently, rechanneling all her anger and frustration to the owner of the van.

"Just look at that. I hate people who park at an angle like that as if they own the road. There's hardly any room for me to get in."

To prove her point, Sara attempted to open the door wide enough to accommodate her small frame. There was barely enough space. Annoyed, Sara moved back and managed to accidentally step on Nik's foot.

Surprised, she swung around. Her body brushed up against his. Again. Electricity swirled through her like lightning down a rod. Unwanted, it was still difficult to ignore.

"Sorry." The apology was scarcely more than a whisper as her voice backed up in her lungs. "You seem to keep getting underfoot one way or another."

She was standing toe-to-toe with him with nowhere to go. Escape was blocked on both sides by either her car or the van. Her door was still open, so backing away from him was out of the question. That left only one way to move. Into his arms.

She looked up at Nik, her eyes large with wonder at the sensations telegraphing through her. Her lips formed a perfect circle. "Oh."

Nik gazed down at her face, as surprised as she was by the mutual jolt. He knew it was mutual by the look in her eyes. For one thing, she wasn't snapping at him. Just resisting.

He realized that he had been unsuccessfully dodging something right from the start. Her. It was time to discover if the sexual tension humming between them was as powerful as it seemed.

Nik wove his fingers through her soft dark hair, framing her face with his palms. "Yeah. Oh."

There didn't seem to be any point in putting this off any longer. He felt the pull within his body, the pull that drew him toward her. Like floodwaters flowing toward the ocean, all his churning emotions had been heading toward this since he had seen her in his kitchen.

"Nik—"

Sara couldn't seem to manage to utter more of a protest than that. Her hands cupped over his, but rather than try to pull them away, she pressed them against his skin. As if to reinforce the contact Nik had initiated.

She had to be losing her mind.

"There you go again," he admonished softly. "Opening your mouth."

It felt as if there was honey in her veins, and she hadn't the strength to pull away from him. From the inevitable. She had no strength at all.

Like a lemming going off to the sea, she thought ruefully, she still had to find out where this was leading her.

Nik lowered his mouth to hers and made a huge discovery.

He didn't know a damn thing about kissing.

First kisses had always been tentative explorations in uncharted territories for him. They were, by turns, interesting, sweet and uncomplicated. What they weren't was explosive. They didn't cause an outpouring of a cornucopia of sensations, tastes, feelings. They didn't involve a complete loss of his sense of direction. And they definitely didn't cause an inversion of the ground with the sky.

All bets were off. He wasn't in Kansas anymore. He was in Oz.

Nik slid his hands away from her face and slipped them around her back. He pressed Sara to him, more to anchor himself to something than for the heavenly sensation the outline of her body created as it fit against his. That was only an added bonus.

Dear God, he'd sampled Harvey Wallbangers that had less of a kick than the taste of her mouth.

She was vulnerable, that was it. There was no other explanation for why she was hurtling through space with the speed of a bullet being fired out of the chamber of a .357 Magnum. From the first moment she saw him, she had thought that Nik was sexy. But that was no reason to feel as if she was a plate of ice cream left out on the porch in the early afternoon.

Sara dug her fingers into his hair, desperately needing to feel something real. This wasn't real, it wasn't happening. It couldn't be happening. His kiss had created a world that was as close to a hallucination as she could imagine it to be.

What had he put into that hospital coffee?

He was glad now that she hadn't listened to him, that she hadn't closed her mouth. The tastes that rose up were sensually arousing as his tongue touched hers. He felt her body dip into his as she moaned.

The sound of her own moan caused a shock wave to vibrate through her body. Sara pulled back, afraid that she would completely lose her identity in the next moment if she didn't.

She realized that she probably looked dazed and wild-eyed to Nik as she shakily drew air back into her lungs.

"Did we just have an earthquake?" she mumbled.

He was reluctant to let her go, but he did. "Felt like it to me."

Sara dragged her hand through her hair, trying to pull herself together. The depth of the passion she'd felt a moment ago utterly unnerved her. Both his and hers. There had been a number of men in her life, but none whom she had ever allowed to matter.

And none had ever kissed her like this.

She'd never experienced anything like it. She'd never longed before, never yearned before where every fiber of her body wanted it to continue, wanted to be taken. Her relationships were always completely superficial, like a drawing on a page. No strings, ever, to tie her down or reel her in. Instinctively she knew that if she ever became involved with a man, really involved, it would be asking for trouble. Relationships hurt. She had learned that from her parents.

The only way to avoid pain was to avoid any sort of actual relationships. And yet here she was, standing hip-deep in trouble.

Sara groped for the feel of the car door behind her. Her fingers slid around the frame.

"I'd better go—".

"Sara—"

Something had happened here just now. God only knew what. Sex, chemistry, attraction, something. Nik didn't want it, or her, just slipping through his fingers before he explored the sensations that had been born in the wake of her kiss. He didn't want her just running off, not yet.

But one look at Sara's face and he knew that there was no way of talking to her now. Something in her eyes reminded him of a wary, frightened child. Maybe it was for the best if they both had a little breathing space, at least for now.

Sara was already getting into her car. Slamming her door, she jabbed her key into the ignition. The car growled to life. She threw it into reverse, her hand shaking.

"You'd better move, Sinclair, unless you want me backing up over you." She hoped that sounded as flippant as she was trying to make it.

Nik had little doubt, as he stepped to the side, that Sara would be as good as her word.

She blasted music all the way to her father's house. She didn't hear a note. It took Sara fifteen minutes to stop trembling. She felt as if her insides were all the consistency of watered-down Jell-O.

Damn that man, she thought. As if she didn't have enough turmoil in her life already.

* * *

By morning Sara had calmed down and had reverted back to her blasé self. She had convinced herself that the reason Nik's kiss had electrified her was that she'd been completely, emotionally overwrought. If it hadn't been for the doubly charged situations she had found herself in, first being summoned by the father who had abandoned her and then having to wait out the results of his surgery, Nik's kiss would have left her completely cold.

Well, maybe not completely, but it wouldn't have felt as if there had been a total upheaval in her body composition.

It was the emotional gauntlet she had just gone through that had contributed to her feeling weak-kneed and palpitating as if she had just dived off a high cliff into ice-cold waters, not the man himself.

It was a good working theory, she thought, getting into her car. And she intended to make it work.

Still, as a precaution, she made certain that she didn't arrive at Sinclair's before the rest of the crew came on duty. Better safe than sorry, at least until she regained her bearings.

She held her breath as she knocked on the back door, and only let it out when she saw that it was Jennifer who opened it.

Katie was trailing after her mother. The ribbon in her hair was slightly askew and drooping.

"Good morning." Sara dropped to her knees and fixed Katie's bow. The child looked like a miniature version of her mother, she thought. Brushing her hand along the little girl's cheek, Sara rose again and headed toward the office. There was a ton of work to do and she was aching to leap into it.

"Boy, you're certainly cheerful this morning," Jennifer commented, following Sara in. "I hear your father's surgery went well. I'm very glad."

Sara dropped her purse into the desk's bottom drawer, then shut it with her foot. She wanted a cup of coffee, and wondered what her first encounter with Nik would be like. She intended to play it very casually, as if yesterday's incident in the parking lot had all been very commonplace in her life.

"Did Nik tell you that?" What else had he shared with his sister? she wondered.

Probably nothing, she decided. She had to give him his due. He didn't seem like the type of man who was driven to talk about his private life.

Jennifer cleared her scattered notes from the desk. "No, actually, Kane did." She saw Sara's puzzled look. "He stopped by to see your father on his way home last night. Did you know Kane and your father work out of the same precinct?"

There had been a lot more that Kane had shared with her last night, things that had Jennifer's heart going out to both father and daughter. But she sensed that Sara wasn't the type who took sympathy easily.

"Small world," Sara murmured. She turned in time to see Nik pass by the doorway. Their eyes met for a moment before he continued walking. "Maybe a little too small," she added under her breath, settling in.

Nik had almost walked into the office, then had changed his mind at the last moment. No sense pushing anything. What would be would be. The philosophy arose from an old song his mother used to sing to him when he was a child.

Part of him still believed in it.

"Hey, Sinclair, any chance of getting a terrific cup of coffee?" Sara called out just as he reached the kitchen.

He stopped, waiting for her to catch up. He smiled easily. So, she was going to play it cool. Well, so could he. "Sure. I'll show you to the coffee urns."

It wasn't in Sara's nature to hide when things made her nervous. The best way to conquer fear of riding was to climb back on the horse that had thrown her. Of course, this time she'd kissed the horse instead of falling off him, but the basic philosophy was the same. If she attempted to stay out of his way, it would only manage to make things worse and blow them out of proportion for her.

Besides, Nik had said that he wanted to be her friend, so that was what they were going to be. Friends. Maybe even good friends. There was room in her life for that. But that was where it would end.

"What happened to my personalized service?" she asked. Nik noted that mischief had replaced the wariness he had seen yesterday in her eyes.

He played along with her mood. "That's for new employees."

Sara fisted her hands at her waist and looked at him, amused. "Well?"

"This is day number two." He held up two fingers. "You're not new anymore."

"Ah, *signorina,* you are here!" As Antonio greeted her, he took Sara's hand and kissed it. His mustache lightly tickled her skin. "I thought perhaps he had scared you away." He nodded toward Nik.

Sara glanced at Nik as he crossed to one of the stoves. "He tried." Nik raised a brow in her direction. Damn, she'd said too much again. "At least someone appreciates me," she quipped flippantly.

"Do some work. I'll appreciate you." Nik turned away. But he was smiling to himself. Neither Antonio nor Jennifer, who had walked into the kitchen just at that moment, missed the expression.

It was three o'clock. The lunch crowd had thinned out and the early dinner crowd was still two hours off. The tempo in the kitchen had slowed considerably. It was as good a time as any, Jennifer thought. She walked into the kitchen.

Nik was experimenting with a new recipe he'd been working on. It wasn't quite going the way he wanted it to. She could tell by his expression. Jennifer debated saving her question for another time, then thought better of it. She loved Nik, but the man needed dynamite lit under him to see things that other people were aware of immediately.

She picked up a packet of saltine crackers from a carton on the worktable as she crossed to her brother. Her stomach was queasy, reminding her of the tiny soul that was forming beneath her heart. "Okay, what's up?"

Another dash of garlic wasn't the answer, Nik decided, staring at the pan before him. It didn't have the taste he was looking for.

Nik looked up at Jennifer, impatient at being interrupted. "In what way? Are you referring to the menu, to the work schedule, to the catering business, to this damn mess that doesn't want to rise up out of the realm of the mundane—what? Be specific, Jennifer, I'm a busy person."

She pulled the red tape off the packet and slipped out a cracker. "You're busy dodging."

Nik moved the pan onto a dormant burner, temporarily surrendering. He pinned Jennifer with a look. "You know, I am strongly becoming convinced that the theory that men and women originated on different planets is absolutely true. What are you talking about?"

She finished the small cracker and twirled the second one in her fingers, her mind on her brother and not the fact that her stomach was lurching. There really wasn't much she could do about the latter, but there might be about the former. "Let me put it in plainer language for you. What's going on between you and Sara?" She punctuated her question with a crunch as she bit into the next cracker.

Nik looked around. The closest pair of ears belonged to Chris and he was busy flirting with Ginger by the exit.

"I'm her boss, she's my employee." Nik decided that he needed something to occupy his mind other than the conversation, and returned the pan to the burner. "At the end of the week a paycheck will pass between us."

Jennifer studied her brother. It wasn't like Nik to deny something that was true. Nik was always forthright, facing everything head-on. Of course, this was probably new to him. She grinned, pleased. "That's not all that's passing between you."

His eyes were not altogether friendly as he looked at his sister. "Meaning?"

Jennifer had watched the two of them the first day Sara had come to work, as well as this morning. Each time they were within several feet of each other there was an underlying current of tension beneath the surface that cut through all the words that flew between them.

"That there's enough electricity going back and forth between you to keep Vegas running for a week."

He kept his expression bland. "I didn't know that hallucinations went along with pregnancy."

"They don't." He wasn't going to talk his way out of this. She cared too much. "You know I don't generally pry into your business—"

"Ha." He reached for the cayenne pepper on the spice rack above the stove.

Jennifer placed her hand on the container, stopping him. "Nik, Julia does that, not me. Give me my due."

He knew she was only being concerned, but he didn't want to be prodded about this, even by family. "All right. So why start now?"

She withdrew her hand. "Because I care." For a second she watched him season the sautéed chicken slices in silence. "Are you going to ask her out?"

He was about to drizzle a handful of finely chopped walnut pieces over the mixture. They fell from his hand in a cluster. "You mean like on a date?"

It was an outdated word for what she had in mind, but for lack of a better start, it would have to do. "Yes."

Nik stirred quickly, attempting to distribute the walnuts evenly. He slanted a look at his sister. "Are you crazy?"

She laughed softly. "You'll have to take that matter up with Kane. Are you?"

He stopped sparring with her. Maybe if she had the truth, she'd understand and leave him alone. A date with Sara was a ridiculous idea, even if the woman's kiss had preyed on his mind all night.

"Every time I make overtures of friendship, she wants to have me castrated. This is not a woman a man takes out on a date."

She'd consumed the last cracker and her stomach was still in revolt. Jennifer crossed to the worktable and picked up another packet. "Brom tells me that she's had a rough time of it."

Nik stopped stirring for a second, considering. It was still no excuse. "That doesn't mean she has to give back in kind."

Jennifer thought about how gentle Nik could be, how supportive. He'd always been there for all of them. The man had a lot of love to give. "I figure you're the one to teach her that lesson." She squeezed his arm.

"I'll think about it."

"Think hard, Nik," she urged softly. "Life is ticking by."

He glanced up at the clock. He was going to have to start getting ready for the dinner crowd soon. "So I noticed."

Jennifer refused to be put off. "I don't want you missing out on what I have. On what Julia has."

He gave the creation in the pan one last stir, placed a lid on top of it and then set it aside to simmer. "Fine, you send Kane and Brom around. We'll go out and do something together."

Jennifer laughed. Nik was hopelessly stubborn when he wanted to be. But he would come around. Or, at least, she hoped so. "You know what I mean. You're the one who taught us all about the importance of family ties, Nik. Go make some of your own."

He thought of Sara and the way she had almost bolted out of the hospital parking lot after he'd kissed her. "The only tie I could manage with Sara is if I bound her up like one of those steers at a rodeo." He walked over to the walk-in freezer to check on the seafood order he had received earlier today.

Jennifer was right behind him. "Maybe she'll surprise you." She stopped short of the refrigerator, waiting for Nik to emerge. "I've been working with her for two days now and I like what I see."

Mentally Nik checked off the amount of seafood he expected to use tonight. "Fine, you go out on a date with her. I'll make your explanations to Kane."

Jennifer grinned.

He slammed the door shut again and looked at her. "What?"

"I don't think you stand a chance."

What were she and Julia plotting? He was sure Julia was the instigator. Jennifer had always been too mild-mannered to push so hard. "Against you?"

She shook her head. "Nope. Against you. I can see it in your eyes, big brother. You like the lady."

Maybe he did, but there was no point in going into that one way or the other. "I also like the Angels. That's not a winning pick, either."

"You'll find a way," she promised. She patted his cheek teasingly, knowing he hated that. "You always do."

He didn't have time for any more games. "Did you come in here for any other reason other than to harass me? Because if you didn't..."

For the time being, she supposed she'd said enough. Nik would undoubtedly take it from here at his own pace. She just didn't want to see him missing out. "Actually, I did want to tell you that the DeCarlo party called to add fifty more guests to their wedding for next month."

Nik nodded, glad to be back on familiar ground again. "The more the merrier."

"The only problem is Sara says we need more money up front before we can go ahead and—"

He raised his hand to stop her before she got any further. "Sara says?" he echoed. Jennifer nodded her head, aware that she had finally lit a fuse. "Since when does Sara dictate terms for anything?"

Jennifer looked up at him innocently. "Well, she is our accountant now—"

"Our *temporary* accountant," he emphasized. "And I don't want anyone from Accountants 'R' Us to suddenly start dictating our restaurant policy. Is she in the office?"

He was already striding past Jennifer, heading toward the hallway.

"Yes. Now, Nik, don't yell," Jennifer warned, hurrying to keep up. "I don't want Katie to think her uncle's gone berserk."

"Then I'd advise you to take her out for a walk. It's time she got some air."

He might have known that if he gave her an inch she'd take out an entire claim. Just because he'd tentatively agreed yesterday to let her utilize a new program—and even that hadn't been a definite yes—that in no way gave her the green light to get any further involved in restaurant policies. She was working for him, not the other way around, and he was going to take great pleasure in pointing that out.

"Sara," Nik announced, "I'd like a word with you."

Sara had just returned from visiting her father in the hospital. It had been a quick, five-minute visit to check on his condition and to assuage her conscience. Five minutes, after all, was all the nurse had originally said was allowed. Sara clung to that. If she stayed too long, things might get said that she had no intentions of saying.

Agitated, confused, Sara was the perfect candidate for a fight. She glanced toward the doorway and saw Nik standing there. Anger creased his brow. He made her think of Thor just before the Norse god let loose with one of his thunderbolts.

Ah, the perfect recipient for a fight.

She smiled at him sweetly. "Something wrong, Sinclair?" she asked.

He crossed the threshold, struggling to keep his temper in check. He lost. "You bet there is."

Thunderstorm, no doubt about it, Sara thought, girding up.

Jennifer took her daughter's hand and led her toward the doorway.

"C'mon, Katie, time to get some fresh air. Uncle Nik is going to make nice with Aunt Sara." As she moved past him, she saw Nik's brow rise. "It's just an expression, Nik," she explained soothingly. But she grinned knowingly as she said it, as if the title she had bestowed on Sara was a prophecy.

Jennifer left Nik and Sara looking at one another like two roosters laying claim to the same barnyard.

Chapter 8

Nik glanced over his shoulder to make certain that Jennifer and Katie were out of earshot. Satisfied, he turned his full attention to Sara. But first he had to shut out impulses that had him responding to her on a very different, very basic level. They had no place in this conversation, perhaps no place in their lives at all.

"Just what do you mean by setting up rules for the restaurant?"

Sara drew her brows together, trying to guess what had set him off like this. Offhand she couldn't think of a thing that she had done that would make him come charging in like a steer on the streets of Pamplona during the annual running of the bulls.

"Excuse me?"

He could almost believe that childlike, innocent expression on her face—if he didn't know better. "Jennifer tells me that *you* don't think we should proceed with catering arrangements for the DeCarlo wedding unless we get more money up front."

"And?" she prompted, waiting. So far, she didn't see what the problem was.

And? Was she being purposely dense, or just baiting him? Either way, it didn't improve his mood. "Where do you get off, dictating what we can or can't do in running our restaurant?"

There was something almost magnetically attractive about Nik when his expression looked so dark and foreboding. And it was exactly that attraction that made Sara break out in a cold sweat. Defense alarms went off.

"I'd hardly call common sense 'dictating.'" She raised her eyes and smiled sweetly. Poetic justice was alive and well. "Careful, Nik, or someone's going to accuse you of protecting your own space."

She was taunting him with what he had lectured her about yesterday. He should have realized that she would, the first chance she got. But she was still wrong. "That's different."

The look in her eyes was gently mocking. She was beginning to enjoy this argument. It was tipping in her favor. "Is it?"

The woman was evoking a mixed bag of emotions from him. He felt like shaking her and knocking some reason into her head. Most of all, he felt like kissing her until they were both senseless instead of just her. "You know it is."

Sara spread her arms wide. "I don't know anything of the kind. Besides—" her eyes held his again as she referred to something else he'd mentioned "—I'm only trying to help."

The hell she was. She was taking yesterday and reversing their roles. "Déjà vu," he said sarcastically.

Sara grinned. "Maybe it is," she agreed pleasantly. "As your accountant—temporary accountant," she amended quickly before he had the chance, though the distinction was more for her own benefit than for his, "I have to call it the way I see it."

She leaned back and assumed what she hoped Nik would regard as a somber attitude. She placed the tips of her fingers together and rocked in the swivel chair. Her eyes never left his.

God, he had beautiful eyes.

She forced her mind back to the little drama she was sketching for him. "Now, the DeCarlos are probably really terrific, trustworthy people who don't even owe interest on their charge cards and pay every bill when it's due. *But—*" she held up one finger in the air "—there are people in this world who will attempt to conveniently 'forget' to pay on time. Or at all. Too many of those and you're overextended. It can happen to anyone, Sinclair. Just read the papers." She gestured toward a folded newspaper Jennifer had left on the file cabinet.

He wondered if she would still be able to talk if someone held on to her hands. She gestured to punctuate almost every statement.

"Don't patronize me, Sara. I'm not a child," he said evenly. "I know that."

"Good." She turned her back to him as she resumed her work. Or tried to. With Nik in the room, it was difficult for her to concentrate on anything. Especially after yesterday.

Sara could feel him standing there, studying her back. It took all she had not to shift restlessly. "Then there's no reason for this argument."

"Except maybe," Nik began, moving around to the front of the desk so that he could face her, "that I don't like hearing criticism—or advice—" he added when she raised a warning brow "—coming from anyone." He decided to be completely honest. "I suppose I don't like being told how to run things even if it does make sense."

There was silence in the room for a moment. Only the low hum of the computer disturbed it. And then somewhere off in the kitchen someone dropped a pan. A few choice words in Italian followed the incident.

"Then we have that in common, don't we?" She lowered her eyes to the screen.

Nik raised his hand, wanting to touch her shoulder. Wanting to touch her. If he did, she'd probably come out swinging. He let his hand fall to his side. "Sara, about yesterday..."

She didn't want to discuss yesterday. At least, not the part of the day that needed to be discussed.

"I appreciate you coming to the hospital and all the noble intentions that brought you there." Her words had come out in a rush. She stopped and looked up at him. "Maybe I overreacted—about everything."

He knew what she was telling him. That what they both thought was in the kiss hadn't been there at all. But he knew what he'd felt. And he believed he knew what she'd felt, as well. She had responded to him far more than just casually. Still, her denial stung.

His eyes darkened. "Maybe we both did."

Why did that hurt? He was only agreeing with what she had said. Sara set her mouth firmly.

"Good." Her fingers flew over the keyboard, typing gibberish. She hoped he wouldn't look over her shoulder when he left. "Another point of agreement. We're progressing, Sinclair."

If that was the case, why did he have the distinct feeling that they were going backward? And why did she sound so brittle, like a drill sergeant complimenting recruits newly liberated from boot camp?

He had no answers, but at least they'd stopped arguing for the moment. Nik decided to quit while there was a truce in force. He had too many details to see to in the kitchen. They were unveiling a new item on the evening menu and he wanted to be sure everything was ready. A new food critic was coming around to the restaurant at the end of next week. Nik didn't have time for personal matters that went beyond his immediate family.

He certainly didn't have the time to wet-nurse a small woman with a very large chip on her shoulder and eyes the color of melted dark chocolate. Even if she did make his blood run hot.

He crossed to the doorway, and then stopped. "Had lunch yet?"

"No. I—" She was about to tell him that she hadn't had a chance to eat because she had gone to the hospital during her lunch break. But she caught herself in time. The less personal details she shared, however minor, the better. "I haven't."

His eyes swept over her. She was wearing a green-and-white-striped tank top and a skirt that was, in his estimation, not that much wider than a headband. It showed off legs that were longer than a person of her stature had a right to have. Legs that made his pulse rate go up far faster than the house wine did.

"Get some. You're too thin."

And too damn attractive.

She raised her coffee cup. Inclining her head, she toasted Nik. "My, but you do have a golden tongue, Sinclair."

She was getting under his skin again in more ways than one. Their truce was in danger of going up in flames. "People come here for my cooking, not my rhetoric."

She laughed as she took a sip of coffee. "And aren't you grateful for that one?"

He started to retort. He knew that things would only escalate again, but he seemed unable to help himself. It was almost as if he had no say in the matter. Worse, it was as if he thrived on this constant conflict that was pulsating between them.

But Sara had already turned away from him and toward the screen. She was hastily deleting something, but he couldn't see what.

Nik thought of the reason he had come charging into the office to begin with. They hadn't actually resolved that. At least, he hadn't.

"I'll have Jennifer call Mrs. DeCarlo and ask for another advance," Nik muttered as he walked out of the office.

Sara smiled to herself as she completed deleting the gibberish she had previously typed in.

"You know, for someone claiming to be such a free spirit, you're just as much of a workaholic as people accuse me of being."

Sara glanced up to see Nik looking into the office. She hadn't seen him since he'd ordered her to have lunch. But she had anticipated him.

She stretched and focused on her watch. It was almost ten. It was hard to believe she'd been in the office by herself for almost five hours. When Kane had come by to collect Jennifer and Katie, Sara had meant to stay only a few extra minutes.

A few minutes had stretched into hours. Though it was just past the summer solstice, the sun had long since retreated from the office like a servant backing out of a queen's room. Sara had absently switched on the desk lamp and kept going.

Just a little longer. She smiled ruefully to herself.

Leaning back in the chair, she arched her back and ran her fingers through her hair, as if that would help clear away the cobwebs on her brain. She saw the flicker of interest in Nik's eyes and it flattered her even though she tried not to let it.

"This is like a good mystery." She gestured toward the files. The pile on the floor now exceeded the pile on her desk. She was making real progress now that she understood Nik's unique method of record keeping. "I want to see how it turns out.

"Besides—" Sara moved the chair around so that she could face him "—I'm *not* a workaholic. It's just that I'm not going to be here that long. I thought I'd work ahead a little so that you'd feel that you'd gotten your money's worth out of me."

It was a lie, but so what? The simple truth was that she liked accounting and right now there wasn't anything else she had to do. But he didn't have to know that. If he knew, it would undoubtedly make him think that he was right.

He'd gotten more than his money's worth all right. And a hell of a lot more than he had bargained for, to boot. She was arguing with him now just for form's sake, he was sure of it.

Nik leaned a hip against the desk, crossing his arms. "You know, I have a strong suspicion that if I said 'day,' you'd say 'night' just because you don't want to agree with me." He did a quick mental check over the past three days. "I don't think we've really agreed on anything since you arrived."

"That's not true." The protest came automatically. And then Sara grinned ruefully as he eyed her. "Well, not entirely, anyway." She lifted her shoulders and let them fall. The tank top moved with her like a second skin and stirred

Nik's imagination. He shoved his hands into his pockets to soothe the sudden itch that arose. "Besides, a little antagonism's good for the soul."

And a lot tended to wear it out. "I'm sure you're the reigning authority on that. "

Sara cocked her head. Her eyes were amused. "Trying to start another fight?"

He shook his head. "Trying to agree with something you said."

She laughed, then began to press a sequence of buttons that would store the last batch of data. "Don't start being agreeable now, Sinclair. It'll ruin that carefully honed image of yours."

Maybe talking to her was an exercise in futility. He picked up the newspaper Jennifer had left for him. He wanted to peruse the food section before going to bed tonight. He liked keeping up on the competition.

Nik started to leave, then changed his mind. He didn't want to go straight home tonight. He wanted to look at Sara in the moonlight.

Perhaps someone had substituted peyote for the cayenne pepper, he mused, retracing his steps. God knows he wasn't acting sensibly. A sensible man would have retreated, glad to escape with his skin intact.

Sara looked over her shoulder at him in surprise. "Forget something?"

Yes, you.

"You know, when I first bought this place," he began conversationally, as if they hadn't just been at odds a moment ago, "I didn't realize how really great the location was."

She raised a brow, wondering what he was getting at. Most people were aware of location before they even inquired about the price of a store or restaurant, unless they were stupid, of course. Nik Sinclair wasn't stupid.

"Scenically, I mean." He nodded toward his left and the back entrance. "The beach is less than half a mile away from the rear parking lot, just beyond the houses. People like to come here for dinner and then top it off with a stroll along the beach.''

She felt uneasy as she resumed storing her material. She had a feeling she knew where he was going with this. And she wanted to go with him, which was what frightened her. She wanted to go *too* much.

Sara didn't look at him. ''At some of the prices I've seen on the menu, that's probably all they can afford to do afterward.''

She was blocking every attempt he made to get by her barriers. Like a well-trained volleyball player, she was slamming the ball over the net every time it threatened to land in her court. Why was she resisting so hard?

''How long have you been a cynic, Sara?''

Her eyes grew distant as she remembered. ''Since I was fourteen.''

He didn't believe her. He thought she was just being flippant. But he would have liked to have met her before she had become so disillusioned. ''What were you like then?''

She roused herself. He was prodding again. Didn't the man ever give up? ''A lot younger.''

He laughed and shook his head. ''Would you have been game to go for a walk on the beach then?''

Sara switched off the machine and ignored the fact that her heart had gone into an accelerated mode. ''I'm game now, if someone would ask me.''

He took her hand as she reached for the computer's plastic dustcover. She raised her eyes to his. She was trying to be brazen, but she was failing, he thought.

''I'm asking.''

She was twenty-eight, for God's sake. Why was her mouth going dry because a man was asking her to take a walk with him along the beach? It only involved sand and water, not a lifelong commitment. Her mouth stayed dry. ''What about the restaurant?''

''Antonio'll handle it. He keeps trying to shove me out of the kitchen every night, anyway. Says he'll lock up.'' A fond smile creased his mouth and Sara suddenly remembered the way it had tasted. ''Personally, I think he's stealing the silverware and selling it off to fund his retirement plan. But I haven't the heart to tell him to go home." He sighed. "He likes to think he runs the restaurant."

And Nik let him, she thought. He took umbrage with her when he thought she was challenging his authority, but he let an old man have illusions and order him around. She liked him for it even though she knew she shouldn't.

"Very understanding of you." Nik looked at her in surprise. Her voice had grown soft, silky. "It might be a whole new light to see you in."

He took her hand again and drew her from her chair. "So, are you game?"

Too game. And too chicken. Maybe it went hand in hand, she thought. "You were serious? About the walk?"

"I was serious. About the walk," he echoed with a gentle smile.

And, I think, about you, God help me.

Sara was very quiet for a second. She'd promised herself not to become emotionally involved with Nik, no matter how tempting the situation might be. And she always kept her promises to herself.

A smile spread on her face as a fresh wave of confidence came from somewhere. She couldn't deny that, though he was a pigheaded son of a gun, she did want to be alone with him. She found him attractive and stimulating, stimulating on more levels than any other man she had ever met before.

What was she afraid of? She had always handled herself before. And she wasn't going to start running now. "Okay, take me to your beach."

Nik kept her hand in his as Sara retrieved her purse from the drawer.

She waited for him while he gave Antonio a few final instructions for the day. It reminded her of a parent briefing a baby-sitter before going out for the evening. And the restaurant was his baby.

He'd probably make a good parent, Sara judged. She'd observed him with Katie. The man who was all business when he donned his apron became all softness and putty in the little girl's hand.

A lot like her own father had been.

The recollection brought with it a painful stab that was sharp.

"You're frowning," Nik noted as he took Sara's arm.

She didn't want him probing into her mind, didn't want him getting any more of a foothold in her life than he had right at this moment. Even that was too much.

"No, I'm not. My face was just relaxing for a second." She patted his cheek. "Like yours does all the time."

He wasn't going to let her bait him. It was clear to Nik that Sara had been thinking of something. Something that obviously bothered her. He wanted to ask her about it, but knew that it would undoubtedly lead to a confrontation. He wasn't up to engaging in another battle of wits with her. All he wanted was to walk along the beach. And, perhaps, to hold her. Nothing more. It seemed like a simple enough desire.

"Don't start," he warned her, holding the rear door open.

"Wouldn't dream of it."

And fish don't swim, he thought.

He led her down a sleepy little residential street that quietly wound its way to the beach. There were single-story houses on either side, little more than cottages, actually. Bathed in the moonlight, even the most faded house looked quaint and appealing. They stood lined up like sleeping doves resting on a branch.

The beach lay just beyond.

The sea was calm, as if it was asleep, as well. It was desolate. There were only the two of them. A sprinkling of anticipation began to filter through Sara's body.

The full moon cast its light on the tranquil waters. The beams danced along the glasslike surface, forming a silvery path that looked as if it would lead straight up toward the moon.

Nik felt relaxed for the first time that day. Perhaps for the first time in a week. They walked along in silence for a few minutes, and he smiled to himself as he looked at her profile. Silence. And Sara. It was a completely new experience.

He began talking because it seemed right. "Sometimes I come here after the restaurant closes just to pull my thoughts together. I like the beach much better at night. It's beautiful and peaceful then. Nobody's yelling or fighting. No stray balls flying by to hit you."

"It looks lonely." She couldn't stop the shiver that slipped over her.

It was natural for him to put his arm around her. He didn't even have to think about it. It just happened. Surprised, Sara looked at him. He kept his arm where it was. They continued walking.

"I might have known you'd disagree." But there was a smile playing on his lips as he said it.

"I'm not disagreeing," she contradicted. "It *is* beautiful. But beautiful things can be lonely."

The sadness in her voice was almost tangible. What was she thinking about? "Are you?"

Sara stared straight ahead. How was it that he always made her say more than she meant to?

"I wasn't talking about me. Besides—" she shrugged carelessly and the strap on her tank top slipped off her shoulder "—I'm not beautiful."

He stopped walking and turned her to face him. Gently he laid his hands on her shoulders. His thumb coaxed the strap back into place. Her skin tingled as if he had stripped her nude. Sara struggled to refrain from trembling. "We're disagreeing again."

A small smile quirked her mouth. "Why does that keep happening?"

His hands remained on her shoulders. Her skin felt soft. He wanted to touch her all over. "Because you're usually wrong."

Even in the moonlight Nik could see the fire reenter her eyes. "I'm—?"

"All right," he conceded, lifting his hands in surrender. There was laughter in his eyes. "Fifty percent of the time you're wrong. The other fifty percent of the time I'm right. Fair enough?"

She began to laugh. He was incorrigible.

When she laughed, when she smiled like that, she took his breath away.

"Better," he whispered, lowering his mouth just a little until his breath was on her face, stirring her emotions, making suddenly tense nerves knit together like fingers laced in prayer. "Much better."

She licked lips that were suddenly parched. This wasn't a good idea. Subconsciously she'd known that even as she agreed to come here with him. Yet she *had* agreed. Was it because she'd been longing to be alone with him, with no one to see them except the moon?

Why was she walking out on a tightrope when she knew there was no net under her, nothing to catch her if she fell? *When* she fell.

Desperate, Sara sought salvation in humor as she took a step back. She felt her heels sinking into the sand. "Does this come under the heading of fringe benefits?"

Gently he brushed his thumb along her cheek and watched desire bloom in her eyes, even as she fought to hold her ground. "Depends on whose you're talking about."

"Mine?" she guessed. It would be the typical male response.

He moved his head slowly from side to side. "Mine."

And then there was no more space between them and no more words to create artificial barriers. His mouth covered hers. The cornucopia burst open instantly, showering him with an even greater spectrum of emotions and sensation than the first time.

He welcomed them all.

Nik pulled Sara to him, locking her in an embrace that was at once fierce and tender at the same time. His blood rushed and pounded through him like the surf during the height of a storm.

Sara didn't even attempt to fight what was happening. She had no strength to do anything but let herself be swept away by the heat of his mouth, by the power of his kiss. Later, when she was back in battle form, when she had her wits about her, she'd do what she could to repair the damage being done right at this instant.

But for now, she reveled in the excitement that seized her as his mouth took hers over and over again, draining her of her very will. She didn't know who or what she was, only that she wanted this sensation to continue. Forever. Longer, if possible.

She could feel the length of his body as it imprinted itself on hers. People weren't supposed to come unraveled just by kissing, she knew that. But she felt like a ball of yarn being batted around by a kitten, unraveling at a prodigious rate.

This wasn't safe, Nik thought. He was on the brink of something, tottering on the very edge. And he was going to fall in.

He had always known that he wasn't the type to do things in half measures. And he wanted her. But more than for just a night. More than for just a week. Commitment was a very real word to him, one he believed in wholeheartedly. Sara had made it abundantly clear that she was only passing through. It would be stupid to allow anything to develop between them.

And yet it seemed, even after such a short while, that he had no say in the matter. Something was happening with or without his consent. And he could only hang on for the ride and hope to be in one piece when it came to its end.

Sara braced her hands on his shoulders, wanting to push Nik away. But somehow she wound up grasping his shirt instead, twisting her fingers into the material as Nik pulled her even closer to him. His long fingers played along her spine until every inch of her vibrated with needs.

Her heart was pounding so hard that it hurt. Her very breath was gone. As his mouth trailed along the column of her throat she felt herself falling in deeper. She was drowning in a bottomless pool of sensations swimming into one another.

Though she didn't want to, Sara struggled to draw back. Stalling for time, attempting to steady her breathing, she leaned her head against his chest. She heard his heart pounding. At least she wasn't alone in this. But it was a small comfort.

This had been even more powerful than the last time. She'd barely recovered before. How was she going to manage to do it again?

She closed her eyes and looked for strength. She didn't find any. Sara couldn't even muster the strength to lift her head.

"So," she managed in a husky whisper, "are you relaxed?"

"No."

Desire and anticipation hummed all through her, begging her to continue. She knew it was impossible.

"Neither am I. I guess that blows your theory about the beach all to hell."

He stroked her hair. In the moonlight it looked almost pitch-black.

"For now." His pulse had stopped doing triple time. Nik ran his fingertips along her arms and felt the slight tremble in response.

Oh, God, if you only knew what you do to me, woman.

For a moment he enjoyed the feel of just standing there with her in his arms. "Sara?"

He felt her breath against his chest as she answered. "Yes?"

He took a chance. If they didn't go forward, they'd go backward. She wasn't the type to stand still. "Come home with me."

He felt her stiffen against him. He was losing her.

"More fringe benefits?"

He moved back so he could look at her face. "Sara, I'm serious."

Her eyes clouded over. "Don't be. Not about me." Sara pulled away from him. "I'm telling you from the start, it won't work."

The wariness had returned. Why, damn it, why? He didn't want to push her, but he couldn't just back away, either. "How do you know unless we try?"

She turned away from him and ran her hands up and down her arms. The night was sultry, but she was suddenly cold. "Because I don't want to try, all right?" Failure only lay at the end of the road.

In his heart he knew it wasn't true. "I thought you were the type who was so unorthodox. Who liked to take risks."

When he reached for her, she moved aside. If he touched her again, she'd give in. And she couldn't. Wouldn't.

"I'll go bungee jumping with you, Nik. Anytime you want. But I won't go to bed with you."

He let out an exasperated breath. He wanted to reason with her, but her resistance made no sense to him. "There's something happening between us, Sara."

"That's *why* I won't go to bed with you. Because there is something between us." Weakening, she spun around and touched his face. He covered her hand with his own and pressed a kiss to her palm.

Sara felt tears forming as she moved away from him. "Leave it alone, Nik."

"Why?" he demanded. "Why?"

She shook her head. "I couldn't begin to explain it to you."

Sara turned and walked slowly back to the restaurant, her shoulders braced like those of a soldier who had been forced to ride into the heart of a battle.

Nik watched her go, then turned and walked in the opposite direction. He had no idea for how long.

She was right. This time walking along the beach didn't soothe him.

It just made him feel lonely.

Chapter 9

The office felt eerily quiet. Jennifer had taken the day off for a long-overdue outing with Kane and Katie. Today there was no constant stream of waitresses stopping by to look in on the baby or to exchange a few words with Jennifer. Rather than enjoy it, for some reason the silence made Sara feel restless.

She missed Jennifer. The woman was incredibly even-tempered. Unlike her brother, Sara thought with a smile. It was odd how you could know a person for only a few short days and feel as if you'd known them forever.

She felt that way about Jennifer. She had no idea how she felt about Nik, other than hopelessly confused. She opened another folder and started typing.

She knew Nik was standing there before she even turned around. She could feel him looking at her. She didn't even try to explore why she knew. She just did.

"Hi." She tossed the greeting in his direction without looking up from her work.

Feeling a little self-conscious that she had caught him staring at her, Nik walked into the office. "I came to see how you were doing."

Actually, that was stretching the truth a little. He had stopped by just to see her. Period.

Sara looked up just as he reached her desk. There was an interesting-looking blue streak running along the length of his apron. She couldn't begin to guess as to its origin. Cooking was as much of a mystery to her as he was.

"Fine, although I miss Katie's chatter." She'd lost her place, and gave up for a moment. "I've gotten kind of used to it."

"She does grow on you." The silence hung awkwardly between them. Nik dragged his hand through his hair. "Well, if everything's all right..."

He began to leave. He felt like an awkward teenager when he was around her. No, that wasn't right, he amended. Even as a teenager he had never felt this way. He'd been a high school jock who'd enjoyed a full and active social life. Conversations with the opposite sex had never been a problem.

Until now.

Sara seemed to knock out all the known parameters of his world as if they were only rotting pieces of wood. So why did he keep coming back for more?

Nik forced himself to stop in the doorway. "Isn't your father scheduled to be released soon?"

"Tomorrow." Her hand hovered over the keyboard as she turned to look at him. "How did you know?"

"I was there when the doctor talked to you, remember?"

He crossed to her again and this time sat down in the chair next to the desk, making himself as comfortable as he could around her.

"What *is* that?" she finally asked, skimming her fingertip along the blue streak. Her hand came in contact with his thigh. Marginally, but it was enough to affect them both.

Nik shifted slightly, suddenly feeling restless. "Blueberry sauce. Chris spilled some prying the lid off a jar. I had the misfortune of being caught in the cross fire." Nik shook his head. "He's got promise, but a *long* way to go." Not unlike he himself had been ten years ago, Nik supposed.

Leaning his elbows on the arms of the chair, he folded his hands together and studied her face. "Need any help bringing him home?" When she raised her eyes to his face quizzically, he added, "Your father."

An amused smile lifted the corners of her mouth. The man never gave up, did he? "I don't intend to sling him over my shoulder and carry him back to his house."

Nik picked up a folder and pretended to thumb through it. The inventory list of last month's condiment order slipped out. "A simple yes or no would work better in this case, Sara." He bent over to pick up the list from the floor and then dropped it on the desk. "Preferably a yes."

"Why?"

Nik stretched his long legs out. He had exactly ten minutes before he had to get back. Chris was about to attempt making a soufflé on his own. "He's probably weak. Getting your father out of the car into the house might not be as easy as it sounds." He paused. "Even for a woman who can do everything."

She didn't have to look at him to know there was a sarcastic smile on his face. Maybe she had been laying it on too thickly. "I guess you think I deserve that."

Nik rocked slightly in the chair, his eyes on hers. "Yes, I do."

She blew out a breath and decided to abandon the pretense of being able to concentrate on anything while Nik was only a foot away from her. "If I'm so irritating, why are you always here, volunteering to help me?"

He liked the slight pink hue that rose to her cheeks when she became annoyed. No cosmetic could begin to approximate the glow.

"Haven't you heard?" he asked mildly. "Some of us are trying to earn our wings earlier these days. No waiting until the last minute or until Jimmy Stewart is about to leap off the bridge."

She stared at him as if he had lost his mind. How did a matinee idol from the fifties get into this discussion? "What are you talking about?"

He wondered if she had ever watched old movies as a child. His father had been an old-movies buff who periodically took Nik and his sisters to revivals and old film festivals when they were growing up, as well as any musical that might have been playing within a fifty-mile radius. It made for a well-rounded childhood.

"A classic Christmas movie. You should rent it sometime and watch." He grinned, leaning forward. "How does it feel?"

"How does *what* feel?" She wished Jennifer was here to take the focus away from her. She wasn't doing well at all, despite her efforts to the contrary. He had completely upended her not once but twice and she was having the worst time getting back on an even keel.

Nik thought of all the times Sara had taken him on a verbal game of hide-and-seek. "To be confused when someone's talking?"

"Not too terrific."

She shrugged, looking for a way to save a shred of pride, of dignity, of sanity. Something. At this point she wasn't sure of anything except that every time she was within spitting distance of Nik, she did. She spat and hissed like a cat that was being cornered. Right about now she felt as if she was standing on emotional quicksand.

She opened another folder and stared at the first page, not making sense of any of it. "It's not my fault if you can't keep up."

"Ditto."

Okay, maybe she had that coming to her. Sara sighed, getting serious. "Really, why are you offering to help me? This is going beyond merit badges and wings."

She really wished he wouldn't try to help. Every time he helped, every time he kissed her, he wedged his way a little farther into her life. And she knew she couldn't afford to have him do that. Reflexively, she fought it. There was a battle raging within her. Part of her wanted what he apparently was offering, but that part was being held prisoner by a steely defense mechanism that was intended to keep her safe.

"Maybe, just maybe, the reason might be," he hypothesized, spreading his hands, "although God only knows why, that I like you, Saratoga Santangelo." She winced.

She should never have filled out her full name on the employee form. "If you really like me, you won't use that name."

"Why? I think it's unique. Like you." He grinned. "Saratoga. It suits you."

She looked away. There was something about his eyes that held her captive. And she wanted to be free. "It reminds me of something I don't want to be reminded of."

He placed his hand over hers. "What?"

Sara extracted her hand, then laid both of them over the keyboard. But she didn't type. "If I talk about it, then I'll be reminded, right?"

Nik shook his head. She was definitely in a class by herself. "For a woman who talks a lot, you're awfully close-mouthed."

Sara just smiled triumphantly. "All part of the mystique."

"All part of the irritation," Nik corrected, but he didn't look annoyed, only bemused, like someone facing a six-hundred piece jigsaw puzzle of Samoyed puppies lost in a blizzard.

His irritation she could easily handle. It was the other part that she couldn't. The part where he told her that he liked her. He wasn't talking about friendship, that much she could see in his eyes.

"Then why—"

Nik framed her face, his long fingers curving about her cheeks. "Because I *do* like you, Sara. A great deal. I don't completely understand what's going on here myself. When I figure it out, I'll let you know. But *until* I do, I intend to go on exploring it. That means I'm going to be seeing you a lot."

She felt her pulse throbbing in her throat like a butterfly caught in a hunter's net. She wasn't sure how she managed to get any words past it. "Lucky me."

"Maybe." He leaned over more. Gently his lips just barely brushed against hers. It felt like brushing against heaven, she thought. "Or maybe we'll both get lucky."

The resistance that had been so strong only a moment ago felt as lax as overcooked spaghetti now. Sara sighed deeply. "All right, I guess I could use some help tomorrow." She glanced at the date that was on the bottom right corner of the computer screen. Something occurred to her. "Don't you work on Saturdays?"

He'd been working seven days a week for a long time. It was time to let go a little. Starting now. If nothing else, if he burned out he'd lose his creative edge, and running Sinclair's meant constant change, constant revamping of menus and alteration of tried-and-true recipes.

"I'm learning to be flexible. Jennifer says it's good for my health and for business." Nik rose to his feet. Time to get back before Chris started another fire in the kitchen. "What time do you want me to pick you up tomorrow?"

She thought for a moment. "Eleven, I guess. He's supposed to be discharged before noon." She looked up at Nik, still uncertain about the wisdom of being around him any more than she had to. "Are you sure . . . ?"

He looked down into her eyes. The pull was there, hard and strong. There was no use denying it. "I'm sure."

Sara felt her stomach flipping over and tying itself in a knot all over again.

Afraid that he'd see more than she wanted him to, Sara turned her chair back to the computer screen.

"Don't say I didn't warn you," she murmured under her breath.

But he heard her.

She was agitated. He could tell by the way she was sitting next to him in the car. Perched as if she expected the seat to explode under her at any moment. But, for a change, he didn't think her state had anything to do with him. She'd been friendly when he'd arrived and their conversation had been pleasant enough, revolving around work, Jennifer and Brom.

Yet there was something in her manner that convinced him she was edgy. She didn't want to be doing this, Nik thought. She didn't want to be going to the hospital to pick up her father.

He realized that, in all this time, she hadn't said all that much about the man. Nik made up his mind to give Brom a call and find out some of the missing pieces to this puzzle.

But he didn't want to wait until tonight. He wanted Sara to tell him. He wanted Sara to trust him. "Do you and your father get along?" Nik saw her shoulders stiffen just a little.

Sara stared straight ahead as they took the off ramp from the freeway. She could see the hospital looming on the horizon just ahead. "I haven't been around him long enough to get along."

Nik eased down on the brake as they came to a red light. Renovating construction was going on to the right, giving the old streets a new face.

He raised his voice to be heard above the jackhammer. "Why's that?"

Sara shot him a look. "You're prying again," she shouted.

He shifted his foot to the gas pedal as the light turned green. "Yes, I am."

She should have gone by herself, as she had first intended. It was just that she'd suddenly wanted a buffer between her and her father on the ride home. This was what she got for being a coward.

"Look, just because you're driving me to the hospital doesn't mean that I have to answer all your questions."

He was definitely calling Brom tonight. "Settle down." To reinforce his words, he placed a gentling hand on her arm, the way he would with an animal that had been spooked. "I'm just curious."

She wished he'd stop touching her. Her skin felt warm just beneath his fingers and she could feel herself wanting things she knew were bad for her. Bad because they would lead to other wants, other desires that couldn't be fulfilled.

She shifted, moving closer to the window. "You know what they said about the cat...."

Nik shrugged as he turned right at the light. "That means I've got nine lives to work with." He glanced at her and grinned. "I'll risk it." His voice grew serious. "After you were out on your own, why didn't you visit your father?"

Sara held on to her purse and stared straight ahead, like a hostile witness on the stand. "I never go where I'm not wanted."

"He said that?" Entering the hospital grounds, Nik guided the car slowly toward the admissions and discharge area. He felt incensed on her behalf. "He told you that you weren't welcome?"

No, he'd never said anything at all. That was the trouble. In all those years he'd never sought her out to talk. "Words aren't everything, Nik."

"Then how did you know he didn't want to see you?"

"I don't want to talk about it anymore, okay?" Talking only aggravated the situation and brought back the pain she had never managed to put to rest or work through. Only lock away.

Nik parked the car near the entrance in a space reserved for compact cars. For a moment Sara didn't move. She sat as if she was bracing herself to face down a demon. Maybe she was, he thought.

Sara turned to look at him. "Do you want to stay here and think of more ways to analyze me while I go—"

He wasn't about to let her face this alone, not the way she felt.

"We'll both go." Nik got out, then rounded the hood and waited for her to join him. "I have a feeling that you need the moral support."

She shrugged indifferently, but inside, she was rebelling against his words. She didn't want or need anyone's help. The day she admitted that she did, she knew she would be in trouble. Because no one stayed for the duration. Her father had proved that to her.

"If it helps you to fill out some good deed requirement list, you can come along to give me moral support. But I can manage perfectly well on my own, so don't think—"

"Sara?" His tone cut through the sea of words like a shark's fin gliding through the crowded waters off a beach.

"That you have to—what?" she demanded finally.

Nik pointed toward the hospital's electronic glass doors. "Shut up and walk."

He made her so mad that she *could* spit. "You know, just because you pay my salary doesn't mean that you can just order me around like that."

"My paying your salary has nothing to do with it. Ever think of running for the Senate? They say that filibusters are really popular there."

She said nothing as she passed him and walked into the hospital lobby. But he could guess what she was thinking.

Nik grinned to himself.

Raymond was sitting on the edge of his bed, dressed and waiting for her when Sara arrived. His room was small and neatly arranged, a carbon copy of twenty more just like it on the floor. Sara had barely even noticed it in her two previous visits. Each time she had left almost as soon as she had arrived, murmuring that she was on her lunch break and had to be getting back.

Coming to see him had assuaged her conscience. Leaving quickly had helped her cope.

Her father looked almost skeletal in his street clothes. Could four days make that much of a difference in a man's appearance? He looked worn and even more shrunken than he had before the operation. For one unguarded moment her heart ached to see him like this. And then she was resurrecting her barriers, shoring up her heart against all breaches.

"I packed," Raymond told her by way of a greeting. His smile looked as if it required more effort than he had to spare. His eyes, mirror images of Sara's, shifted to Nik. A question rose in them.

Nik moved forward and took the man's hand in his. Raymond did his best to grip it firmly. It was more difficult than he liked.

Nik took in the stubborn set of the jaw, the proud brown eyes. The man was Sara's father, all right. "Hello. I thought I'd help Sara bring you home. I'm Nik Sinclair, Sara's boss."

"He's taken the term to heart," Sara flung over her shoulder.

She looked in the closet to see if her father had left anything behind. A single wire hanger swayed slightly in the breeze she had created by opening the door. She closed it again.

"It's only temporary, though." She had to keep reminding herself of that before she became too complacent. This was *all* only temporary.

Nik shoved his hands into his pockets as he stood back, out of the way. Caught in the silent cross fire, he tried to understand exactly what was going on between Sara and her father. It was almost as if their roles were reversed. Sara was the angry parent while Raymond behaved like the contrite child.

She felt Nik's eyes on her. He was doing it again, she thought, annoyed. He was analyzing her. She turned toward her father. "Has the doctor been here to see you yet?"

Raymond held up a bulging envelope that was lying on the bed next to him.

"He came by an hour ago to give me my discharge papers." Because it was less painful to look at Nik, Raymond addressed his words to the other man. "I'm a free man." He handed the envelope to Sara. "The nurse said to ring for her when you got here so that she could bring a wheelchair."

Sara looked up sharply, the envelope hovering over the mouth of her purse. Her eyes shifted to her father's legs. "Wheelchair? You can't walk?"

"Sure I can walk." He waved a disparaging hand in the air, annoyed at what he considered the entire dehumanizing process of being in a hospital. "It's some damned hospital policy to take away our dignity. Just like with those drafty hospital gowns they make you wear. Slit straight up the back to rob you of your privacy."

Nik straightened. He jerked a thumb toward the door. "I'll go get the nurse."

"No." Sara placed her hand on Nik's arm, stopping him. "I will."

His first impression was that she just didn't want him doing anything for her. But one look at her face made him realize that the reason she was racing out into the hall ahead of him was that she didn't want to be alone with her father. The realization hit him. That was why she had agreed to his coming along with her in the first place. She didn't want to be alone with the man.

Sara hurried out of the room. Nik looked after her and shook his head.

"Have you known my Sara long?"

Raymond's question had Nik turning away from the door. My Sara. Nik wondered what Sara would have had to say about that.

He felt sorry for the man.

Nik sat in the single chair next to the bed. "No, my brother-in-law recommended her. Brom Culhane," Nik explained.

Raymond's gaunt face stretched into a smile. "Brom." He repeated the name fondly. "How's he doing these days?" Sara's father nodded toward the closed door. "Sara didn't say very much about him." He shrugged self-consciously, his eyes bright. "I've kind of lost touch with everyone over the years."

The man looked so eager for news Nik didn't have the heart to brush him off with a few token words. He searched his mind for something he could tell him. It turned out to be a great deal more than he had realized. They were still talking when Sara returned.

She reentered the room with a nurse's aide directly behind her. Holding the door open as the young woman pushed in the wheelchair, Sara was surprised by the sound of voices. Her father and Nik were talking as if they were old friends exchanging anecdotes. Her father was actually laughing. Sara pressed her lips together.

She didn't know exactly why hearing Nik talk with her father annoyed her, but it did. Ruefully she realized that, in her own way, she had wanted Nik to be on her side. And there were sides drawn in this, very clear-cut sides. She was on one and her father was on the other. And there were never going to be any peace talks.

"Wheelchair's here," she announced needlessly. Nik rose from his seat as the aide lined up the wheelchair next to the bed.

Raymond turned to look at Sara. "You didn't tell me that Nik was related to Kane."

I didn't tell you a lot of things, because you never asked.

"I didn't think you'd be interested." Her voice was polite, but completely devoid of feeling. "I have no idea what you're interested in anymore."

Sara picked up her father's suitcase, her mouth grimly set.

Nik glanced at Sara as he helped Raymond into the wheelchair. Raymond seemed like a basically decent man. Just what the hell was Sara's problem? Nik knew he was going to have to find out before they could make any headway themselves.

When they arrived at the house, Nik found himself just taking over. For once, Sara let him.

As Nik helped her father into the house and then into the bedroom, Sara busied herself in the kitchen making coffee. She took an inordinately long time measuring out the crystals and pouring cups of water into the urn. If she couldn't keep her mind busy, at least her hands were occupied.

She wished she had never come here. Why couldn't she have just made up an excuse, told her father that she couldn't get away? Why had she come all this way just to put herself through all this again?

Because part of her had never gotten over his rejection. She had buried it, but not forgotten it. She'd loved him dearly once and there was a part of her that yearned to reestablish their old relationship. To do that she needed to do the impossible. She needed to forgive him.

Maybe subconsciously that was why she had come, to find a way to forgive him. But she wanted him to know how much he had hurt her, wanted him to squirm for what he had done. Most of all, she wanted her father to apologize. Because she wanted him to tell her why he had walked away from her the way he had.

Grow up, Sara. Not everything has a happy ending.

"You're making a mistake, you know."

Startled, Sara dropped the measuring cup, and a shower of dark crystals spilled on the colorless vinyl floor. Muttering, she picked up a sponge from the sink and began wiping up the mess. She looked up at Nik, her eyes just the slightest shade dangerous. "No, I don't know, but I'm sure that you'll tell me."

He took the sponge from her hand and rinsed it, then squeezed out the water. He envisioned her neck in his hand in place of the yellow sponge. "What's going on between you and your father?"

"Nothing." She added the last measuring cup of coffee crystals into the receptacle. "Absolutely nothing."

She said the words with such finality it should have been the end of the conversation. But it wasn't. She might have known that it wouldn't be. Nik didn't seem to respect boundaries or privacy.

"No, it's definitely something." When she wouldn't turn around to face him, he laid his hands on her shoulders and turned her toward him. "Sara, he's sorry for what he did."

Sara lifted her chin. A stubborn look entered her eyes. "I don't really care."

She might be fooling herself, but she wasn't fooling him. "Oh, yes, you do." She struggled to shrug him off, but he wouldn't let her go so easily. He had to get through to her somehow before it was too late. For all of them. "You really care. Otherwise, you wouldn't be acting like a spoiled brat."

The dark look in her eyes would have warned off a lesser man. "You're going a little too far, Sinclair, don't you think?"

"No, I don't think I've gone far enough." He nodded toward the rear of the house. "There's an old man in there who needs you. He's just come face-to-face with his own mortality and he's scared."

Nik wasn't saying anything to her that she hadn't already thought of. But it didn't change anything. "There's nothing I can do about that."

"Maybe not," he conceded. "But you can show him that you care."

Where did he get off, lecturing her? She yanked her arms free. With the kitchen counter at her back, her eyes blazed as she faced Nik. "For your information, that old man who needs all this loving you're talking about ripped my heart out when I needed him. I can't just come skipping back to him and say everything's fine and dandy."

Nik slowly measured out his words. Didn't she see how counterproductive her feelings were? How destructive? "So where's it going to end?"

She set her mouth firmly. "It already ended."

She didn't believe that, he decided, studying her. "I don't think so. You're still here," Nik pointed out. She began to answer, but he wouldn't let her. "I think you just don't know how to take the first step back."

Her expression was entirely impassive. He had no idea what she was thinking. "And if I never do?"

His eyes met hers. "I don't think you're that stubborn. Or that cruel." She let out a small huff of breath. "It's easy, Sara. All you do is put your foot down on the path, just one at a time." He cupped her cheek so softly, tears nearly welled up in her eyes. "He needs you, Sara."

Her voice was hoarse when she answered him. "I don't need a guilt trip, Sinclair."

She wasn't going to put him off. "You need something, Sara. Something has to break up that dam you've built inside of you or you'll never be free."

She didn't like him making it sound as if she was in some sort of bondage. "Free to do what?"

His eyes were caressing her face. She could almost feel his touch along her skin. "To love anybody again."

"You, I suppose," she whispered.

A smile played on his lips. "Doesn't sound all that bad to me." His fingertips curved along her face. "This schism between you and your father is eating you up inside. You've got to get rid of it, clear it out."

He had to make her understand. Otherwise, when it was too late, she'd never forgive herself.

"Look, Sara, life's short, shorter than we think. I thought my parents would be around forever. They weren't." Regret filled his voice. "There were things I said to them, things I did that I wished I could have taken back after it was too late—"

"You?" She looked at him incredulously. "The choirboy?"

He laughed at the label. He was light-years away from that. Especially back then. "I don't have those wings yet."

He kissed her forehead lightly. Sara couldn't help thinking she had never felt anything so sweet. Damn him for being sweet. She liked it better when they were arguing. She knew how to handle herself then.

"I know what I'm talking about. Don't waste time being angry or hurt. Talk to him," he urged. "Tell him what you feel."

Sara dug in stubbornly. "I don't feel anything."

"Then tell him that, too." He had to be getting back. Nik crossed to the living room. "But work it out. I'll see you on Monday."

Sara followed him to the front door. A flutter of panic began forming in her stomach. She didn't want to be alone with her father. Nik had dredged up fresh emotions, disarming her. How was she supposed to cope with this situation? "You're leaving?"

Was that sorrow? He would take anything he could get. "I have to." He ran a finger along her lips. "Miss me a little bit. It might be good for us." His eyes looked over her head toward the back of the house. "But right now, you need to be alone with him."

He closed the door behind him.

Bewildered, confused, Sara slowly walked to her father's room. She stood in the hall for a long time, debating with herself. Finally she knocked lightly on his door.

"Dad?"

He was lying so still on the bed that for a moment, she thought he was asleep. But then he turned his face in her direction, his eyes only half open.

"Can I get you anything?"

He smiled and slowly shook his head. "No, but thanks for asking."

Sara nodded as she slipped out of the room again. "Sure."

Maybe she'd taken the first step after all, she thought, closing the bedroom door behind her. But she was still going to need time for the others. A great deal of time.

"Damn you, Nik Sinclair, for messing me up all over again," she whispered as she went back to the kitchen. She needed a strong cup of coffee. Badly.

Chapter 10

The telephone rang three times before Sara finally realized that there was no one in the office to answer it. Engrossed in her work, Sara had forgotten that Jennifer was out catering a party. One of the waitresses had taken Katie out for a walk, so the room was empty except for her.

She let it ring again, but no one at the front desk picked it up. Apparently there wasn't anyone there, either, she thought, irritated. The shrill noise wouldn't let her concentrate.

Didn't this thing ring in the kitchen as well? Where *was* everybody?

Sighing, Sara marked her place with her fingertip on the column of numbers she was inputting, and leaned over to pick up the receiver. Her hoop earring clanked against the earpiece as she cradled the telephone against her shoulder.

"Sinclair's," she murmured absently. "How may I help you?"

There was a momentary pause on the other end of the line. Then a deep male voice asked, "Sara?"

"Yes." She frowned. It didn't sound like her father. Who would be calling her here? "Who's this?"

The laugh was resonant. He hadn't called to talk to her, but now that she was on the phone, Brom was delighted. "Your favorite cousin, last time I checked."

"Brom." Sara sat up, the long column of numbers temporarily forgotten. She grasped the receiver in her hand again as she pictured her cousin sitting in his office. "How are you?"

"I'm fine. The more important question is, how are you doing?"

Idly she ran her finger along the bottom of the monitor. She thought of her father. "As well as can be expected." Her mind shifted to Nik and took on a completely different tone. "You didn't tell me that your brother-in-law was pigheaded."

So Jennifer had been right about the situation when she'd called Julia yesterday. Something *was* up between the two. He smiled to himself. Couldn't have happened to a nicer pair.

"I thought I'd leave that as a surprise. Besides, as I remember it, you're pretty damn stubborn yourself. I figured you'd hold your own against him."

Yes, but it wasn't easy. She didn't feel like admitting that, even to Brom, with whom she had shared all her girlhood secrets. She began keying in another set of numbers. "I always do."

He was going to have to leave for the casino shortly. Brom decided to get to the point of the call. "Is he around?"

"Nik? Probably." She hit the Enter key and smiled as another screen materialized. "He's never far off from his pots." She moved her chair away from the desk. "I'll get him for you."

"Thanks." Brom realized he hadn't asked Sara about her father's condition. He was slipping. "Wait, how's your father doing? Did the surgery go well?"

Things felt a little less awkward between her and her father, but still no less painful. She twisted the cord around her finger. "Perfectly. He came through the operation with flying colors."

Brom heard things in her voice that weren't being said. There had been a time when he had known Sara very well. "And you?"

She laughed cryptically. "I've got some colors of my own." Scars, mostly, she thought, but there was no point in dragging Brom into it. She'd cried on his shoulder enough as it was, all those years ago.

He knew how sensitive she was beneath the banter and the ready wit. "Hang in there, Sara."

Sara felt a little self-conscious. "Don't waste time worrying about me. I'm completely resilient." She hurried on before he could ask anything further. "I'll get Nik for you."

She laid the receiver down on the desk and went in search of Nik.

Sara pushed open the door to the kitchen and looked around. Antonio and Chris were conferring by the worktable. "Anyone seen Nik?"

Antonio jerked a thumb toward the walk-in refrigerator. "In there. He's talking to the vegetables."

"Of course," she murmured under her breath.

Sara stopped at the entrance of the huge refrigerator. Nik was standing inside, muttering to himself as he scanned the selection of vegetables on the shelves before him. He exhaled and she could almost see his breath forming.

"Damn."

He wrinkled his nose when he was angry, she noticed. It took the edge off. An amused smile lifted the corners of her lips. "What's the matter?"

He half turned, surprised to see her there. He gestured at the shelves. "I distinctly remember ordering kohlrabi."

Sara wouldn't have known kohlrabi from a cold rabbit, but she assumed that it wasn't there.

"Throw extra parsley on the plate. Nobody'll miss it." She heard Chris trying to stifle a laugh behind her.

But Nik didn't appear to be amused. He leveled a steely look at her. "It's pretty easy to be cavalier with something you know nothing about."

His statement only served to make her look triumphant. "I hope you're listening to yourself and taking notes."

He'd have to substitute Swiss chard until he could get a delivery, he thought. It wasn't the biggest tragedy. Running out of lobster would have taken that prize. At least this week.

When he looked up she was still there. "Why are you standing in the refrigerator doorway, annoying me?"

She nodded toward the hall. "Because Brom's on the phone. He says he wants to talk to you, although why is beyond me."

Nik walked out of the refrigerator and shut the heavy steel door behind him. "Why didn't you just say so in the first place?"

"I kind of liked listening to you curse at the vegetables." She grinned as she moved aside to let him pass. "It's nice to see you get annoyed with something else besides me, even if they are inanimate objects."

He filed away the look on her face. There was no tension evident, merely humor. It seemed that the only way they were going to carry on a conversation where she wasn't freezing up on him or retreating was if she was needling him, Nik thought.

He could put up with that. For the time being.

Nik crossed to the desk in the office and picked up the telephone. "Hello, Brom? What's up?"

Brom had begun to wonder if anyone was ever returning to the phone. His impatience evaporated at the sound of Nik's voice. "I'm calling your bluff."

Nik had no idea what Brom was referring to. "What bluff is that?"

"You promised to come up here and give the restaurant a proper once-over now that the new staff is finally in place, remember?"

Nik moved aside to let Sara sit down at the desk. He watched absently as she began to type in numbers that aligned themselves into columns on the blue screen. "Yeah, I—"

"Did," Brom concluded for him. "A.J's asking when her Uncle Nik is coming up to see her. It's been a while, you know."

Nik cradled the phone between his neck and shoulder as he picked up a list for next week's meat and poultry order. He began to leaf through it. "A.J's six months old. She can't talk yet."

Brom's laugh contradicted Nik's assumption. "She's a miniature Sinclair woman. She'll be talking by the time you get up here."

"Probably," Nik agreed.

Nik looked at Sara, toying with a thought. Maybe she'd be more relaxed at Tahoe, around Brom. Antonio wasn't going on vacation for another three weeks and Chris was coming along well, albeit slowly. Perhaps a break this weekend wouldn't be such a bad idea, after all.

"Just a second," he said into the receiver.

He leaned over Sara and pulled the desk calendar to him. He flipped two pages, scanning each intently. There was nothing special planned on either date. No large parties booked. Nothing out of the ordinary. Antonio could handle it without any difficulty.

Nik replaced the calendar, sliding it next to Sara's elbow. "Okay, Brom, you're on for this weekend."

"Good. I was thinking in terms of having everyone come up," Brom elaborated now that the first part of his plan was falling into place. "Think you can drag your sister and that husband of hers up?"

He knew Jennifer didn't need an excuse. Unlike him, she wasn't wedded to the restaurant. Hers was a fuller life. He glanced at Sara.

"I'm very persuasive when I have to be." Sara made a face at him as if to contradict his statement. "Besides, they'll want to see the baby."

So far, so good, Brom thought. Now for the most important part. "And Nik—"

"Yeah?"

"See if you can get Sara to come up with all of you, as well. It's kind of tough for her, being around her father, dealing with old wounds. I think she really needs to get away."

"My sentiments exactly." Nik remembered the questions he wanted to ask Brom about Sara. He hadn't had time to call him before, but he couldn't do it now, with Sara sitting right here. He made a mental note to talk to Brom once he arrived in Tahoe.

He looked directly at Sara as he made his promise. "Consider it done."

Brom smiled to himself. He knew he could count on Nik. "Good, I'll have a car come around to pick you up at the airport. Just call me back when you know what flight you'll be taking."

"Will do. 'Bye." Nik replaced the receiver on the cradle and then rotated his neck to get rid of the stiffness.

Sara had pretended to be busy working during the call, but she had listened. They both knew she would.

"Consider what done?" she wanted to know. The look he had given her when he'd said it warned her that something was up.

He dropped the list on the desk. "Brom wants me to bring you with us when we visit."

She didn't think she particularly cared for his wording. "You make me sound like a box of candy you're supposed to pick up at the airport."

He lifted a brow. "Not at all. Candy's sweet. A box of dynamite might be more appropriate a comparison," he corrected. "Will you come with us?"

She shrugged. She certainly wouldn't mind seeing Brom again, but she didn't care for being backed into a corner. "I might be busy."

Nik cupped her chin in his hand and turned her head until she was looking up at him. His eyes searched for a different response.

"Will you come?" he repeated.

Why did she have this feeling that her whole life might change if she agreed? It was just a weekend. A weekend with a whole entourage of people. And Brom. She had always felt safe around Brom.

So what was the problem?

Nik, a small voice whispered in reply.

She blocked the voice out. Sara leaned back in the chair and dragged her hand through her hair.

"Why not?" she agreed gamely. "I always like seeing Brom."

"Good. Unless something unforeseen happens between now and the weekend, we'll be leaving Saturday morning." He began to walk out of the room, then hesitated in the doorway, suddenly realizing that there might be an obstacle. "Is your father up to being left alone?"

Sara nodded. Raymond Santangelo was a hard man to keep down. He had already been up and about for short periods of time.

"He can spend a couple of days by himself." She looked at Nik pointedly, just so that he remembered. "He'll have to soon enough, anyway."

Nik nodded, but made no comment as he walked out of the room. Sara thought she saw him frowning, but she might have been mistaken. At any rate, it wouldn't have changed anything. As soon as she felt her father was well enough, she was leaving. She had to.

True to his word, Brom had the limousine waiting for them right at the airport. When his chauffeur, Harold, opened the rear door, Sara was surprised to see that Brom and Julia were seated inside. The baby, drooling and animated, was between them, sitting in her car seat.

Julia laughed, pleased at Sara's expression. "Surprise."

Nik was directly behind Sara, and gently urged her into the car, his hands on her hips. Sara tried not to think about how much she liked having his hands on her. The feelings she was experiencing right now were all wrong. They weren't going to lead anyplace. She couldn't let them.

"Julia couldn't wait for you to arrive," Brom explained to them, "so she decided to hold the reunion in the limo."

Holding Katie's hand, Jennifer followed Nik into the car. "Goodness, she's grown so much," Jennifer cried, looking at the baby. She tickled A.J.'s toes. The infant wiggled them and giggled as Jennifer scooted over to let Kane climb in.

"And you haven't," Julia commented as she looked Jennifer over for telltale signs of her pregnancy. Jennifer was still as slender as she ever was.

"Soon," Jennifer promised, mechanically glancing down at her waist. "All too soon I won't be able to see my feet. Only my stomach."

Julia sighed wistfully. "I'd give anything for that sort of view." But she had A.J., thanks to Jennifer's selflessness, and she would forever be grateful to her sister.

Katie sidled up to Brom. "Got candy, Uncle B'om?" She looked up at him hopefully.

A charmer, just like her aunt and her mother, Brom thought. "For you, always." Brom dug into his pocket and presented her with a multicolored sucker. Katie accepted it with the same sort of awe that a woman displayed upon receiving her first bouquet of flowers.

Kane watched his daughter eagerly rip off the cellophane wrapper. He took it from her and shoved the sticky wrapper into his pocket.

"She'll get your car dirty," he warned Brom.

Brom wasn't about to let something so mundane as worrying about his car being dirtied interfere with Katie's pleasure.

"So, we'll clean it." Brom ruffled Katie's hair and she grinned up at him, her lips already outlined in bright, sticky pink. "As long as the lady's happy."

The baby squealed and Katie went on licking loudly. Voices melded like an orchestra tuning up for a performance as questions flew back and forth in the car.

Sara suddenly felt overwhelmed by what she felt were the natural sounds of family surrounding her. It took her back across the years, when family outings were a regular event for her family. Any given Sunday a large number of them would converge in someone's backyard, or at a park. Uncles and aunts and numerous cousins as far as the eye could see. Or so it had seemed at the time.

Nostalgia brought with it a pang that tightened around her heart.

Sara looked at Brom. She could see by the look in his eyes that he knew what she was thinking. He gave her a reassuring smile and leaned forward in order to be heard better. "Good to see you again, Sara."

An amused smile creased her lips. "You saw me two weeks ago. I've only been in Newport Beach for twelve days."

"Is that all?" Nik asked incredulously. Sara gave him a dirty look that only egged him on. "Feels like forever to me."

Sara poked Nik in the ribs with her elbow. Nik had the good grace to wince as everyone else laughed.

"Everybody in?" Brom scanned both sides of the stretch limo. Jennifer and Katie were on his side, while Kane, Nik and Sara sat opposite him.

"Unless you're expecting someone else," Kane answered. He tested the door next to him to make sure it was properly closed.

Brom turned and tapped on the glass partition that separated the chauffeur from the passengers. When the man turned, Brom gave the signal. "Okay, Harold, take her back to the house."

"House?" Nik raised a brow quizzically as he looked at Brom. "I thought you said we were going to tour the restaurant."

"All in good time, Nik, all in good time," Brom assured his brother-in-law. He grinned secretively as he exchanged looks with Julia. "I've got a surprise for you."

Nik eyed Brom suspiciously. He wondered if there was something wrong at the restaurant that Brom was trying to break to him slowly. After all, Sinclair's/Tahoe was part his.

"I'm not sure I like surprises."

"You'll like this one," Julia promised him as she strapped A.J. securely into her car seat.

"All right, what's the surprise?" Nik asked Brom as he walked into the sprawling ranch house.

"I've got a baseball game lined up for us to play." He checked his watch. "In about half an hour. You'd better hustle."

"Baseball?" Nik echoed in disbelief. The sport, once so important to him, was the farthest thing from his mind these days.

Brom grinned at the stunned look on Nik's face. Nik had probably forgotten that they shared a passion for the game. "I told you that I get together with a bunch of guys regularly." He narrowed his brows comically. "We play some very serious ball."

Julia walked in behind them, carrying the baby. "Very serious." Julia echoed, lowering her voice to approximate Brom's. Her whimsical expression told Nik that she was humoring Brom.

A fondness sprouted within Nik as he remembered his college games. Still, he was more than a little rusty. "I haven't played in years." There had just never been enough time.

Nik's protest failed to impress Brom. "Good, then you can play on the other team." Brom grinned broadly, as if he was anticipating the outcome of the game. "I told you to pack old clothes," he reminded Nik as Jennifer and Kane entered the house.

The instruction had seemed a little odd at the time. "I thought maybe you wanted us to do some cleaning," Nik cracked.

"Maybe later, after you lose. Now change your clothes. They're probably all waiting for us on the field now. Addison Park, remember?" Brom asked Sara.

Sara remembered. She nodded her head as a bittersweet feeling wound its way all through her again. That was the site of the last family outing she'd ever attended with her parents.

Nik looked uncertain as he stood, debating. "I don't know about this."

"Yes, you do," Julia assured her brother. She placed her hand on his back and shoved him toward one of the guest rooms. Brom followed behind her, bringing Sara's suitcase as well as Nik's. "Once a jock, always a jock."

Nik shrugged and let himself be pushed along.

"Your room's right next to his." Brom placed Sara's suitcase inside the door.

She merely nodded as she entered. She was trying to brace herself for the event ahead. It would seem odd if she didn't go along and yet, going to the park, remembering happier times wasn't going to be easy for her.

She wished Brom had picked out another place.

"And this is your room. Now hurry up," Brom instructed. "C'mon, you, too, Kane."

Kane raised a brow. He'd been following with their two suitcases and was caught completely unaware by this new twist. "I don't play baseball."

"You'll learn," Brom promised. "We're one man short."

Nik grinned as he closed the door. There was no arguing with the man. And maybe he didn't really want to. Once, before reality had chewed away at his dreams with sharp, pointy teeth, he had entertained thoughts of trying out for a professional ball club. He had a pretty distinguished record behind him both in high school and college.

But once his parents had died, he'd put aside his dreams and shut them out of his life. There were his sisters to care for and responsibilities to live up to. Baseball was a dream others could go on to pursue, not him.

He grinned to himself. It would be good to have the feel of a bat in his hands again.

As per Brom's instruction, Nik had packed the oldest shirt he owned, a jersey that had two small holes bitten out of it, courtesy of an overactive washing machine. He pulled it on now. The jeans he took out of the suitcase were equally worn, with one knee threatening to break through the thin webbing of white threads at any moment.

When Nik walked out into the hallway again, he almost collided with Sara. She looked like a teenager in her white shorts and hot pink T-shirt. All she needed was a ponytail.

His eyes swept over her legs. He'd hate to see them dirtied, sliding into home plate. "Are you playing?"

All through school Sara had been hopelessly inept when it came to team sports. She shook her head emphatically as she leaned against the wall. "Nope. Your sisters and I are strictly the cheering section."

Nik braced one hand against the wall as he looked down at her. There was a skylight directly overhead and it bathed her in sunlight. He began to think of a different sport than baseball.

"Which side are you cheering for?"

Her eyes were mischievous as she raised her chin. "I haven't made up my mind yet. Let me see how well you play, first."

Jennifer emerged from her room down the hall. "The coach at college thought that Nik was the team's most valuable player." Glancing first at Sara, Jennifer gave her brother a very supportive wink as she passed them and went on.

Nik knew Jennifer had something on her mind other than the game. And so did he.

Sara shrugged, unimpressed. "Must have been a pretty poor team."

The light played on her lips and he wondered if there was going to be any more through traffic in the hallway to interrupt him. "UC Irvine had a very good baseball team that year."

She smirked, her dark eyes teasing him. "If you say so."

He braced his other hand on the wall, bracketing her. Sara's eyes held his, waiting. "Did I ever tell you that you have an irritating smirk?"

"Probably." She raised herself up on her toes, teasing him with the nearness of her mouth. "A ballplayer with something to prove always plays a lot better."

He could feel her breath on his face, on his mouth. His hands flattened on the wall and he inched a little closer to her. "And since when did you start coaching?"

She could feel the heat from his body. She tried not to let it affect her. Or at least not show him how much it did.

"Since now. I've decided that you need someone in your corner, since everyone else will probably be rooting for Brom's team."

"Oh?"

His mouth looked incredibly tempting and she wanted nothing more than to touch her lips to it. Sara mentally groped for a lifeline and found none.

"Sure. It's his house." Feeling oddly light-headed, she gestured vaguely toward the front of the house, where she assumed Brom was waiting. "Let's see what you've got, Sinclair."

He looked into her eyes. "All right, but I want you to remember that you were the one who asked."

Her throat tightened, almost cutting off all available air. Sara refused to surrender to the jittery little hum that traveled through her like a precursor to an earthquake.

"I remember everything. It's both the gift and the curse of having a photographic memory. Now stop talking and let's see some action."

She was going to add "out on the field" but she never had the opportunity. Nik was already touching off an explosion within her as he lowered his mouth to hers.

There was no immunity. Unlike inoculation, there was no way she could protect herself from him by having kissed him before. No tolerance had been formed, no antibodies filled her to take the edge off what was happening to her. What happened each time he kissed her.

The world flipped over. Day became night and she was catapulted light-years away from a ranch house in Tahoe to a world of fire and heat. Mardi Gras in outer space, she thought, clinging to Nik's shirt.

It took everything she had not to let herself drift through the region permanently. With her head spinning, she pulled back. It was only a small consolation that Nik was breathing as hard as she was.

"God, if you can play baseball only half as well as you can kiss, I don't think that Brom's team has a prayer of winning."

Nik ran his thumb along her bottom lip and had the pleasure of feeling her shiver against him. "Is that a compliment?"

Sara shrugged. "I always call them as I see them." Nik pinned her with a scrutinizing look that drew out the lie like a magnet pulling out a pin. "Well, *almost* always." She placed both her hands on his chest and pushed him away. "Now get out there and play ball."

Once at the park, Sara settled in beside Julia and the baby. Exercising supreme effort, she purposely shut out the barrage of splintered memories that were trying to break through. This was Nik's day to relax and she wasn't going to spoil it, or insult Brom's hospitality by allowing the sadness to get the better of her.

Sara glanced around at the wives and children who'd come to join in the recreation. Blankets were scattered all over the perimeter of the playing field like so many multi-colored lily pads floating on a lake.

Brom had thought of everything, right down to providing hot dogs, sodas and popcorn. And right afterward, there would be a picnic lunch.

Jennifer dropped down next to them on the grass. Katie made a beeline for the hot dogs.

"He goes all out, doesn't he?" Jennifer asked her sister.

Julia nodded, but it was Sara who answered. "Brom never did things in half measures. It was always all or nothing." She squinted as she looked for him out in the field. Brom was playing shortstop this inning. "Brom likes to bring passion to everything he does."

Julia only smiled to herself, silently agreeing.

Nik was the third man up to the plate. Sara cringed a little, hoping that he wouldn't do too badly. Maybe a bunt or a walk to get him on base. She didn't want to see him strike out his first time up.

Without realizing it she crossed her fingers and tensed, watching his every movement.

The pitcher threw once, and then again. Each time Nik swung, he came in contact with air as the ball whizzed by him into the crouching catcher's mitt as if it contained some sort of homing device.

Sara shut her eyes.

Jennifer nudged her. "You can't see that way."

"That's the whole point," Sara murmured, opening one eye hesitantly.

And then suddenly Sara jumped to her feet, stunned. Belatedly, she began cheering as the third time the pitcher threw to Nik the ball connected with the bat. A resounding smack splintered the sultry afternoon air and the ball was launched into a huge arc that flew far beyond the outfielder's raised glove.

Julia was applauding madly. She and Jennifer exchanged looks, remembering other games played in professional-looking stadiums. Julia cupped her hands around her mouth. "You've still got the magic, Nik!"

Yes, Sara thought, remembering the interlude in Brom's hallway, he did.

Chapter 11

The baseball game ran a full nine innings, spanning what seemed to Sara an endless two and a half hours. By the end of it, both sides were more than willing to call it quits.

Brom took the towel Julia offered him, wiping his face as he sank onto the grass. He was the last to join them at the picnic. Julia had packed a huge red-and-white tablecloth that looked as if it could have covered a mess-hall table. It easily accommodated them all.

Brom eyed Nik good-naturedly. Nik had homered twice during the game, the second one a grand slam in the bottom of the eighth.

"And to think I invited this guy up to play." Brom shook his head.

Kane lay sprawled out on the grass, his head cradled in his laced hands. He felt exhausted and extremely grateful that the game was over. "C'mon, Brom, a gambler's supposed to lose gracefully."

Brom never frequented his own tables for purposes other than social. Success in business was all that he asked of Lady Luck. He'd never longed for her to blow on his dice.

"In case you've all forgotten, I never gamble on anything other than a sure thing." Dropping the towel to the grass behind him, Brom reached for Julia's hand and curved his fingers around it. Words weren't necessary between them.

Or for Sara, who looked on, a touch of envy slipping through her like thread through the eye of a needle.

Brom nodded toward Nik as he addressed his case to the others. "I thought I was asking an old, out-of-shape ex-jock for a friendly game of baseball. I had no idea I was getting Hank Aaron."

Jennifer laughed as she dug through the ice chest and found Kane's favorite brand of beer. She tossed him the can. He caught it easily.

"Now you make a catch," Brom complained. Kane had missed an all-important ball that had helped the other side score.

Kane shrugged, pulling the tab. "You should have been throwing beer cans, not balls."

"It wasn't that bad," Jennifer soothed.

Brom shifted over toward the ice chest. "Not bad?" He helped himself to a beer. "You call losing fifteen to six not bad?"

Julia never understood what the fuss was over sports. She shrugged. "It's not like you lost a hundred and twelve to three."

A red rubber ball plopped directly before Nik's feet. He looked around and saw a blond boy, no more than four, running eagerly toward him, his arms outstretched. Nik tossed the ball to him. He was pumped, he realized, and he loved it.

"That's basketball," Nik pointed out. Julia merely lifted a shoulder, unconcerned about specifics.

Brom thought the matter over. "You don't play that, too, do you?" he asked Nik.

"Nope." In college he'd always been too wrapped up in baseball to go in for any of the other sports.

"Good." Brom nodded, pleased. A glint entered his eyes. "Next time you come up, we play basketball."

"Hey, this is Tahoe. Don't you guys believe in a friendly game of poker?" Kane protested, spreading his hands wide. A little foam emerged from the can and he drank it quickly before it spilled on the grass. He was a lot better at cards than he was at running around and sweating.

"If all else fails," Brom conceded. "How's your game?"

"Fair to middling," Kane answered easily.

"Uh-huh, famous last words." Brom knew confidence when he saw it. "I think we'll stick to basketball as our next game of choice."

Nik closed his eyes as he stretched out on the grass. "We'll talk." Jennifer's voice had him opening his eyes again quickly.

"Katie!" Jennifer rose to her knees, calling after her daughter. Katie had scampered away, chasing after a white butterfly that refused to accommodate her by getting caught. "Come back here. I don't want you wandering off."

Katie looked over her shoulder at Jennifer, as if weighing her mother's words against the allure of the butterfly. The butterfly won.

Jennifer scrambled to her feet. "That girl. You have to keep your eye on her all the time."

"Like her mother," Kane said fondly. "Sit, I'll get her." He handed Jennifer his beer before going to retrieve his pint-sized would-be entomologist.

Jennifer pressed the cold can against her throat as she watched Kane chase after Katie. Seeing her father coming toward her, the little girl squealed and began to run in the opposite direction. Kane snatched her up in his arms and then swung her around until it seemed as if her giggles filled the air.

The others understood Jennifer's immediate concern and shared it. She flushed slightly as she looked at Sara. "I guess ever since the kidnapping, we've all been a little edgy about Katie, even in a place like this."

Sara nodded. No explanation was necessary. Brom had filled her in when she had stopped by to visit before arriving in Newport. He had told her how Jennifer's daughter had been kidnapped from the hospital when she was only

three days old. Kane had been the police detective assigned
to the case. Touched by Jennifer's plight, Kane had broken
police department regulations by allowing her to come with
him as he tracked Katie down.

And along the way he had broken a few rules of his own.
By the time the trail had led them to Brom's door, Kane,
who had lived his entire life in shadows, had stepped into the
light and fallen in love with Jennifer.

Sara thought that Brom's story was no less dramatic.
When his first wife had been unable to conceive, Brom and
Alexis had decided to adopt. Ultimately they had gone a
private route when the more conventional method kept
stonewalling them. The man handling the private adoption, a once-trusted friend, had turned out to be part of a
ring that stole babies from hospitals around the country.
Alexis had died suddenly of ovarian cancer just a few weeks
before Katie was placed in Brom's arms.

Instantly in love with the infant, Brom had made up his
mind to go through with the adoption. His plans had
changed abruptly when Jennifer and Kane had shown up to
claim the baby. Because she could see how much he loved
Katie, Jennifer had invited Brom to visit them anytime he
wanted.

It was in the hushed, romantic atmosphere of Sinclair's
that he had first met Julia. A few breathtakingly turbulent
months later he had married her.

And where was her story? Sara wondered with an envious pang she was ashamed of. Her cousin's story, as well as
Jennifer's and Kane's, had almost fairy-tale qualities to their
endings. Both couples appeared to be living happily ever
after.

Appeared.

But appearances or not, Sara knew that it wasn't going to
happen to her. There were no happy endings, real or imagined, in her future. She wasn't made for a relationship. She
was afraid to even consider undertaking one. Afraid of the
consequences.

Because of what she had seen and what she had lived
with.

To discover that her parents' happy marriage, something she had wholeheartedly believed in, was all only an illusion perpetrated for her benefit had made Sara lose faith in her own abilities to perceive things, to see things as they really were and not the way she wanted them to be. She didn't trust her own judgment. And she didn't want to repeat her mother's mistakes.

And yet, she wanted . . .

This wasn't the time, she upbraided herself.

Sara took a thick roast beef sandwich out of the hamper and began eating slowly, trying to block out her thoughts.

The park was alive with noise. Everyone whom Brom had invited had come prepared for a picnic after the game. There were children playing, parents laughing. . . .

Like the old days, she thought, when she believed happiness was everlasting.

No matter how hard she tried to evade them, her memories continued to find her, a determined little army with pointed lances aimed at her heart.

Sara raised her eyes from her sandwich as Kane returned with Katie in tow. He plopped the girl down next to her mother and flanked her with his long legs as he sat down.

Turning, Sara was aware that Nik was studying her again. And he looked as if he could read her thoughts.

"This is good," she told Julia suddenly, holding up her sandwich. "What kind of dressing did you use?" She didn't know blue cheese from ranch, but it was something to say.

"I didn't make it," Julia answered.

"It's from the restaurant," Brom informed his cousin. "House secret." He winked at Nik.

A challenge. This he was more than up to. "I bet I can guess." Sitting up, Nik moved closer to Sara. He slid his fingers down along her wrist to hold her hand steady and then took a bite of her sandwich. He felt her pulse race beneath his thumb.

Who would ever have thought that having someone mooch her food could turn into an erotic experience? Little quivers of excitement went hurtling into her stomach from all directions.

She needed a cold shower, Sara thought restlessly. And another cold dose of reality wouldn't hurt the situation, either. She needed both and more, because all she could think about was running her hands along Nik's smooth, muscular back and kissing him again. Never mind that the man had just played a hard game of baseball in eighty-five-degree weather and was undoubtedly sweaty as hell.

It didn't change a thing. She still wanted him. Wanted to touch him. Wanted to make love with him the way she had never wanted anything else before.

Sara cleared her throat, wishing she could rid herself of her feelings as well. Her hand dropped limply to her lap, the sandwich forgotten. She looked at Julia. "Got anything cold to drink?"

Julia handed Sara a soda out of the ice chest. The lady had it bad for her brother, Julia thought. She wondered what she could do to help things along.

Nik would have gone on eating out of Sara's hand if no one else had been present. Eating out of her hand and progressing on to sample the taste of her skin, the flavor of her lips.

But there would be another time, and soon, he promised himself. For now, he'd enjoy the company of his family. If nothing else, it seemed to set Sara at ease, and that was an accomplishment.

Nik looked at Brom confidently. "You're using Russian dressing with a light cream substitute, a sprinkling of cayenne pepper and a pinch of garlic for taste."

Kane shook his head, refusing to believe Nik was serious. "You're bluffing." He unwrapped a sandwich himself and took a bite. It was flavorful, but nothing telegraphed itself to his palate. "Nobody's that good."

"Brom?" Nik waited for his brother-in-law to vindicate him.

Brom shrugged, mystified at Nik's ability. "I don't know. I'm going to have to check with Josef, but it sure sounds right."

Jennifer didn't need any verification from a third party. "Never mess with Nik when it comes to ingredients and food," she told Brom and Kane. "The man knows no equal."

Julia unscrewed a jar of apple sauce for A.J. She dipped a spoon into it and, bracing herself, raised the spoon to the baby's mouth. A.J. stuck her tongue out and did battle with the spoon.

"Or so he likes to think," Julia put in.

Nik laughed and shook his head as he took his own sandwich from the hamper. "Same old Julia."

Sara took a bite out of her sandwich, her mouth covering where Nik's had been only minutes before. It wasn't possible for her to taste his lips on the bread. So why did she think she did?

"I think I really like your sister," Sara decided out loud.

"You would. You're two of a kind." Both women seemed to get a perverse pleasure out of needling him, Nik thought.

Sara raised her sandwich in a silent toast to Julia as the latter turned to look at her.

Julia thought she saw something in Sara's eyes that she recognized. A wariness. The same sort of wariness that had once been a part of her own world until Brom had slain her dragons and made the nightmares go away. She wondered what Sara's demons were and if Nik was the one who could make them die.

She'd seen the way her brother looked at Sara. Perhaps he didn't even know it yet himself, but he was taken with the woman. More than taken. If she didn't miss her guess, Nik was halfway in love with Sara.

Julia mentally reviewed the sleeping arrangements and smiled to herself as she coaxed another spoonful of apple sauce between her daughter's messy lips. She was glad she had placed Nik and Sara next door to each other. Proximity always helped move things along.

She only hoped that Nik wouldn't be slow on the uptake.

The picnic went on for another two hours and then, as if by mutual consent, the party broke up. The other men on Brom's baseball team and their families took their leave.

Within fifteen minutes the park was quiet. Sara looked around and shivered.

"Are you cold?" Nik asked, surprised. The sun was hot.

"No, I was just thinking."

"About what?" he coaxed.

Behind him, Kane was helping Jennifer fold the table-cloth while Katie dashed back and forth beneath the canopy they had temporarily formed. Brom was taking the basket back to the car as Julia changed yet another diaper. Despite all the activity, he and Sara might have been alone for all the attention Nik paid to the rest of them.

Sara ran her hands along her arms, remembering. "What a great park this used to be."

"Used to be?" He looked around. The park was clean and well kept. He could see the lake just beyond a stately row of trees. There were barbecue pits strategically scattered about to the left of the playing field. "Looks pretty good to me now."

She blinked and then smiled. Turning to him, she nodded. "Yes, I guess you're right. It still is." She started walking toward the car, determined to shake off her mood. "I had no idea you played that well."

Nik laughed as he slipped an arm around her. "Neither did I."

They stayed at Brom's house long enough to shower and then change. Leaving the children with the housekeeper, Brom took everyone to Casino Camelot. There they had dinner in the restaurant that Julia had designed, and then took in a show afterward.

Kane settled back comfortably in the limousine and draped his arm around Jennifer's shoulders. He wondered how he had managed to live all those years without her. He knew he couldn't do it now. She was as much a part of him as his soul. The soul she had helped him find.

He looked at his brother-in-law. "I'll give you one thing, Brom. You certainly know how to entertain your guests."

"It's my business." Brom smiled expansively, content that everyone he cared about had enjoyed themselves tonight. He had a thriving business, a beautiful, loving wife, a daughter he adored and a family he could always count on. Life, he decided, didn't get much better than this.

He gathered Julia closer to him as he looked at his cousin. Sara sat opposite him, beside Nik. She didn't look entirely comfortable. Brom detected the slight tension outlining her body, as if she was fighting some internal battle with herself.

Stop fighting, Sara. You'll only lose if you win, he thought.

Brom smiled at her encouragingly. He didn't want Sara to miss out on all this. This was the kind of life she was meant for, not the nomadic one she had adhered to. He wanted her to experience that sense of belonging that he had because of Julia and the baby. But he knew he couldn't show Sara the way. She was going to have to find it on her own.

Brom glanced at Nik. Maybe they could find the way together. If he didn't miss his guess, Nik and Sara would make an excellent pair.

Harold brought the limousine up the winding path to Brom's front door. Brom took Julia's hand as he got out and helped her from the car. The others followed close behind. "Thank you, Harold. I won't be needing you any longer tonight."

Brom pressed a series of numbers on the keypad at the front door, then unlocked it. He stepped aside and let everyone file by.

"It's been a long day and I've got more planned for us tomorrow." He looked at Jennifer and Kane. "Why don't we call it a night and turn in?"

"Sounds good to me," Kane agreed. He laced his fingers through Jennifer's. Katie was safely tucked away in the nursery with A.J. That meant that the rest of the night was theirs. He was looking forward to it.

Sara felt restless, as if she was a Thoroughbred standing at the starting gate, waiting for the gate to open. Except that the end of the race was a foregone conclusion. She knew she'd never get to sleep feeling like this.

"I think I'll raid your refrigerator if you don't mind." She looked from Julia to Brom. Julia nodded her permission. "I don't feel much like sleeping just yet."

Brom gestured toward the kitchen. "Help yourself. My house is yours."

Sara flashed a grateful grin. "At least that hasn't changed." Raised next door to one another, they had practically lived in each other's houses while they were growing up, until Sara moved. "Night, everyone. See you in the morning."

She avoided looking at Nik as she passed him.

"Nik, can I see you a minute?" Kane drew Nik aside in the living room. "I'll be there in a minute, Jennifer," Kane promised his wife.

He waited until everyone else had left the room.

"What's wrong?" Nik perched on the edge of one of the sofa's arms, waiting.

"Nothing. I couldn't help noticing the signals going on between you and Sara."

"You mean like walk and don't run?" Nik quipped. "Mostly don't walk," he added.

"Exactly." Kane felt a little awkward. It wasn't his style to butt in to other people's business. His personal inclination had always been to guard his own privacy. But living within a family, a real family, had taught him that there were times when interfering was necessary. If you cared.

"I don't know if this means anything to you but, working as a detective, sometimes I stumble across information that becomes useful later, like the piece of a puzzle you can fit in only after other pieces are in place."

Nik looked at him, confused. "Are you trying to tell me something about Sara?"

"Maybe, in a way." Kane stumbled along the unfamiliar terrain. "This is actually about her father, Raymond."

Nik nodded. "I've met him." He crossed his arms in front of him. "Go on, I'm listening."

Kane shoved his hands into his back pockets and began to pace around the room as he spoke. "Raymond Santangelo's a hell of a guy. I've known him for about three years and you couldn't ask for a better cop. But he's got this gambling problem. Had, actually," Kane amended. "From what I know, he hasn't bet a penny in almost a year. Up until then, he played the horses whenever he could. Blew everything he had at the track. That's why his second wife left him."

"Second wife?" Nik hadn't realized that Sara's father had been remarried. Or divorced.

Kane nodded. "The one he married after Sara's mother. Anyway, one night, while we were on a stakeout, he talked a little more than he probably would have under normal circumstances—stakeouts can get awfully boring."

Nik had little doubt that no matter how bored he became, Kane would never divulge anything personal unless he fully meant to.

"Santangelo told me that he left his first wife because he didn't want his daughter finding out about his gambling problem. He didn't want to look like a weakling in her eyes. When he couldn't seem to lick his problem, he thought that it was best to sever all contact with her under the circumstances rather than to have her find out."

Nik blew out a breath. So she had no idea why her father had disappeared. That would explain Sara's hostility toward the man. "Obviously Sara didn't agree."

"He had no way of knowing that. He did what he thought was best." Kane shrugged, looking at his brother-in-law. "I don't know if that helps you any—"

Nik rose from the sofa. "What do you mean, helps?"

"Nik, I *am* a detective." Kane's chiseled features softened as he grinned. "And a man. I've been there before myself, standing in your shoes, confused as hell about a woman because she tied me up in knots inside." He thought of Jennifer, waiting for him in bed. He moved toward the doorway. "Only difference was, I didn't think I was good enough for her." He laid his hand on Nik's shoulder. "That's not your problem. But we've all got hurdles to leap over before we can reach the finish line." He dropped his hand and crossed the threshold. "She's a hell of a prize if you can win her. Night."

"Night." Nik nodded vaguely in Kane's direction, his mind already on Sara. "And thanks."

"Don't mention it."

They parted company in the hall, Kane going to his bedroom and Jennifer, Nik toward his room and restless sleep. As he turned in the hall, he glanced toward his left. There was light coming from the kitchen.

Sara.

Nik debated. Maybe he felt like conducting his own late-night raid on the refrigerator. Or on the raider.

He walked into the kitchen and found that she had opened the French doors that led out onto the patio. Julia had told him that it was her favorite place to have breakfast. In the distance he could see the lake. Beams of moonlight strummed long, slender fingers along the black waters, flirting with them.

Sara was sitting at a glass-top table, twisting the stem of a wine goblet in her fingers. Nik couldn't remember seeing anyone look so sad before.

Sara looked up, sensing his presence a moment before Nik walked out on the patio. "Can't keep away from the kitchen, can you?"

"Occupational habit." He dropped into the seat next to hers. "Actually—" his voice softened "—it wasn't the kitchen that lured me."

She smiled over the rim of her goblet. "Very sexy line."

He laid his hand over hers. "I don't do lines, Sara. Life's too short for that."

She sighed, closing her eyes. Suddenly she felt very tired. Maybe it was the wine, although she'd only had a few sips. Or maybe it was the tension, finally taking its toll on her.

"Oh, I don't know. Sometimes, when you take it one day at a time, life starts to feel like some sort of an endless entity, stretched out before you."

He wanted to understand her. "I thought you had a good time today."

"I did." She smiled sadly, catching the moonlight in her glass. "Maybe too good."

Nik sighed, feeling like a man in a foreign country without any maps, any road signs. "I'm back to needing subtitles again."

Sara bit her lower lip. Maybe she owed him an explanation, before he thought she was completely crazy. "It reminded me a lot of the picnics I went on as a kid. Especially since Brom was there." A faraway look entered her eyes. "It reminded me of how wonderful I thought life was."

"It still can be."

His voice was warm, coaxing. Maybe he still believed that, she thought. But she didn't. She shook her head as she cupped the goblet between her hands. "No."

"How can you be so certain of that?

"I grew up."

Nik leaned forward, searching for answers in her eyes. "What's that supposed to mean?"

She felt her defense mechanism activating, but she couldn't stop it. "It means that I know good things don't last, no matter how much you think they will or how much you want them to."

Nik refused to accept that. More, he refused to let her accept it. "Look at Brom and Julia, or Kane and Jennifer." He gestured toward the house impatiently, struggling to keep his voice low. "It doesn't look as if it's going to end for them, does it?"

"No, but . . ."

Her voice trailed off as she lifted her shoulders and let them drop again helplessly. He didn't understand, she thought, and she couldn't make him understand. There were times she couldn't completely understand it herself. But she couldn't shake the feeling that failure waited for most relationships at the end of the road.

So with all this going against it, why did she want to be involved with Nik? It didn't make any sense. She pressed her hand to her head. She felt as if she was going crazy.

He had to find a way to break down her resistance. "My parents were happy until the day they died."

The look on her face was envious. "Mine weren't. I just thought they were."

They were at an impasse, but he wasn't about to surrender. "So what are we looking at?" His eyes probed hers. "Never trying to grab at happiness because there's one failure in the way?"

She rose, leaving her goblet on the table. She walked to the edge of the patio and looked out. Her hands curled around the white wrought-iron fence that surrounded it. "You don't understand."

Her eyes fluttered shut for a moment, absorbing his nearness, his scent, wishing she wasn't emotionally shackled the way she was. "How can I when I don't understand it myself? I just know I'm afraid, too afraid to take the step."

"Don't be afraid." Gently he turned her around to face him. His eyes caressed her face, weakening her resolve. "I won't hurt you, Sara."

She shook her head, trying to resist him. Trying to resist herself. "That's what you say now, but—"

He wouldn't let her finish. "That's what I *mean* now. They're not just words, Sara." Slowly he trailed his fingers along her bare arms. Needs sprang up within her to mark his path.

She closed her eyes, absorbing his touch. "I know, but—"

He laid his fingers against her lips. "No, there is no 'but.'" He dropped his hand. "Trust me, Sara. Trust yourself."

She shook her head, fear licking red-hot tongues through her as if she was standing in the center of a veritable inferno. "You don't know what you're asking me to do."

"Yes, I do." His voice was soft, gentle, soothing, even as his touch inflamed her. "I'm asking you to take a chance. The same chance I'm taking." He searched her eyes for understanding. "I'm not asking you to do anything that I'm not asking myself."

She tried to pull away, but found she had no strength. "You're confusing me. I can't think."

He smiled. "Good. Maybe if you stop thinking you'll give yourself a chance to feel." He took her hand and placed it over his heart. "What do you feel, Sara?"

"Your heart. It's got a good beat. You're very healthy," she quipped, desperately trying for humor.

He wouldn't let her talk her way out of this. It was too important to both of them.

"There it is, Sara—my heart. In the palm of your hand. What are you going to do about it? Are you just going to walk away from it? From me?"

He was undermining her resolve like acid eating through a thin layer of tissue paper. "Did you major in philosophy, as well?"

"No, Sara." Nik pulled her into his arms, fitting her against him. "Just life."

And then he kissed her. Kissed her the way she had been waiting for him to do all afternoon. And skyrockets went off, right on cue.

She was lost.

Chapter 12

Sara had no time to rally against him. No time to build up her armaments. No time and no will.

She felt as if she was melting against Nik like heated mercury even while she knew that she should be pulling away from him.

Running away.

Yes, running. She had absolutely no defenses within her grasp to fight this hot onslaught of his mouth on hers, this plundering of her very soul.

She didn't want to fight it.

His body twisted against hers, absorbing the full measure of her frame as it pressed along the length of his. Nik was hard and rigid against her. Desperate, she searched for indignation, for anger, for something, damn it, that would help.

There was no help.

His mouth was tangy and sweet and overpowering, reducing the structure of her barricades to rubble. They crumbled pitifully.

She couldn't get enough of him. She knew she had to stop. If this was just good sex, then maybe she could accept it. But it wasn't. There was so much more to it. And she knew she couldn't handle it.

Sara thought she was losing her sanity.

Drowning in him, going under for the third time, she somehow managed to drag her head back. Her pulse was breaking the sound barrier as it throbbed all through her body, demanding satisfaction.

"Wait," she implored. She pressed her palms against his chest. They felt as forceful as twigs trying to keep back the wind. "We shouldn't be doing this here." She looked over her shoulder at the darkened house. "What if someone sees?"

He thought of Julia and Jennifer. They had their fingers crossed so hard, hoping something would happen between Sara and him, that he was surprised they could dress themselves in the morning. Brom had made it clear that he hoped Nik could fill the void he felt was in Sara's life. As for Kane, even he had tried to help things along by telling him about Sara's father.

Nik ran the back of his hand along her cheek, exciting them both. "If they do, they'll probably throw a party and have us married before morning."

"No!" Sara snapped out the word, pushing him from her as she took a step away. The wrought-iron rail at her back prevented any further escape.

She was really frightened. Why? What did she see when she looked at him? He had to understand.

"Don't worry, I won't let them bring a preacher around." Nik slipped his hand over hers. His strong fingers rubbed her skin slowly, sensuously. He saw passion struggling to break through in her eyes. "Come on, I know just the place to escape from prying eyes."

She didn't want to escape from prying eyes. She wanted to escape from him. And herself. Sara shook her head. "No—"

Suddenly she was airborne, effortlessly swept into his arms. Surprised, she could only stare at him. She tried to find her voice in order to demand her release. The words wouldn't come. Her arms betrayed her as they slipped around his neck for support. Struggle though she did, she *wanted* this.

"What are you doing?"

Nik grinned, walking into the kitchen. He pulled the terrace doors closed after them. "If the mountain won't come to Mohammed, Mohammed is just going to have to carry the mountain to where he wants it to be." Still holding her, he left the kitchen.

"And where's that?" Sara's throat was dry, tight as she asked the question. Her body hummed, yearning. She felt desire growing at a prodigious pace.

"My room."

His bed. Heaven.

What was the use of fighting? She knew that she was destined to end up there. She'd known when she had boarded the plane this morning. Perhaps she'd known since she had seen him in the kitchen, a rugged, gorgeous-looking man communing with something in a copper pot.

With a sigh that bordered on surrender, Sara laid her head against his chest. She felt Nik's heart beneath her cheek. She knew it was silly, but it made her feel secure. Warm. Safe. She hadn't felt that way in years.

Nik only smiled to himself as he crossed into the darkened hallway.

Sara prayed everyone in the house was asleep and that no one would see them. There was no strength left in her to resist. Not against him. Not against herself. And certainly not against the inevitable.

The door to his bedroom stood open. Nik crossed the threshold and then eased the door closed with his elbow. It clicked into place as the latch bolt slid into the strike plate.

The soft, almost imperceptible sound reverberated in Sara's head, echoing like the sound of a cell door being closed.

Suddenly she came to life, squirming in his arms. "Put me down, Sinclair." She cloaked herself in a few precious shreds of anger. It was a desperate attempt to deny the almost violent needs racking her body. "I'm not a sack of meal you can just carry off at will."

Too late, Nik thought as he set her down. *It's too late for both of us.*

Wariness rimmed with panic entered her eyes. "Sara." His hands whispered along her arms. "There's nowhere to run."

And nowhere to hide.

She knew that. That's what made it all so frightening. She couldn't escape this. It was as if she was glued to the hardwood floor. "You're really making this hard for me."

"Yes, I know." There wasn't a speck of remorse in Nik's voice.

She felt like a prisoner. And he was the jailer. Him and those eyes of his that saw through her. "Damn hard."

He began to coax her mouth open with his own. His lips were firm, seeking. His tongue outlined her lips. A flurry of small, teasing kisses just barely touched her mouth, like butterflies flirting with the tips of the summer grass. He heard her sigh as she wound her arms around his neck. Her body adhered to his.

She searched his eyes. He knew, damn him. He knew. "I want you, Nik. God help me, but I do."

His hold tightened around her. His smile was gentle. "I never say no to a beautiful lady."

A frenzy spun through her. If this was to happen, it had to happen quickly, so she could outrun her thoughts, her fears. She tugged at his shirt, pulling it free from the waistband. Anxious, her fingers fumbled.

Nik captured her hands in his and pulled them aside. She looked at him, confused. Didn't he want this?

"Slowly, Sara, slowly," he cautioned. "Savor it, like a gourmet meal."

For a fleeting moment passion was tempered with humor in her eyes. You could take a man out of the kitchen, but never the kitchen out of the man. "Is that how you think of yourself? As a gourmet meal that you've graciously consented to serve to me?"

She didn't understand yet. He shook his head as he crooked a finger beneath her chin and lifted it so that her eyes met his.

''No, that's how I think of *us* and what there is between us. Something special. Something really out of the ordinary.''

There were explosions going on inside him, coupled with an urgency he'd never known before. But as much as he wanted to take her this instant, he knew that he had to go slowly, or not at all.

Tonight was something he wanted her to remember. Always. Tonight would be the cornerstone of the foundation he intended to lay for them. The memory would be something for Sara to cling to when she began fearing that nothing lasted.

This would last.

But he had to convince her, and that took time.

Nik lifted her hands to his lips and softly kissed each one in turn. He watched her eyes change and darken until they were almost black, like deep, rich Swiss chocolate.

Releasing her, he slid his hands along her sides and then slowly inched his palms along the swell of her breasts until he reached her shoulder blades. And the zipper that ran the length of her dress.

Sara sucked in her breath as she felt the zipper begin to part along her bare back. Deftly, Nik guided it down slowly. He pressed only the tip of his finger against the tab, moving it lightly down the delicate slope of her spine. Heat flashed along her skin, marking the path. She shivered as the zipper separated completely.

Needs slammed through him as Nik brought his mouth down on hers again. He molded her body to him, attempting to absorb the sensations that were skimming over her.

The thin shoulder straps drooped in submission, slipping down her warmed skin. Nik's hands wove a spell over her as he caressed her back. His own heart hammering, he skimmed his lips over the hollow of her throat. Then his mouth, hot and moist, moved from one shoulder to another.

Sara arched against him, desperate to draw in every last shred of sensation that Nik was creating for her. Her body felt like a blazing inferno, the very core of a steam engine. She was going to explode at any moment unless he took her.

"Now," she cried hoarsely against his mouth. He swallowed the word and tasted the desire in it. Sara's fingers dug into his shoulders, frantic for the feel of him. "Now."

Nik cupped the back of her head in his hand, tilting it away. Her mouth was mussed from the imprint of his. His stomach knotted. "Shh."

He stepped back and her dress floated away from her torso. She was nude from the waist up. Reverently, as if he was worshiping at the altar of a goddess, Nik molded his hands around her breasts. His thumbs teased the pink edges until they hardened, rigid with desire.

Unable to bear the separation, Sara moved against him. Passion flared in his eyes, spurring her on. Only half lucid, she undid the buttons of his shirt and then peeled it from his body. She wanted to feel him against her. Like a creature needy for warmth, she wanted to feel the heat radiating from his body to hers.

Again he stopped her. She was moving too fast and he could only restrain himself for so long. Exercising the patience he had inbred into his life to the limit, Nik laid Sara on the bed and buried his head at her breast. His tongue moved quickly from one peak to the other as she gasped and twisted, her hands grasping for him.

Her skin shone, damp with moisture as she pulled him to her. He loomed above, a fraction out of reach, trying to memorize her face the way it was now, at this instant. Her eyes were almost wild, dazed. There was no wariness, no barriers.

For now, she was his.

Later they would work on forever, he thought. This moment, he had now. Wanting to rip the last barriers away, Nik forced himself to go slowly. He pulled her dress down the long, tantalizing length of her legs, dragging her panties along with it. It all fell in a colorful heap at the foot of the bed.

Her skin was golden, her limbs supple and graceful as she tangled them around him, eager, wanton. Sensations pleaded for release.

"You're still dressed," Sara protested in frustration.

"Not for long."

Nik undid the belt and pulled off his trousers quickly, never daring to take his eyes from hers. She might disappear if he did.

Completely nude, they tumbled onto the bed together, lost in one another.

Her mouth was hot on his, searching for things that had no name, feelings that had no form. She only knew she wanted to continue to lose herself in him. To take and be taken until there were no coherent thoughts left in her mind, no protest left in her soul.

Anticipation had Sara spiraling upward to the first climax. He needed only a little to drive her over. The slightest touch to her core did it.

Nik watched in fascinated awe as she bucked and twisted, digging strong fingers into his back.

She tried not to scratch him as she literally scrambled back over the edge. Her breathing was short, labored as pleasure dashed over her like the pounding surf during a typhoon.

Sara sighed long and hard as she sank, limp, farther into the bed. It felt as if she had fallen for miles, when she hadn't even moved.

Opening her eyes, Sara saw Nik smiling just above her face. She looked at him, a half question forming in her eyes.

He was energized by her very reaction. "Lady," he promised, "you ain't seen nothing yet."

The journey began again with a jolt. His hands were clever as they lightly slid along her moistened core, teasing, promising, then moving back until she whimpered. And then he plunged his fingers inside to work her up into a frenzy again.

Stars exploded in her head as she was thrown into the center of the hurricane. Agony and ecstasy entwined eternal hands and held her captive together.

She wanted it to stop.

She wanted to die this way and never have it end.

She was magnificent, he thought, watching her. And he was only human.

His first goal had been to pleasure her, to show her what could be. To make her understand how important she was to him. But he could only hold himself back for so long. He wanted desperately to be inside her, to join with her and be one.

Ever so gently Nik rolled over onto her, then propped himself up on his elbows. He felt her part her legs for him and then arch against him in mute supplication.

He didn't need any more.

Nik drove himself into her. A moan echoed in his throat as she sheathed him eagerly, desperately, her hips cradling against his. Framing her face as he kissed her, Nik moved his hips, coaxing a mirror rhythm from hers.

Together they began a ride that neither of them was destined ever to forget.

Weakened, humbled, stunned and very, very content, Nik crumpled onto Sara, too exhausted to do anything else. He felt her heart beating wildly, like the wings of a hummingbird, against his chest.

From somewhere he found the strength to brush a kiss along her hair. It drained him. It was another moment before he could ask, "Am I too heavy for you?"

"No." She murmured the word and it rippled against his shoulder, stirring excitement within him even as he lay in a state of total collapse. Too much would never begin to be enough.

"Good," he muttered. "Because I can't move."

"Neither can I." She liked the feel of his weight on her. Sara allowed her hands to play softly along his back. It felt every bit as strong and muscular as she had fantasized it would be. "If there's an earthquake now," she mused aloud, "they'll find us like this."

He tried to lift his head, and decided against it. Not yet. He wanted to stay this way just a little longer. "I've got no problems with that."

She smiled, and he could feel her lips curving. It tickled his skin. A warm feeling began to spread through him again.

"They could bury us in the same coffin," Nik proposed, as if considering the matter. "It'd be a lot cheaper that way."

It was so absurd she laughed. "You're macabre."

The slight movement of her belly as she laughed excited him. Nik felt his strength suddenly, miraculously returning.

"No, just practical." He raised himself on his elbow to look at her. "Sometimes."

Light from the single lamp in the room played along his face, leaving half in shadow. It made him seem a little unreal.

Just like this feeling inside her.

"But not now," she guessed.

"Most especially now."

She didn't understand. "And what's practical about this?"

He maintained a straight face, but his eyes gave him away. "Well, it *was* the only practical solution. If we hadn't made love tonight they would have had to come and lock me up by morning."

She felt herself smiling. "And why would they have locked you up?" She tried to tug a sheet up over her breasts. Nik held on to it firmly, foiling her as he grinned as mischievously as any boy.

"Because I would have gone completely insane from wanting you."

She doubted that very much. "Oh, it's been that hard for you."

Nik traced the slight dimple in her cheek that formed with her arch smile.

"It's been that hard for me." He was smiling, but there was something very serious in his tone. And then the look shifted again and his eyes were completely roguish. "Speaking of which . . ."

She could read his mind. Perhaps because it echoed her own. She could feel desire beginning to swell and fill her veins again. Still, she couldn't give in so easily.

"Isn't this about where you have a cigarette and then roll over and go to sleep?"

He shook his head. "Not my style. First of all, I don't smoke."

Nik gathered her to him so that there was absolutely no space between their bodies. He felt her stirring in latent anticipation and his own body responding.

"And second, I'm definitely not sleepy." His fingers drifted along the swell of her hips, lingering, caressing, inspiring. "That only leaves us with one thing to do."

She found that she could still tease, still give as good as she got. The knowledge pleased her. "Whip up a new recipe?"

Start with one man, one woman, add in spice, lace with love and hot, sultry sex. Simmer for an hour. Serves two for a lifetime.

A smile lifted the corners of his mouth as he thought of this particular recipe finding its way into a cookbook. "In a manner of speaking."

"Speaking," she repeated solemnly, as she raised her head and then brushed a fleeting kiss over his lips. "You want to talk?"

He was already balancing himself over her, anticipating the feel of her body, soft and giving, hot and demanding, beneath his. He slowly moved his head from side to side. "The farthest thing from my mind."

Sara felt herself melting, and struggled to keep her mind from falling into the same burning abyss. "What is on your mind?"

"You, Sara."

Nik kissed her lips once, then again, a little more deeply. He felt her responding instantly. It was almost as if they had always been like this, reading each other's needs, responding to each other's desires.

And perhaps, in some other time and place, they had been. Soul mates, predestined for one another.

"You," he repeated just before his mouth took hers in earnest.

Sara parted her lips, eagerly admitting his tongue, suddenly hungrier than she had been the first time. She cinched her arms around his neck, eager to return in kind what he was giving her.

The minutest glimmer of a thought, before all thought dissolved again, had her knowing that this couldn't possibly last.

Nothing good ever lasted.

But for tonight, just for tonight, she could pretend that it did.

And for tonight she could love him the way she wanted to be loved. The way she had wanted to be loved all of her life. Everlastingly. Tonight she could pretend that the word *forever* had a meaning.

Liquid quicksilver turned to molten lava in her veins as Sara ignited beneath his touch. She inflamed them both.

Before dawn nudged aside the darkness with strong fingers of light, Nik knew that whatever came, whatever else lay out there waiting for him, he was never letting Sara out of his life again.

Chapter 13

Fourteen years had gone into forming who and what she was. Fourteen long years. Sara couldn't just change all that overnight, even though part of her fervently wished that she could. She couldn't just open herself up to the relationship, to Nik.

But she could treasure what had happened for its own sake.

It had been an incredible night. One that she knew she would remember forever. She stirred against Nik, wondering if he was awake yet. Light was flooding the room through the filmy white curtains. It had to be at least seven, if not later. It was time to get up and go back to her room before anyone saw her.

She didn't want to move.

Just a few minutes more.

Sara slipped her hand over Nik's chest. Her fingers drifted over the light sprinkling of sandy brown hair even as pointed daggers of fear began to slowly rip along the edges of her mind, depriving her of peace.

She sighed.

Nik felt her breath swish along his skin. He'd been awake for a while now. Perhaps he hadn't actually slept at all, just dozed a little. He hadn't wanted to disturb her by moving. The feel of her body against his was something he cherished far more than comfort.

Now that she was awake, Nik shifted so that he could look at her. He studied her face for telltale signs. "Regrets?"

She nodded slowly. "Two." She held up an index finger. "That we did it." A second finger joined the first. "That we didn't do it sooner."

Maybe it was the early-morning fog on his brain. "Isn't that two different sides of the same coin?"

His assessment was truer than he thought. The smile on her face was tinged with a sadness she wasn't fully aware of exposing.

"Yes, but it's the same coin." She realized that she was being too serious and giving away too much. Her tone lightened. "I never claimed to be an easy woman to understand."

And that sentence would get his vote for the understatement of the year.

"That you didn't. " He positioned himself farther up on the bed until he was leaning against the headboard. "But then, I don't make hamburgers. I work with sirloin."

Some of the sadness melted as she laughed. "Is everything a food metaphor with you?"

He considered her question seriously. "Basically. For instance." His green eyes darkened slightly as he trailed his fingers along the plane just above her breasts. "Your skin's like fresh whipped cream."

His voice was low, seductive. She felt herself slipping into it as if it was a tub of scented bathwater.

"Whipped cream topping off a cup of hot chocolate on a cold winter's day. To be savored while curled up in front of a roaring fire at a ski lodge."

She managed to rouse herself, and then smiled at him. "Sounds good."

His eyes made love to her. "Tastes even better."

Nik pressed a kiss to her arm and languidly worked his way up her shoulder. Sara's head fell back as she drank in the exciting rush he created within her. But the sensation was dueling with her reborn fears. The match between them was almost even.

Almost.

The scale began tipping in Nik's favor.

Sara struggled to keep her mind clear. She couldn't be found in his room like this. "Nik, it's almost time to get up."

Nik raised his head until their eyes met. "Exactly what I was thinking."

The man was impossible. What was worse, he was destroying her resolve. She wanted to stay here with him like this. Forever. Sara tried to push him back but there seemed to be no strength in her hands. "Everyone else'll be up, too."

Nik concentrated on her ear. It was small and delicate and tempted him to nibble on it, like a perfectly designed hors d'oeuvre.

"They're an inventive group. They'll find something to do."

With a sudden burst of willpower Sara sat up, though she would have far preferred sliding down onto the bed with him. She grasped the sheet and pulled it around her breasts.

"I have to get back to my room," she insisted.

She was right. He couldn't rush this just because he knew, in his heart, that it was right for both of them.

Nik leaned back on his elbows. "Spoilsport."

He was teasing her now, but she couldn't lead him on. "Nik, I'm not any good at relationships."

Distress tinged her features. Nik pretended not to see in hopes that it would disappear again. "Could have fooled me."

He wasn't taking this seriously. "No, I mean really. I always mess things up somehow."

He didn't want to hear about a string of former lovers. If he didn't know about them, they didn't exist. What mattered most was now. And the future. And them.

"Past history." He waved it away as if it were a mere fly buzzing about his head. "Clean slate. Fresh start. With me." He took her hand and held it firmly though she tried to pull it away. "With me, Sara," he repeated. "We've already got a head start. Let's just see where this'll go."

Nowhere, she thought, but refrained from saying anything. He'd find that out for himself soon enough.

When he released her hand Sara rose, still wrapped in his sheet. Sara dragged her hand through her hair and wished he wouldn't look at her. She could probably haunt houses right about now. "I need a shower."

He glanced over toward the bathroom. The idea of soaping her body sounded pretty good from where he sat. "We could save time by doing it together."

She was busy gathering her clothes together. "We wouldn't save anything if we did it together."

She gasped in surprise as he grabbed her waist and pulled her to him. Nik kissed her hard, reminding her of what the night had been all about. "Except maybe, my sanity."

Why did he keep insisting on turning her knees to rubber like that? She drew her body away. She couldn't think when he held her so close. "We already saved that last night, remember?"

He shrugged, unfazed by the reminder. "My sanity's very fragile."

She gathered the pile of clothing into her arms again, this time maintaining her distance from him.

"It'll have to fend for itself." She crossed to the door, the ends of the Roman toga she had fashioned out of the sheet trailing after her on the floor. "See you in an hour, Sinclair."

Nik sighed dramatically as he fell back on the bed. "If they haven't locked me up by then."

It was all too tempting to lie down next to him and recreate last night. But she held her ground. "I'll chance it."

Opening the door, Sara looked furtively around the hall. She felt like a teenager trying to sneak back into her house after curfew.

Satisfied that the hallway was empty, she slipped out of Nik's room and into her own.

It felt as if the weekend had just raced by. More than that, Sara thought as the plane taxied down the runway, it felt as if this weekend had happened to someone else, not to her. The events had been too idyllic, too wonderful. The aura that had been created by it all, the baseball game, the picnic, the night of passion followed by the brunch party Brom had surprised them with, just couldn't last. She could already feel it beginning to fade.

Only pain lasted. Happiness dissolved like soap bubbles blown into the air. Bright and shiny rainbows one minute, gone the next.

When the plane finally came to a halt in the Newport Beach airport, Sara knew the adventure was over. She had to regain control of herself. It was time to take a tight rein over her emotions again before things got way out of hand.

If they hadn't already.

Her father was going to recuperate soon. When he did, she would leave, Nik or no Nik. It was a pattern she had followed all of her adult life. She always knew when to leave. When things looked as if they were getting too serious. Too much for her to handle.

They deplaned and entered the terminal. Sara was barely aware of what Jennifer was saying to her. Something about work. Katie was being cranky and whimpering, interfering with the conversation Sara wasn't really paying attention to.

Kane picked his daughter up and she curled against him. It was hours past her bedtime.

"See you in the morning," Jennifer said over her shoulder as she hurried out with Kane to the parking lot. Home for them was only a couple of miles away.

Sara picked up her suitcase.

Nik reached for it, his hand covering hers. Sara wouldn't relinquish her hold. Nik let go. He knew that they had taken another step backward. "I'll take you home, Sara."

They walked through the electronic doors that had eased open as they approached. "No, that's okay." She looked toward the line of taxis that stood waiting for fares, even at this hour. "I'll just grab a cab."

Stubborn to the end, he thought. "When I was a kid, my mother always taught me to return anything I took and put it in the exact same place where I found it. If I didn't, she read me the riot act."

Sara gave him an irritated look. Why couldn't he just let her retreat? "Your mother's not here, you're not a little kid anymore and I'm not a thing you have to return to its proper place."

Nik tugged on the suitcase. "Humor me." A glint entered his eyes. "Or would you rather I reverted to food metaphors again?"

Sara released the suitcase, raising her hands in surrender. "Heaven forbid."

What was the harm? So he'd drive her home. So she'd be alone with him in a small space for a little while. What was the big deal? She could more than handle herself.

At least, she had before.

"Okay." She nodded as she began to walk toward the parking lot where they had left his car. "You can take me home."

How did she always manage to sound like a queen commanding her subjects? "I can die a happy man. My wishes have all come true." With his suitcase beneath his arm and hers in his hand, Nik took Sara by the arm as they walked. In his opinion, it was well worth the juggling act.

It was dark and there weren't that many people around. Sara began to regret her capitulation. "I said okay to a ride, not sarcasm served up hot."

He saw his Mustang and motioned her toward it. "All right, no sarcasm served up hot." He stopped next to his car, setting the suitcases down. His eyes washed over her, making her yearn for last night. "What would you like served up hot?"

You. Sara looked away as he opened the trunk. "Nothing."

Nik deposited the suitcases and shut the trunk. The smile on his face told her that he had read her mind. But at least he had the good grace not to say anything.

Accepting a ride home from him *was* a big deal. She realized it almost the moment she sat in the car next to him. Once the car door was closed, the space between them felt nominal. Intimate.

She didn't need this, she thought, staring at the road ahead. Her insides felt jittery, as if she were a child anticipating her first recital. Except that there wasn't going to be a recital. There wasn't going to be anything and she knew it. The weekend had been an aberration. This was what her life was supposed to be like. Singular. She had made the choice to spend it alone a long time ago.

She didn't want her mother's sorrow to become her own. No man was ever going to walk out on her. No man was ever going to break her heart.

That meant no surrendering to longings or desire. Nik represented both.

She'd been much too quiet on the way home. He was afraid to guess what she was thinking. Nik turned down a dark residential street. Streetlights and an occasional porch light illuminated his way.

He glanced toward her. "When can I see you again?"

Her fingers knotted together in her lap. She held on so tightly the tips began turning white. "Tomorrow, at work, I'll be there bright and early, as usual."

Nik had trouble controlling his anger. They'd come too far to begin playing games again. "That's not what I meant and you know it."

She searched for ways to put him off. Her own survival depended on it. If she allowed herself to get in any deeper, she wouldn't be able to pull herself out. He didn't understand. No one did. He was already getting annoyed with her. It was always like this. Next, the arguments would come. And then the tears. It was better to be alone. No pain, no gain didn't pertain to relationships.

Sara's voice hardened. "You mean for another tussle in bed?"

Nik's hands grasped the steering wheel hard. He pretended it was her throat. How could she reduce last night to those terms? "Was that what it was to you?"

"Yes." She looked down at her fingers and slowly unknotted them. "No."

When she raised her head again, the look in her eyes was defensive. It wasn't as if she hadn't warned him. He knew what he was getting into. "Look, I told you I wasn't any good at relationships."

He took another turn, this time to the left. There was contained fury in his voice. "Why are you trying so hard to prove it?"

"So I won't—so you won't get hurt," she amended quickly, cursing herself for the slip. She slanted a look at him.

They both knew she was afraid of being hurt, but Nik played along. "My hide's a good deal thicker than you think."

"Impossible," she muttered, trying to sound flippant.

"And I won't hurt you." The promise was soft but none theless binding.

She smiled ruefully in the dark. "You already are," she said quietly.

By causing fissures in her walls, by making her break her own rules, by making her feel something for him, he was already causing her pain.

She pointed to the left, anxious to get away. "We're here." She unfastened her seat belt and wound the purse strap around her hand. "You don't have to stop at the house. I can get out right here on the corner."

She was acting like an idiot. "Why don't I just push you out as I drive by and throw your suitcase out after you? That way I won't have to come to a stop at all." He couldn't remember a recipe, no matter how difficult, ever trying his patience the way she was.

He pulled the car up to the curb before her father's house and got out. Wordlessly, struggling to keep his temper in check, he rounded the back. Unlocking the trunk, Nik took out her suitcase.

There were a hundred different things he wanted to say to her. He wanted to ask why she was jeopardizing their future together. He wanted to lash out at her for her stubbornness and her determination to kill what was flowering between them. He wanted to demand to know what the hell she was so afraid of.

But he said nothing. He merely handed her the suitcase.

Nik slammed the trunk closed. "I'll see you in the morning."

She nodded, taking the case. Sara avoided his eyes. "Right." She began to walk away.

Nik stood looking after her. "Love doesn't have to hurt, Sara."

She stopped, her shoulders stiffening. She didn't turn around. "It doesn't have to," she agreed. "But it does."

And then she walked away.

It wasn't until she heard his engine start up again and then fade away that she played back his last words in her head.

Love doesn't have to hurt.

Love? Had he just told her that he loved her? No, it wasn't possible. Love didn't happen like a flash fire in a pan. It—

Had, she thought. Sara let her barriers down long enough to admit it to herself. Love had happened just that fast, just that overwhelmingly. If not for him, it had for her.

Oh, God, she was in trouble.

She felt numb and confused as she put her key into the lock and let herself into the house.

It took her a moment to realize that the lights were on in the living room. Her father was sitting in the beige-and-brown recliner, looking through the magazine section of the Sunday paper. He let it drop when he saw her come in. "Have fun?"

She crossed to him quickly. "Are you all right? Is something wrong?" She tried to remember where she had put away the surgeon's phone number.

Raymond smiled at her display of concern. "I'm just fine, Sara."

She let out a sigh of relief, her adrenaline draining from her. Her eyes narrowed. It was almost eleven o'clock. He father had always been a firm believer in going to bed early "What are you doing up?"

He moved the lever on the recliner. The footrest disappeared as he sat up. "Waiting for my daughter to get in. You said you'd be back tonight," he reminded her.

She frowned. He needed his rest. "You shouldn't have stayed up."

Having her fuss over him was something new. He let himself enjoy it for a moment. "I liked staying up waiting for you." Raymond thought of his daughter's teen years. " missed out on doing that."

Not tonight, Dad, I can't handle this tonight. Restlessly Sara shifted the suitcase to her other hand. "You missed out on a lot of things."

"Yes, I know." He wanted to take her hand, to ask for giveness, but he didn't know how. He was just beginning t learn how to forgive himself. "And you have no idea how sorry I am about that."

Sara's expression grew distant. "No, I don't. I haven't th faintest idea how sorry you are." She remembered how she had finally come to terms with it all, how she had hardened her heart. Or tried to. "I didn't think you were sorry at all."

"Then you thought wrong."

Sara turned from him. Raymond reached for her hand stopping her. She was surprised at how much strength there was in his grip. He had always held her so gently when she was a child. Now it felt as if he was holding on for his very life.

His eyes implored her to believe him. "Not a day went b when I didn't miss you. I have always, *always* loved you Sara."

Her eyes were cold, but she could feel them misting Damn, she didn't want to cry now. Not now. "You had very funny way of showing it."

He smiled disparagingly. "I thought I was showing it th only way I could."

She pulled her hand away. Her anger flared red-hot. "By deserting me?" How could he insult her by talking such nonsense? "By making me feel that my father, the man I loved more than anyone else in the world, didn't care about me anymore?"

Raymond shook his head. He suddenly felt very old. "That wasn't the way it was."

"Then how was it, Dad?" she demanded, her voice rising. "How was it for you? For me it was lousy." Tears began to fall. "Other kids had fathers they could spend time with. Fathers to talk to. Fathers to give cards to on Father's Day."

Sara wiped away the tears angrily with the heel of her hand. She didn't want her father thinking that she was crying over him.

"I didn't even have an address." She looked at him accusingly. "I didn't even know where you were. Just somewhere in California."

"I was right here all the time. I sent child support checks every month." That much money he always put by. Despite his obsession, he would never have cheated Sara of her due.

Sara shrugged, annoyed with herself for letting loose like that, letting her emotions free. "I found that out later. But Mother said you moved without a forwarding address. She said the envelopes the checks came in had a different postmark on them every month."

Raymond offered her his handkerchief, but she refused it, sniffing instead.

The pain refused to remain buried any longer. "The first year you disappeared out of my life, I called information, hoping to track you down by your phone number. I was going to call and yell at you for leaving, but you weren't listed anywhere." She bit her lip to stem the flow of fresh tears that threatened to come. Sara remembered sitting in her room with a road atlas she had bought. "I called information in every city in Southern California that I could find."

His conscience shot steely arrows of guilt through him. "I'm a cop, Sara. We like to stay unlisted. You remember."

She swallowed. The lump in her throat was huge. "Yeah, I remember."

He didn't know what to say. He only knew he had to say something. He was losing her. "Sara..."

There was no use in going around and around about this. The past was behind them, leaving an inky black mark in its place. Nothing her father could say would change what he had done to her. He had shut her completely out of his life for his own selfish reasons. Because he wanted to start a new life without her. That was what her mother had told her when Sara had asked.

And what Sara believed, because there was no reason not to.

Sara shrugged indifferently, dismissing the conversation. "I'm tired, Dad. I'd like to go to bed now. And you should, too," she added as an afterthought.

He had let silence plead his case for too long. Raymond caught her by the arm, imploring her to stay. "No, I have to explain."

She'd fought too many emotional battles today to remain polite. Her resolve broke.

"Explain what?" she lashed out. "That I was a reminder to you of your mistake, just like I was to Mom? I don't want to hear it." She tried to pull away, but he wouldn't let her.

She had to hear the truth, no matter how painful it would be for both of them.

"No." Raymond raised his voice. "You're going to listen."

She yanked her hand free, accidentally knocking over the suitcase. She hardly noticed it. "You can't talk to me like that. You haven't the right to play father now after all these years."

"Maybe you're right." Raymond let his hands hang at his sides, but his eyes held her in place. "Then listen to me because you're fair."

She sighed as she dragged her hand through her hair. She was crazy for letting him talk her into this. "All right. Talk."

Raymond began to pace, agitation fueling his steps. Now that she was listening, he wasn't certain he had the right words at his disposal.

"I didn't break off contact with you because you reminded me of a mistake I had made." He laughed softly to himself at the irony of her accusation. "Hell, Sara, you were the only thing about my life that was good and clean. I stopped seeing you because I thought it was for your own good—"

"My own good?" she echoed incredulously. "How can you *say* that?"

He shrugged, looking away. "Vanity, I guess. I didn't want you to know what a weakling your old man was."

He had completely lost her. "I don't understand."

Raymond looked at her then and she found herself pitying him. She tried to lock the sentiment out, but it seeped through. "Maybe I should start by explaining your name."

He had told her about that. Time and again. It had been her favorite bedtime story. Didn't he remember? "You named me after the place where you met Mom."

"Yes, but it wasn't Saratoga the city. It was the racetrack."

Just the way the kids at school had always teased her. "Go on," she said quietly.

He drew a long breath. His mouth felt dry, but he pressed on. "We met when she was standing in line in front of me at the two-dollar window at Saratoga. We were both betting on the same horse." He smiled ruefully. "The horse won. I told your mother she brought me luck. She confessed that she had never placed a bet before. She had come with her girlfriend on a lark." Shame entered his eyes. "For me, betting wasn't a lark, it was an obsession."

Sara could see that the admission was difficult for him. He stuck his hands in his pockets and pressed on like a tired mountain climber trying to reach the summit.

"I managed to get it under control for a while. But then I started playing again. Nothing big at first. It still got the better of me. I won big a few times and then I was hooked all over again. I started betting more and more, until I was betting money I didn't have." He sighed heavily. "We had to sell the house."

Sara could only stare at her father, stunned. Everything was falling apart. Just as it had then. "That's why we moved? You said you wanted to go to a different neighborhood."

"I would have said anything to keep you from finding out the truth. For a while I honestly thought I could get my betting under control, but it was controlling me. Underneath it all was always that hope, that dream that I could get all the money back that I had lost and set us up for life."

He turned and stared out the window, unable to face her any longer. He was afraid of what he would see in Sara's eyes.

"One day your mother said that I loved gambling more than I loved her. That if I did love her more, I would have stopped gambling when she asked me to. She didn't understand that I couldn't." A streetlight cast a pool of light on his front lawn. He stared at it, remembering the pain his decision had cost him. "I didn't want to leave her trapped in a marriage where she felt unloved. I agreed to get a divorce on the condition that she would never tell you about my gambling."

Sara thought back over the years. So many things made sense now that had seemed odd at the time. How could she have been so stupid, so blind?

He looked at her reflection in the window. "For a year I fought it, hoping that we could get back together again, become a family. But there didn't seem to be any use. I couldn't stop going to the track. So I dropped out of your life. I didn't want you to be disillusioned about me."

She wasn't the only one who had been blind. "Don't you see? Your turning your back on me was what disillusioned me. So, you have a problem—"

"Had," he corrected firmly, finally turning around. There was pride in his voice. "I joined Gamblers Anonymous. I've stayed away from the racetrack and betting for almost a year now." A familiar smile quirked his lips. Sara recognized it as her own. "I don't even allow myself to watch "Mr. Ed" reruns on cable."

Sara didn't know whether to laugh or to cry. All those years of blaming herself, of lying awake at night, trying to figure out what it was that she had done wrong to make him leave. They had all been wasted. It hadn't been her fault at all.

Hesitating, Sara forced herself to make contact. She laid a hand on her father's shoulder. He covered it with his own. When he looked at her there was gratitude in his eyes.

She was still angry at him, angry about the years that he had allowed to be cast away. Years neither one of them could ever get back.

Raymond searched her face and saw the beginning of forgiveness there. He felt like crying himself.

"It wasn't you I pushed away, Sara. It was myself."

Nothing would ever remove the sadness from his eyes, Sara realized. He had been hurt just as much as she had by all those empty years.

"But I've paid for it." Raymond opened his arms to her, but made no move, still afraid. "And I'm not pushing anymore."

Sara moved into his arms, embracing him. And this time she let the tears flow freely.

Chapter 14

Nik drove up to the curb and shut off the engine. For a moment he just sat in the car looking at the house bathed in the light of the late-afternoon sun. Sara's car was in the driveway. That meant she was home. Good. He hadn't called ahead because he was afraid she'd leave.

Nik unbuckled his seat belt.

It had been an exceedingly hectic week. He'd hardly had time to draw two breaths in succession. There had certainly been no time for any meaningful dialogue between himself and Sara. Any words they might have exchanged on the subject of last Saturday night would probably have deteriorated into a shouting match, given his harried state and Sara's wariness. For a whole week, when he did have any time to talk to her, Sara had quipped and bantered, keeping him at bay. Like a circus animal trainer who cracked her whip and held up a chair between herself and the lion, Sara had been warding him off with her sharp tongue.

It was as if their night of love and discovery hadn't even happened.

But it had, and he was resolved to make her face it. Face it with him. Whatever there was standing in their way, keeping her from him, Nik intended to blow it out of the water. He wouldn't have come as far as he had in his own life if he had meekly accepted the inevitable, or bowed readily to defeat when the first shot was fired.

If anything, he thrived on adversity. And Sara was as adversarial as they came.

Nik pocketed his keys, still watching the house for some sign of her. "This is war, Saratoga Santangelo, and I'm about to fire another salvo at that sweet little broadside of yours."

Determined, Nik intended to fight any way he could to get through to Sara. Dirty if necessary. His first line of offense involved food and Sara's father.

Nik got out of the car and circled to the trunk. It was filled with food—entrées, desserts, everything that was necessary to prepare the type of feast that would bring tears to the eyes of the most hardened critic of Italian food. Kane had mentioned to him that Raymond had a weakness for Italian food, and Nik had gone to work.

Nik decided to begin the battle slowly. Carrying a covered dish of cannelloni, he walked up to the front door and rang the bell.

He rang twice before the door finally opened. Sara stood in the doorway. She was barefoot, wearing a baggy T-shirt and frayed cutoff shorts that were cut so high on one thigh it had him tightening his grip on the handles of the serving dish.

Sara was annoyed at the instant flutter that went through her at the sight of Nik on her doorstep. There wasn't anything she could do about it. But she could manage to maintain a cool, flippant expression even though her pulse had accelerated like an adolescent's at the sight of her first crush.

Sara leaned one hand against the doorjamb, blocking his way. She glanced at the covered dish and raised a questioning brow. "I already gave at the office."

Nik had seen the momentary flicker of desire in her eyes. It was all the encouragement he needed. "The office decided to give something back."

Stubbornly she remained fixed in the doorway. "Why aren't you at the restaurant, Sinclair? It's only six-thirty."

Nik nudged her aside with his shoulder. Sara reluctantly stepped back and let him walk in. "It's Saturday."

That wasn't an answer. Jennifer had told her that Nik worked six days a week and half days on Sunday most of the time.

She fisted her hands at her waist, challenging him. "You took last Saturday off."

"I'm becoming decadent." Nik looked around the room, but didn't see Raymond. He nodded toward the right, taking a guess. "The kitchen this way?"

"Yes, but—"

Nik was already leaving her behind. She picked up speed, reaching the kitchen at the same time he did.

Why was he bringing her food? "We're not a charity case, Sinclair."

He ignored the antagonistic tone of her voice. For some reason Sara was afraid of him. He intended to find out why.

"You told me about the extent of your cooking, remember?" He placed the casserole on the counter and mentally cleared off space for the rest of the things he had brought with him that were still in the car. Sara was going to have to move the blender and the toaster, but that was about all. "I figured your father must be starving right about now."

Pompous ass, they were doing just great without him. Who did he think he was, barging into her house—her father's house, she amended quickly, realizing her slip—and—and—

Raymond walked into the room behind them. "Sara, who was—" He stopped as he realized that Sara had company. He looked at Nik's face. Recognition was immediate, but the name lagged a minute behind. "Nik, isn't it?"

Crossing to him, Nik took Raymond's hand, shaking it. The older man looked a great deal healthier now than he had the last time Nik had seen him. Maybe Sara wasn't as bad a cook as she claimed.

"Yes. How are you?" Nik asked.

Sara couldn't get over the fact that the two men were acting as if they were old friends instead of practically strangers. What gave Nik the right to just waltz into her private life like this?

"Fine." Raymond's leathery cheeks spread in a warm smile as he glanced at his daughter. "Sara's been taking good care of me."

Sara shifted in place, uncomfortable with the compliment. They'd made headway since last Sunday, but there were still some things between her father and her that had to be worked through. It took time to mend breaches, even under the best of circumstances and intentions. It didn't help to have matters announced to the whole world. Or to Nik.

"Nik thinks I'm starving you to death." Sara gestured at the casserole dish. "He's obviously brought you a care package."

The tolerant smile on Nik's face fanned her temper. Just as he knew it would. He liked her better when she was angry. She tended to act on impulse then. And he could work with that.

"She told me that the extent of her cooking abilities was to burn things. I figured she was keeping you alive on those little frozen food packages you boil and serve." He nodded toward the refrigerator.

Defensive, Sara moved over and leaned against the refrigerator. Any minute, the man would start taking inventory. She didn't feel like being subjected to any criticism.

Damn, it was bad enough having to deal with her own edginess when she was around him at the restaurant. Why did he have to bring that tension here? Wasn't she going to have any peace from him?

Sara raised her chin, her eyes narrowing. She was spoiling for a fight. "And if I was?"

Nik viewed frozen food in the same light that he thought of fast food. Unfit for human consumption. "It's a good way to become malnutritioned."

Raymond knew a fight in the making when he saw one. He quickly crossed to the counter. "Let's see what Nik brought us, Sara."

"His nose, which he's sticking into things again." Sara folded her arms in front of her chest as she turned away from both of them.

Raymond flushed slightly as he looked at Nik, then took care to tread very cautiously. This was harder than maneuvering through a booby-trapped minefield.

"You'll have to forgive my daughter, Nik. I'm afraid that being cooped up all day with me is making her a little testy."

Sara gave her father a sharp look. "I can make my own apologies, Dad."

Nik's expression was agreeable as he waited. Sara remained silent. "Well?" he prodded her expectantly.

She gave him a saccharine smile. "When I think an apology is necessary, you'll hear one."

Raymond sighed as he moved toward Nik. "She always did have a stubborn streak," he confided.

Any minute now he was going to pull out baby pictures of her, Sara thought, her fuse dangerously low.

Nik nodded. "I kind of suspected that." He moved toward the doorway. Confronted with Sara and her microshorts, he'd forgotten all about the rest of the food in the trunk.

Sara raised her hand like a student in class and waved it before both men. "I'm standing in the same room with you, gentlemen. There's no reason to talk about me as if I were dead."

"Dead people are docile," Nik pointed out. "No one can ever accuse you of being that." He nodded toward the front door. "Want to help me?"

"Leave?" she suggested, bringing a touch of eagerness to her voice.

"No." His voice was mild, patient. It had an inverse effect on her temper. "I've got more food in the car."

He glanced over his shoulder to see that Raymond had let curiosity get the better of him and was lifting the lid on the serving dish. The older man looked as if he had suddenly fallen in love.

"Cannelloni," Raymond whispered with a reverence that was usually reserved for the interior of churches.

Kane had been right, Nik thought.

He grinned, pleased. "I always enjoy cooking for an appreciative audience." Nik turned to Sara and took her arm, ushering her out. "I have eggplant parmesan, manicotti and cannolis in the trunk of my car, plus an assortment of vegetables."

"Cannolis?" Raymond's eyes shone as he replaced the lid on the dish.

"Two dozen, freshly made," Nik promised as he walked out of the kitchen. He discovered that he didn't have to drag Sara with him. She was bearing down on him of her own volition.

Her hand on his shoulder, she pulled him around to look at her once they were outside the house. Her eyes were like two dark arrows, aimed straight for his heart. There was no mistaking them for Cupid's arrows, he thought. They were more along the lines of poison-tipped darts.

"Are you out of your mind?"

"Possibly," he conceded. A sane man would have retreated by now.

She didn't have the patience for word play today. He was crowding her, and she lashed out.

"Why are you trying to kill my father?" she demanded. "The man just had an angioplasty. In case you don't know what that is, that's a procedure intended to rectify a heart blockage caused by too much fat buildup. Fat, as in what you're offering to feed him."

He unlocked the trunk. It popped open, giving Sara a clear view of the interior. There was enough in there to feed three people for a week. The man was moving in!

"I know what an angioplasty is," he said mildly. They were going to need to make two trips, he decided. He didn't want to drop anything.

Nik was obviously two tacos short of a combination plate. Sara gestured at the trunk, anger seeping from her very fingertips. She hadn't traveled all this way and gone through emotional hell just to indulge her father and see him back in the hospital in six months or less.

"If you know what an angioplasty is, how can you bring him all this in good conscience?" He was using her father to get to her, that's why. "Or don't you have one?"

His smile hardened around the edges. "My conscience is alive and well, Sara." He moved several things aside, arranging them to facilitate removal. "I'm not a short-order cook, Sara. I'm someone who's studied the art of preparing meals. The key word here," he emphasized, "is *art*."

She was far from convinced. "The key word here is annoying."

He didn't have time to stand and argue with her all day. Though it was the tail end of the afternoon, it was still hot and the food would spoil if he didn't get it into the house. "I know how to prepare Italian food using low-fat products."

She shivered, thinking of her last experience with something bearing that label. She eyed the contents of his trunk dubiously. "And still make it taste like something other than rubber?"

Nik removed a large box from the trunk and handed it to Sara. The box felt surprisingly light in her hands. Sliding the lid aside, she looked in to see four rows of cannoli neatly arranged. Chocolate-sprinkled cream peered invitingly out of both ends. She felt her mouth watering despite herself.

"And still make it taste like something other than rubber," Nik assured her.

She shut the lid again. "This I have to see."

Nik took out a large pot and hefted it toward the front door. "I was counting on it." His words drifted over his shoulder.

Sara followed him into the house. She just bet he was, she thought.

Nik took over the kitchen like a liberating World War II general marching into formerly enemy-occupied territory. Sara and the sauce both simmered as, for the next hour, Nik reheated the main dishes and prepared the pasta salad and vegetables he had brought with him.

The man was everywhere. Everywhere she didn't want him to be.

Sara finally occupied herself by setting the table. She looked at Nik grudgingly as he pronounced his manicotti "perfection." No wonder he never wore a chef's hat. He probably couldn't find one that was big enough to fit his head.

With a clang, Sara laid down the knife she was holding. "You have a way of taking over, don't you?"

He glanced in her direction, amused. "Only familiar territory."

Placing the fork on the other side, she turned and looked at him. "That would apply to the kitchen and the food."

What was she getting at? "Right," he agreed slowly. He added a dash of oregano to the sauce, then tasted it. Good.

She was tired of shadowboxing. "So what are you doing, butting in to my life?"

He replaced the lid on the pot and checked on the spaghetti he was preparing as a side dish. He intended to give Raymond a smorgasbord of food to choose from. The rest would be leftovers to be eaten over the course of the week. "I don't follow."

She didn't like talking to the back of his head. Abandoning the table, she walked over to him by the stove. "That's unfamiliar territory."

Now they were getting to it, he thought. Still, he went on as if the conversation only marginally held his attention rather than completely, the way it actually did. "Not entirely. I just thought I'd keep you from making any mistakes you'll regret later."

She thought of last week. It should never have been allowed to happen. It had made her too vulnerable. "I already have."

Knowing the way her mind worked, anticipating her answer, hearing it shouldn't have hurt. But it did.

Nik maintained an impassive expression. "I was referring to you shutting your father out of your life. Last time I looked, you seemed pretty intent on doing that."

Unable to deal with the way he was looking at her, Sara went back to setting the table. It was amazing how much mileage she could milk out of something so simple. "Well, we've come to an understanding since then."

Now that Nik thought of it, Raymond had looked a little more at ease. And the air hadn't been charged with the same degree of tension as when he'd brought Raymond home from the hospital.

If anything, it seemed as if that tension had shifted completely so that it now surrounded him and Sara. "I'm glad to hear that." Nik sprinkled grated cheese into the sauce.

She yanked the refrigerator door opened and took out a small bottle of wine. "Which is more than you and I have come to, it seems." She slammed the refrigerator door shut again.

Nik looked up from the dish of eggplant he was arranging. His eyes seemed to touch hers. "I'm working on it, Sara. I'm working on it."

And undoing me. She looked away. "We're working at cross-purposes."

"Maybe," he agreed. For a moment he abandoned what he was doing and crossed to her. "I have a solution."

Sara moved to the other side of the table as she folded another napkin and slid it next to a plate. She chewed on her lower lip. "What?"

He wanted to nibble along her lip the way she was doing. The taste of her mouth returned to him in vivid waves. "Come and join my side."

She raised her eyes just for a moment. "You're overbearing."

He grinned, making no move to return to what he'd been doing. "When I have to be." He moved in front of her again. "Some people call that tenacity."

Sara set down the last knife and fork. There was hostility in her eyes. He had invaded and wasn't leaving. "I call it royal pain."

Somehow, she wasn't exactly sure how, Nik had managed to back her up against the counter. Suddenly the kitchen seemed a lot smaller to her, and he was filling every available space.

Nik lifted his hand and lightly swept it over her hair. It was hard to believe that he could be so gentle one moment, so infuriatingly abrasive the next. "Then let me make the pain go away, Sara."

She licked her lips. The very sheen tempted him.

"*Then* you'll be leaving?" Her voice was so shaky she was ashamed of herself. It reflected what was happening to her internally.

"Not on your life." Nik searched her face for a moment, looking for something that insisted on remaining hidden. With a sigh he stepped back, giving her room. "Tell your father dinner's ready."

Sara walked out of the room, though she wasn't completely sure how. Her insides were vibrating like a tuning fork. All systems were screaming Mayday. And the plane was going down.

Because he had embraced discipline as a way of life, Raymond ate in moderation. But he sampled everything. His abundant appreciation was evident in every bite he took and savored.

He looked at Nik, seated across the table from him. "This is wonderful." Raymond took the smallest sip of wine to wash down the last of the tetrazzini. With harnessed gusto he turned to the cannoli. "I thought that food like this was out of my life forever."

Raymond sighed as he let the dessert melt on his tongue. "If you were a woman, Nik, I think I'd be proposing right now."

If he were a woman, she wouldn't be hip-deep in trouble right now, Sara thought belligerently.

Feeling that anything she said would only be used to serve Nik's purpose somehow, Sara had elected to eat in silence. It seemed as if Nik and her father hardly noticed her verbal withdrawal. They talked all through the meal. They'd found common ground in the fact that they both knew Kane, and had gone on from there to cover baseball, cooking and police work.

She hadn't seen her father this animated since she was a child. No doubt about it, she thought grudgingly. Nik was good for her father.

Just bad for her.

As was his habit with things he prepared, Nik had eaten very little. "No need for anything as drastic as marriage," he said with a laugh, then nodded at the counter behind him. "There are plenty of leftovers for you, and I'll give you all the recipes." He wasn't normally so generous with his original recipes, but he made an exception this time. "I promise that your doctor will approve of every single one."

Raymond eyed the plate of cannoli, but knew that one had to be his limit. With a heavy sigh he laid down his fork.

"Recipes won't do me much good," Raymond confessed ruefully. "I'm not very handy in the kitchen. And Sara—" He glanced toward his daughter and his smile was reminiscent of the ones she had once been so used to. Approving and loving. "Well, Sara has other attributes."

Nik raised his glass to his lips, his eyes on hers. "Yes, I know."

Sara looked down at her cannoli, debating whether to eat it or throw it. He had no right to do this to her, to invade her life and make her feel as if everything was being turned upside down.

The suggestion in his voice had her muscles contracting. In the past week she'd worked so hard at severing the tie that had been formed that one night. She'd almost deluded herself into thinking she could do it. Now here he was, reigniting the bonfire within her even as he was stoking her anger.

Raymond pushed himself away from the table. His chair scraped along the vinyl floor. "Well, all this good food has made me feel really sleepy. I'm afraid a tired old man is going to have to withdraw."

He began to rise, but Sara reached over and caught his hand.

"No." Damn, did that sound as panicky as she suddenly felt?

Leaning, Nik picked up Raymond's plate and set it on top of his own. "Sara," he reproved mildly, "your father knows what's best for him."

Sara saw traces of the smile Nik was struggling not to let show. She bit her lip to refrain from saying something in front of her father she might regret. She'd have to wait until they were alone to give Nik Sinclair the dressing down he deserved.

Raymond rose to his feet and shook Nik's hand. "I can't tell you how wonderful all this was for me. Really wonderful," he echoed.

"You can stop by the restaurant any time," Nik told him.

Raymond had approached each new dish with almost equal gusto. But Nik had paid close attention and noted that the man had favored one slightly above the others, taking seconds of the small portions he had allowed himself.

"I'll whip up another plate of tetrazzini for you," Nik promised as he stood. "On the house."

"Thanks, I might just take you up on that." Raymond stretched, then crossed to the doorway. Nik was gathering silverware together. "Don't worry about making too much noise—washing the dishes, I mean," he added with a transparent grin Sara could have killed him for. Sold out by her own father. "I sleep like a rock once I'm in my bed."

Sara, still seated, shut her eyes. She felt as if her father had just placed a For Sale sign on her body and waved it at Nik. At least he hadn't offered a dowry, she thought cynically.

Raymond looked from Nik to his daughter. He could only hope. "Well, good night." He withdrew.

"Night," she muttered darkly without looking in his direction.

"You know," Nik mused out loud, stacking plates on top of one another, "this might be a whole new way to go at the restaurant." He rolled the idea over in his head seriously. "We could have a separate menu for people who have to

watch their fat intake." He looked at Sara. "As my accountant, what do you think?"

Sara grabbed the plates and all but sent them crashing as
she set them in the sink with a thud. "As your *temporary*
accountant, I think that you're overextending yourself by a
hell of a margin."

He was actually considering doing it. Her meaning eluded
him. "Do you think so? Seems to me that the restaurant—"

She swung around to look at him. "Here," she said
fiercely. She enunciated every word, in case he somehow still
missed her meaning. "I think you're overextending yourself by being here like this."

The hell with cleaning up the kitchen. He could do it later.
Right now there were other things that needed cleaning up
a lot more.

Something in his eyes when he looked at her told Sara she
should be running for higher ground. The floodwaters were
definitely coming.

She stood nailed to the floor.

Throwing the dish towel down, he pulled her to him so
suddenly the air whooshed out of her lungs as their bodies
made sizzling contact.

"You think that's overextension?" The look in his eyes
was half amused and half threatening in the promise they
held. "You ain't seen nothing yet."

Sara tried to push him away. Damn, she wasn't a weakling. Why did her arms feel like useless rubber bands now?

"The last time you said that—" she began and then got
no further.

He sure as hell hoped that old man slept as soundly as he
claimed, because he knew that there was no turning back
from this point.

"Yes?"

Words were sticking to her mouth again. And she couldn't
force herself to look away from his eyes. It was as if they
held her very soul captive.

"You took me to bed."

He cupped her cheek with his hand and gently brushed his fingers along the skin. "There's something about familiarity that breeds a feeling of security."

Panic, cold and hard, seized her. Panic that he would make love to her here and now. Panic that he wouldn't. "But not for me."

"Then we won't make it all that familiar," he told Sara.

Each time they made love, Nik promised himself, it would be different. An exploration to find something new in territory that was well-known and well loved.

What was she doing? How could she just capitulate this way? Sara scrambled to regain ground.

"But—"

Whatever else she was going to say melted away like snowflakes on a hot stove as he put his hands on her. Nothing more, just that. His hands on her shoulders and his eyes on hers.

And she was his.

She knew it was weak and that she would live to regret it. But she had already made up her mind to leave within a week. Her father's doctor's appointment was on Friday. He was recovering rapidly. She could see it. There was no excuse to remain any longer after that.

This one last time, she let herself give in to what she'd been yearning for all week. This madness of the blood that was no good for her.

He pressed a kiss to her neck. Shards of pleasure slashed recklessly all through her.

"Where's your room?" he whispered against her throat.

"In the back." He felt her words vibrate along his mouth, exciting him.

Her father's room was off the living room and faced the front of the house. "Then we won't be disturbing your father." It wasn't a question.

She could only shake her head mutely. The only one he would be disturbing, ultimately, was her.

Chapter 15

He'd thought that the first time would be the most impor
tant and that nothing else could ever compare to it. He was
wrong. Each time he made love with Sara would be just as
precious, if not more so, than the last, no matter how long
he lived.

No matter how many times he made love with her.

Nik wanted to give her the world, wrapped up in shiny
paper and bound in bright ribbons.

He had only himself.

It didn't seem nearly enough. He wanted to give her
something special, to somehow wipe away the sadness, the
tinge of distrustfulness in her eyes that always lingered there
even when passion shone, full bloom.

He wanted to make her his. Forever.

Nik closed Sara's bedroom door behind him. He didn't
bother turning around. He couldn't take his eyes off Sara.

He could hear her breath catch when he touched her face.
It was impossibly erotic.

Softly, as if she would melt at the slightest contact, he
brought his lips down to hers. Her sigh of acceptance had

his blood surging through his veins like the end of the *1812 Overture.*

Urgency battered him like waves against the shore, demanding satisfaction.

But he managed to maintain control. He swore to himself that she would never know anything but kindness from him. Someone had obviously hurt her. He was never going to chance Sara confusing him with that man, even for a moment. He'd leave her rather than risk that ever happening.

Where was the strength that she was so proud of? Where in heaven's name was her resilience? Why did everything dissolve to liquid when he touched her? Why did she silently vow to relinquish everything she believed in, everything she knew to be true, just so that he would touch her again?

She was betraying herself for the price of a kiss.

Sara had no answers. And the questions were fading. All she wanted was for Nik to make love to her, to make love *with* her. To completely surround her until he was her walls, her ceiling, her floor.

Sara almost cried with joy as she felt his hands move over her body, caressing her, revering her. Making her burst into flame as he gathered her to him.

If she was any closer she'd be through him, and yet, it wasn't close enough.

It would never be close enough.

She dug her hands into his shoulders, trying to absorb him as his mouth laid siege to hers with an abandonment she reveled in.

Nik cupped her head and drew her away. He looked at her, his own breathing ragged and echoing in the silent room. The rise and fall of her breasts against his chest was driving him crazy.

"Oh, God, Sara, this was all I could think about all week. Just being with you again like this."

Sara vainly sought control. He had it all. "Before or after you seasoned the Stroganoff?"

Nik slid his tongue along her ear and enjoyed the shiver it evoked. From both of them.

"Before," he swore, his breath hot along her skin. "Way before."

Dear God, she was going to make a fool of herself and tear his clothes off right here and now. She wanted him. Wanted to be with him. Joined for all eternity. "No food metaphors?"

Her voice was thick with desire. It matched his own. "None. Nothing but you, Sara." He looked into her eyes and saw his reflection there. He was her prisoner. "Always you."

She would have sold her soul to believe that. But she knew better.

Knew...

She didn't know anything except that she needed him. Now.

Nik slid his hands down her spine. Bunching the hem of her T-shirt in his fingers, he began to lift it from her body. Sara raised her arms for him, her eyes never leaving his. There was such love there, it made her ache.

It fades, Sara. Love fades. Promises fade. Her mother's voice echoed in her brain.

Nik tossed aside Sara's shirt. "You're not wearing a bra," he murmured even as he cupped her breasts in his hands.

Her skin tingled, first hot, then cold. "I never seemed to get around to putting it on this morning."

He felt intoxicated by her scent. It was strong and arousing. Her body flowed through his hands, hot, moist, ready. He caressed, coaxed, worshiped. Her shorts snapped open readily beneath his fingers just as she tugged at his jeans.

Hands urgent, seeking, shed clothing quickly. Material fell to the floor and tangled, a silent prophecy.

Both nude, they tumbled onto Sara's bed, arms and legs entwined as their lips were sealed to one another. Hearts made silent promises, beating wildly as they rolled together. Each sought the comforting feel of the other. Each wanted to please and thus be pleased.

His mouth was everywhere, causing tiny earthquakes along her body.

She tasted of desire, dark and alluring. He could have feasted on her for a year and never sated his appetite. He filled himself with her until all that he tasted, smelled and felt was Sara.

She felt his tongue flitter teasingly around her nipple, hardening it instantly. As she moaned, he moved to the other breast. Agony and ecstasy played for control of her, each winning, each taking.

She was almost gasping now as she arched against him. She desperately wanted to do this to him, to make him spiral off into the darkness, searching for the light, just as he did to her.

But he was too quick for her. Too quick and too clever, and she could only hang on to the sides of the roller coaster that had her soaring up and then plunging down.

Her stomach quivered as she felt his mouth trail along her skin. Stars burst through her brain as she felt Nik bring his mouth to her very core. With a muffled cry she felt herself free-falling through space, riding the crest of an explosion. Nik needed only to touch her to set them off.

All he had ever needed to do was touch her, right from the beginning.

Sara grabbed fistfuls of her comforter as Nik wove his magic again. And again. She felt herself hurtling upward and then slowly being let down. She was in a million pieces, bright and glowing like the stars in the sky.

Her arms felt limp. *She* felt limp. It was all she could do to pry her eyes open and look at him. Gravity was fighting her for control of each lid.

It took her a moment before she found the strength to even form words. "Are we still on earth?"

"Just barely."

Nik's body whispered against hers as he slid along the bed until his face was level with hers.

He loved looking at her, loved seeing the different emotions play across her face. Wonder, desire, need. And ecstasy. Ecstasy had to be his favorite. Because he had created it for her, offering it to her like a bouquet of the rarest of roses.

He brushed the hair from her cheek. "The next time," he promised, "we're going to make love someplace where there isn't anyone else around."

There isn't going to be a next time.

Sara tried to focus her mind on what he was saying. "Why?"

He rolled on top of her, balancing himself on his elbows. Looking into her eyes. "Because I want to hear you call out my name when I make love with you."

She slid her tongue slowly along her lips. She saw raw desire flame in his eyes. "Nik." It was barely a whisper. It was all she could manage.

He shook his head, curling his fingers along her cheek. "With more feeling."

She smiled then. It was so genuine, so guileless it took his breath away. "That would require more air in my lungs, and you stole it from me."

"Then we're even."

He laced his hands with hers as he positioned himself over her. Sara parted her legs for him, her heart hammering wildly in anticipation.

His mouth covered hers when he entered her. Nik felt her sharp intake of breath on his tongue, tasted it in his mouth.

It excited him beyond belief.

He couldn't help himself. He'd sworn that he would make love to her slowly, patiently, but he broke his promise to both of them. Passion rose up and seized him so tightly in the palm of its hand that all he could do was give in to it.

The rhythm it evoked took him and he rode her hard. That she met him movement for movement only increased his ardor.

In a final burst over the summit, they found their salvation together.

Exhausted, Nik could only muster enough energy to slide to the side so that he wouldn't crush her. The way he felt right now, his elbows couldn't even begin to support his weight.

Please, I want this feeling to go on. Please.

But even as Sara prayed, she could feel the euphoria leaving her, taking with it its protective cloak. The cloak that kept reality away. She shivered.

He could feel her withdrawing even though she hardly moved. *Why, Sara? Why?*

Nik turned his face toward her and managed to keep the concern from his eyes. He pressed a kiss to her forehead. "That was a nice overture. If you give me a minute, the curtain will go up on the main performance."

Their eyes inches apart, Sara stared at him incredulously. She felt as if all of her had been reduced to the consistency of overcooked tapioca pudding. Not being a physical weakling, she'd assumed that he would be in a similar condition.

"You're kidding."

Nik grinned at the unabashed wonder in her voice. He managed to raise himself up on one elbow. The vantage point served to inspire him. He had a better view of her this way. And he would never tire of looking at her.

"There are two things, I promise you, that I will never kid about."

She ran the tip of her finger over his lips. "Food," she guessed as a smile lifted the corners of her mouth.

He barely nodded. "And making love with you." He pressed her fingers to his lips and kissed them with such feeling that desire was instantly reborn in her. "Not necessarily in that order."

He believed it, she thought. At least for now. And for now, so did she.

Tomorrow there would be other truths, the way there were for her parents. The way it was for her mother. But tomorrow was still a long way off. And she still had most of tonight.

Sara slipped her hands around his neck. "Put your money where your mouth is."

He laughed softly, gathering her to him. "I'd rather put my mouth where you are."

She shifted her hands through his hair, memorizing every moment, every texture, every taste, and filing it away. For tomorrow and all the empty tomorrows that would follow. "Nobody's stopping you."

For now, she thought silently.

And then Sara ceased thinking at all.

"Pretty good news, eh, Sara?" Feeling like a million dollars, Raymond leaned back in the car and let a sigh of relief escape.

Sara had just spent the past forty-five minutes with her father at his cardiologist's. The doctor had given him a very favorable prognosis. From all indications—after the extensive tests that had been performed both at the hospital and in his office—it appeared, Dr. Brice told them, that Raymond Santangelo would probably outlive him.

Sara grinned. There was no need to feign her relief. "The best."

Raymond watched the scenery pass by with the renewed appreciation of a man who had been given a second chance. When he thought of the years he had wasted...

But all that was in the past. He had the rest of his life to enjoy things.

He turned to Sara. "I don't mind telling you that I was pretty worried back there." He saw concern crease Sara's brow, and he hurried to explain. "I mean, I was feeling okay, but you never know...." His voice drifted off as he thought about it.

"I was feeling pretty much okay before the operation, too. Right up until the last week or so." A self-deprecating smile curved his lips as he remembered. "I guess, looking back, it was a pretty lucky thing I talked to Madigan."

Sara eased her way out of the medical complex and turned onto a main thoroughfare just as the signal turned red. "Kane?"

Raymond turned to see if any policeman was in sight. His daughter's driving methods weren't exactly orthodox. "Yeah. Nik's brother-in-law."

She wondered if it was her imagination or if her father had placed extra emphasis on Nik's name. "What's he got to do with it?"

"Everything," Raymond said emphatically. "He's the one who made me go to the doctor." He laughed dryly. "Gave me the option of going on my own or going on report. He doesn't mince words."

Sara brought the car to a semihalt at the red stop sign, glanced both ways and continued going. Her father frowned at the California stop, but he was feeling too good to reprimand her.

"No, he doesn't," she agreed. "I guess I owe him my thanks."

Raymond laughed as he thought of Kane's receptiveness to that. "His kind doesn't take well to being thanked. Just like Nik." He stole a look at his daughter's profile. "You know, with this clean bill of health the doctor just gave me, maybe we could take Nik up on his offer."

Sara raised a brow in her father's direction as she entered the residential tract. "What offer?"

"You remember," he coaxed. "To stop by the restaurant for some tetrazzini. We're all out." Yesterday he had finished the last of the leftovers from the food that Nik had brought him.

Sara nodded, vividly remembering everything about that evening. She smiled at her father. "You're free to do anything you want, Sergeant Santangelo."

Raymond looked at Sara wistfully. "I thought that maybe we could go as a family."

She felt a touch of guilt for what she was planning. "You and me?"

His response was immediate and eager. "Yeah." *And Nik.* When Sara didn't answer, he sighed. "I guess that's not much of a family."

She wondered if her father was feeling genuine remorse, or if perhaps, just perhaps, he was attempting to manipulate her.

In any event, she answered honestly. "I told you once, Dad, just the two of us would have been more than enough for me.'' She smiled as she looked at him. She was glad she had come. Glad she had made her peace with him. ''It still is.''

''Then it's a date?''

Sara shook her head. Her mind was made up and she couldn't allow herself to change it. Or to postpone what what she had to do. It was going to be hard enough as it was. ''No.''

''But—''

Sara took a deep breath, fortifying herself for what she was going to say. ''I said I'd only stay until you were well.''

''Um, you know—'' he rubbed his chest in small, concentric circles ''—there *is* this tightness in my chest that I didn't want to mention.''

Sara grinned. ''Uh-huh. You're a great cop, but a lousy actor, Dad.''

Raymond laid his hand on her arm. Even his touch implored her. ''Stay, Sara.'' When she turned to look at him, he said, ''This isn't acting.''

She knew that. And there was an ache in her heart because she had to refuse him. ''I can't.''

They had made their peace. It wasn't him she was leaving. ''Is it Nik?''

Eyes back on the road, Sara nodded solemnly. ''Yes.''

He didn't understand. Everything he'd witnessed had told him that they cared about one another. He knew Nik cared about Sara. It was evident in the way he looked at her.

''I would think he'd be a reason to stay.''

''Maybe,'' she agreed, trying not to think about Nik at all, ''if I were like everyone else.''

Sara turned into her father's driveway. She shut off the engine, but neither of them made a move to leave the car.

Touching her cheek, Raymond turned her face until she looked at him. ''I've always thought of you as special, Sara,'' he said gently. ''But not stupid.''

''And you think leaving Nik is stupid.'' She wasn't asking. It was a foregone conclusion. She could tell by her father's expression.

"Hell, yes." He couldn't say it emphatically enough. "Men like Nik don't grow on trees."

A smile quirked Sara's mouth as she remembered another conversation, pressed in the pages of time. A conversation that had gone on to form the rest of her life. "That's what Mom once said about you."

Raymond suddenly understood. "Sara, don't let my mistakes mess up your life."

Too late, she thought. All she could do was smile in response.

Raymond took both of his daughter's hands in his. He suddenly felt very helpless. "Everyone's different, Sara. Nik isn't me. Nik doesn't have private demons he's a slave to."

It wasn't a demon she was worried about. She could handle flaws, *expected* flaws. It was the inevitable that terrified her. Seeing Nik walk away from her someday would be more than she could bear.

But her father's declaration had her curious. "How do you know?"

Raymond shrugged. "I had him checked out."

Sara looked at him, stunned. "You what?"

It had seemed like a perfectly natural thing for him to do. "Hey, I'm still on the force, with a lot of connections. Kane gave Nik a glowing report, which is saying a lot for Madigan."

He couldn't read her expression, but he couldn't back out now, even if he wanted to. "Maybe I wanted to catch up on playing 'Dad.' I finally got a chance to butt back in to your life, Sara. Don't have me butting out again."

Uncomfortable, Sara opened the car door and got out. "It's a lot more complicated than you think."

Getting out on his side, Raymond looked at his daughter over the roof of the car. "I can't tell you what to do, Sara."

There was no hostility in her voice, only resignation as to what she had to do. "No, you can't." She walked toward the front door.

Raymond followed her. "But there comes a time when people should stop weighing everything and just take a chance. Something like this might not come again."

She could only make the connection to what her father had espoused before. "You mean luck? Gambling?"

"No, I mean love and yes, gambling. In a way." Falling in love with someone was a gamble. He knew that. "One thing I've learned, Sara, and I learned it a little too late—" he placed his arm around her shoulder "—love's the only game in town that's worthwhile."

For a second she enjoyed the feeling, the closeness that existed between her and her father at this moment. But her mind was already made up. Still, she didn't have the heart to tell him yet. Tonight. She would tell him tonight. When she packed.

"I'll think about it."

"Good." He took out his key. "Think really hard." He unlocked the door and crossed the threshold. "Parents don't want to see their kids make the same mistakes that they did."

"Don't worry," she said quietly, "I won't."

The third time he looked up, Nik realized that he was watching the clock on the wall like a nervous apprentice chef babying his first soufflé. Sara had said that she was taking her father to the doctor first thing in the morning. It was now after eleven. How long did "first thing" take?

Had something gone wrong? The phone hadn't rung. Was he hoping for too much, thinking that she'd call if she needed someone to lean on?

Muttering to himself, he picked up a ladle and stirred the bouillabaisse he had simmering on the stove. When he glanced up in the direction of the clock again, he saw Sara walking by the entrance.

Surprised that she didn't stop in the kitchen to talk to him, his fingers went lax. The ladle slipped into the huge pot.

"Damn!" Nik made a grab for the spoon. The handle was hot. He yanked his hand back. He'd singed it like a novice. It did nothing for his temper.

Antonio looked over Nik's shoulder, amused. "New ingredient?"

Nik wrapped his fingers in the corner of his apron. They stung and throbbed, but his mind was elsewhere. He nodded toward the pot. "Just get it out."

Using a pot holder, Antonio caught the top of the ladle and drew it out of the pot. He laid it on the stove, then looked at Nik's hand. "I would put some ice on my hand if I were you."

"That's not where it hurts." Nik headed toward the hall.

"Then I would marry her," Antonio called after him, "and take care of that pain, too."

Easier said than done, Nik thought.

He stopped in the office doorway. Sara sat with her back to him. He could tell by the set of her shoulders that something was wrong. Did her father need to go back in for more surgery? Had the angioplasty not taken?

"Sara, what's wrong?"

She swung around. She wasn't ready, she thought, her pulse quickening. She would never be ready to say these words.

And yet, she had to.

Sara forced a smile to her face. "Oh, Nik, just the person I wanted to see."

Her voice was strange, Nik thought. Strained. As if she was addressing a stranger she didn't want to talk to. Why?

He sat on the edge of the desk and took her hand. Whatever was wrong, they could face it together. "How's your father?"

Sara flexed her fingers and drew her hand away. "He's fine." She looked up at Nik, reminding herself that all this was for the best. For both of them. No broken hearts to mend down the road, because there wouldn't be any road. "He should be back to work in about six weeks." She smiled, but her heart wasn't in it. "Sooner if he has his way."

"That's good." Why was this sudden feeling of panic clawing at him, making him waltz around her with empty chatter? Damn it, *what was wrong?*

Sara ran her hand over the discs that were neatly boxed in a see-through holder on the desk. "I've gotten all your records brought up-to-date."

He watched her face, waiting for an opening, waiting for a clue. "Congratulations." He measured out the word slowly.

Words began coming in a rush. Sara rose to put distance between them. It felt as if the office was closing in on her. As if her world was closing in on her.

"And I transferred everything to a different program." She twisted her fingers together, hating herself for fidgeting. "It'll make keeping track of the accounting much simpler for you. I've left directions for Jennifer to follow."

Nik didn't move. "You can explain it to her when she comes in tomorrow."

"I'm afraid that's impossible." She said the words to the file cabinet.

"Why?" His voice drew her back around to face him like a woman under a trance.

Sara forced herself to look at him. She owed him that much. "I won't be here tomorrow."

Chapter 16

Silence hung heavily between them, oppressive and sticky, like an endless Louisiana summer night.

"The day after, then."

His eyes were angry, accusing. She couldn't make herself look away. Guilt warred with fear. "No, I won't be here then, either."

Nik gripped the edge of the desk on either side of him. "Why?"

Each word felt as if it weighed a ton as she forced them from her mouth. She hadn't expected it to be easy, but this was awful, beyond anything she had imagined.

"I'm leaving first thing in the morning. Today's my last day here."

Nik pressed his lips together. His voice was low, tense, like a cat crouching to spring. Sara braced for a verbal attack.

"I see. Just like that?"

How *could* she? he thought. She loved him. He knew she loved him. He wasn't the type to delude himself, to imagine things that weren't true just to feed his own ego. She *did* love him. How could she just turn away and leave?

The accusation in Nik's voice made Sara defensive. She knew she had to push hard if she was going to push him away. "Look, Nik, I don't like permanency. I thought that was understood. I like moving around, I like change. Frequent change."

She took a deep breath, but she was going to need more than oxygen to fortify herself, to provide the courage to say what she had to say. "You knew that this was just temporary." She waved a hand around the room, taking in the computer, the office. Them. "We both agreed to that."

They had agreed on a lot of things, albeit silently, he thought. He searched her face for a clue as to why she was suddenly fleeing, but there was a shield up, keeping him out.

"That was before things began going so well." He pinned her with a look, daring her to deny it. "Until you came along, I didn't think I could give up control." He allowed just the tips of his fingers to glide along her cheek. He saw the muscle there quiver. "I find that I can. Very easily."

Sara moved aside. She couldn't allow him to touch her again. Her resolve would break if he did. "That's very flattering, but I think it's time for me to get on with my life."

Her words couldn't have hurt more if they'd been tiny sharpened knives. "I thought that was what you *were* doing."

Until she had come into his life, he hadn't thought that he would ever fall in love. But he had. Deeply. He was prepared to beg her to stay if he had to. It wasn't his style, but this was about more than pride. This was about a lifetime. Sara had heaped those words at him for a reason. She was trying to chase him away. He couldn't let her.

Coming up behind her, he placed his hands on her arms. "Sara, I want you to stay."

She closed her eyes and told herself she wasn't going to cry. "I can't."

His voice was hard when he spoke again. "Can't? Or won't?"

She shrugged out of his hold, but couldn't force herself to look at him. Her voice was cool. It was the performance of her life. "The bottom line is the same. I'll be gone."

The door slammed behind her. She hadn't realized that the sound could be so jarring. Or that her decision would cause her such pain.

Sara crumbled into the chair like a marionette whose strings had been cut. Forcing herself to move, to do *something,* she switched on the computer. There was still some last-minute work to finish up. Pride wouldn't let her leave before that was done. She never left things unfinished.

Except her own life.

The words she had spoken to Nik had tasted raw, foul in her mouth when she'd uttered them. But they had to be said. She had to get away, now, before she couldn't at all. Before it was too late.

The screen before her opened, waiting for a command. Tears made her lashes heavy, blinding her. Sara blinked them back, then rubbed her streaked face with the heel of her hand. Focusing on only her work, going on automatic pilot, she hit a combination of keys. The message on the screen asked her to please wait.

"I can't," she whispered. "I can't."

It wasn't easy this time, picking up and going. Not like all the other times. She'd never been this entangled before.

She'd never been in love before.

Sara leaned her elbows on the desk and covered her mouth with her fingers, holding back a sob that threatened to escape.

Maybe just this once, she could—

No.

Her fear that their relationship would progress to its natural conclusion outweighed everything else. Above all else, she didn't want to experience the pain she had seen in her mother's eyes.

It had been bad enough to endure her parents' divorce as a child. To watch her own marriage disintegrate, as she knew it inevitably would, would totally destroy her. She couldn't risk it. Sure, she could hope that it wouldn't end up the way so many other marriages had, but all the hope in the world wouldn't insulate her heart, wouldn't keep it from breaking, if Nik left her.

Her hands felt icy. It was as if all the blood, all the life had drained out of her. She rubbed her hands on her jeans, try-ing to get the circulation moving.

But what would get circulation moving again in her heart?

This was for the best. It was, she insisted adamantly. She had made up her mind a long time ago that it was better to do without love than know what it was to love someone, to be loved by someone and then be deprived of it. Sara knew that she couldn't have coped with Nik walking away from her. If he looked at her someday and said he didn't love her anymore.

It was better *this* way.

So if she was doing the right thing, why did it feel so wrong?

The message on the screen read Error, Try Again.

''A lot you know,'' she whispered, her throat raw with tears she was holding back.

Nik had avoided her all day.

Sara had seen him only once today, and he had looked the other way. A part of her, a small, childlike part, had hoped, had wanted him to grab her by the shoulders and shake her until she changed her decision.

It was all just a fantasy, just like their nights together had been. If he had tried to talk her out of it, she knew nothing would have changed. She would still leave at the end of the day. She had to.

But, oh, God, she wanted to feel that he did love her.

Better this way, better, the computer seemed to hum as Sara typed in the final line.

She stared at it. That was it, she thought. Finished. Ev-erything was up-to-date and running. She was finished. She'd left clear notes for Jennifer to follow when she took over. There was no reason for her to linger at Sinclair's any longer.

No reason at all. Leaning over, Sara switched off the computer.

Get up, Sara, it's time to go.

Sara remained seated in front of the computer.

She cursed Nik's soul for doing this to her. Every other time when she'd left a job, it was to go to something else. She'd always felt as if another adventure would be waiting for her on the horizon. A new start. Anticipation would pump through her veins. She would look forward to whatever lay ahead, always forward. Never back.

Now she felt as if she was fleeing, running *from* rather than running *to*.

There was nothing to run to anymore. Her life was behind her. Nik had brought her face-to-face with the pattern her life had taken on and she didn't like it.

Sara took a deep breath and squared her shoulders. *The man has got you turned inside out. You'll be a basket case inside of a month. Time to hit the road, Sara, girl.*

"You okay, Nikolas?"

Antonio placed his hand on Nik's arm. Concern etched its way into the fine lines about the man's mouth and eyes. He had watched Nik bang pots and snap at people and then apologize all through lunch and dinner. There was just so much pain a man should be required to take.

No, no, he wasn't okay, Nik thought belligerently. He'd lost his temper this morning and then told himself that maybe this was for the best, after all. Let her go. Who the hell wanted to love a crazy woman, anyway? Eight hours later the answer was still the same. He did. .

Nik turned angry eyes on Antonio, hardly seeing the man. "Yeah, why?"

Antonio thanked his patron saint that he wasn't the recipient of the harnessed fury he saw in Nik's eyes. He had never seen Nik like this.

"Ginger said that she was leaving today. Sara," Antonio added needlessly. He nodded toward the hall and the office beyond.

Determination made the planes of Nik's face stand out. He knew what he had to do. "She thinks she is."

Nik glanced at his watch, even though he was standing directly in front of the clock. She was still in the office, despite the fact that her workday had ended hours ago. She didn't want to go any more than he wanted her to.

Antonio looked from the doorway to Nik's face. There was a fight brewing. "You want me to lock up?"

Nik stripped his apron off like a retired gunfighter about to put on his holster. His eyes never left the doorway. "Yeah."

Antonio caught the apron Nik tossed aside as he strode out of the kitchen. "The best ones are not gotten easily, Nik."

"Then she must be a hell of a prize." But then, he already knew that.

Nik glanced at Antonio over his shoulder. The other man smiled and held up his thumb in the universal signal of confidence.

"My money is on you, Nik."

Let's hope that's enough, Nik thought.

As he approached the office Nik forced himself to calm down. Sara had taught him things about himself he hadn't realized. In arguing against the need for her services in the first place, and then resisting the revamping of his accounting program, he'd finally been forced to see that he'd been too obsessive about controlling all facets of the restaurant. The grasp he had maintained on it had been his way of coping with his parents' death. It was his way of trying to be in control of life in general. The restaurant was his microcosm and he was the ruler.

But it wasn't that easy. Nothing ever was.

He realized that he couldn't control his own fate. But he sure as hell had an option in choosing the path he took through life.

And he wanted it to be with Sara.

It was time to smell a few roses. Nik fully intended to smell them with her at his side.

His temper sufficiently under control, Nik looked in. Sara was still in the office. She was just sitting at her desk, staring at the computer screen. The computer wasn't on.

Here goes everything.

Nik walked in. "That was me, four weeks ago." He swept his hand to include both Sara and the dormant computer. "Except at the time, there was this miserable white line running across the screen." He dragged his finger along the monitor to illustrate. "Telling me that I had killed the program."

She had barely refrained from jumping when Nik walked in. She managed to compose herself. She had to.

If she just kept talking about business, she could get through this.

"I don't think you can kill this one. It's geared for the busy executive who doesn't have time to fool around with a lot of steps."

"Nothing like not having to fool around with steps." He eyed her for so long she almost screamed. "You about ready to go?"

Was he going to push her out the door? Had she hurt him that much that he wanted to be rid of her as soon as possible?

Sara searched his face. There wasn't a single trace of hurt evident. Her heart sank even deeper into the abyss it had fallen into.

But there was something there, in his eyes. Something she couldn't quite understand.

Nameless, it made her nervous.

"Yes, as a matter of fact, I am." She pushed away from the desk. "Everything's all here, just the way I found it." She indicated the file cabinet. "Just neater."

Fumbling inwardly, Sara picked up her purse. She clutched it against her like a poultice whose function was to suck out the poison from a wound.

She cleared her throat. "Well, I'd better go tell everyone goodbye."

Sara turned toward the door. Nik caught her arm, stopping her. Sara looked at him quizzically, confused. There were so many signals bouncing within the confines of the room she didn't know which one to believe.

Nik's expression was mild, as if he were talking to a casual acquaintance. "Why don't we take a walk on the beach first?"

It was dark on the beach. Dark and intimate. Just like the first time. Sara knew she should just refuse. "Why?"

Nik shrugged carelessly, glancing over his shoulder at the window. His hand remained on her arm. "It's a nice night."

Sara tried to dig in. She knew being strong was her only hope. She shook her head. "I don't have the time, Nik—"

His fingers moved along her arm, creating tidal waves within her. Resistance began to drown.

"After tonight—" he looked at her meaningfully "—you'll have all the time in the world. We both will."

Maybe he wasn't as unscathed by her leaving as she'd first thought. Panic began erecting building blocks of trepidation within her.

Sara bit her lip uncertainly, torn between common sense and needs. "Nik..."

If nothing else, he still knew how to goad her. "Afraid?"

She raised her head, her eyes narrowing. "No," she lied.

"Good." He ushered her out into the hallway. The faint shuffle of retreating footsteps told Nik that Antonio had eavesdropped on them. He didn't care. Privacy wasn't an issue. Winning Sara was. "Then let's go."

Rather than walk through the restaurant to the front door, Nik led Sara out the back entrance. Maybe privacy *was* an issue, he thought. He didn't want to share her with anyone else.

He wasn't saying anything, just walking. The quiet was making her crazy. She felt like a settler waiting for the Indians to attack at dawn's first light. Nerves were tangling into an intricate web within her.

Say something, damn you.

He just continued walking beside her.

Sara swallowed. She shouldn't have come. "I also arranged your files so that it will be easier for you to pull up records when you have to pay taxes."

Nik didn't even look at her. His profile was impassive. "Very efficient of you."

Sara looked down at the sand beneath her feet. Tiny drifts swarmed around her sneakers with each step. "I thought so."

The conversation fell, stillborn, right next to her feet in the sand.

She wanted to hit him. She wanted to run back and get into her car.

She didn't know what she wanted.

The silence hung on as they walked. The sea, mildly restless, teased the shoreline like a flirtatious Southern belle, lifting skirts of foam before retreating. Somewhere in the distance Sara heard a girl giggle.

She squinted, trying to discern shapes in the moonlight. She saw two teenagers, a boy and a girl, running on the beach some distance from them. The boy was chasing the girl. Laughing, she was no match for him. When he caught her they both tumbled down on the sand, oblivious to everything but each other.

Aching, remembering, Sara looked away.

Moonlight outlined her profile. It had been all he could do not to take her into his arms from the first moment they had been alone. Nik continued walking and stared straight ahead. He'd hoped that some sort of magic words would occur to him to make her change her mind.

But nothing came.

He stopped and turned to her, blocking her way. "Marry me, Sara."

Sara blinked, certain she had misheard. Praying that she had misheard. *Don't make me say no.* "What did you say?"

Uncertainty rippled through him, like the winter wind through the top branches of a tree. She was going to say no. He could feel it. "Marry me, Sara."

Instead of answering him, Sara turned away and began to cry.

Nothing hurt more than the sound of her sobs. Nik forced her around to face him again. Anger and pain mingled in his words. "I asked you to marry me, not jump off a cliff."

She sniffed, desperately trying to brazen her way through. "Same thing."

His eyes swept over her face. *Why?* He didn't understand. And he wasn't going to let her go until he did. "Do I frighten you that much?"

She shook her head, her eyes downcast. "No. *You* don't."

His patience was at an end. "Then—?"

Sara raised her eyes to his face again. "The future does."

Was it just a matter of terminally cold feet? He almost laughed. "Sara, nobody knows what the future holds. But that doesn't mean we can't try to grab a little bit of happiness along the way."

He didn't understand the huge, bottomless fear that existed within her. And she didn't have the words to make him.

"I can't. The consequences are too great."

Nik threw up his hands as his voice rose. "What consequences?" Out of the corner of his eye he saw the two teenagers withdraw.

Lowering his voice, Nik struggled to be understanding. "Sara, if there was someone in your life who hurt you, tell me," he implored. "I need to know who I'm fighting, *what* I'm fighting, because damn it, I *am* going to fight." He took her into his arms. "I'm not letting you leave my life like this."

Sara couldn't talk. Instead, she buried her face against his shoulder. Silent tears wet his shirt. Nik held her close, stroking her hair. "If some man—"

She had to stop this, she upbraided herself. "It wasn't a man. Not entirely."

Nik thought of his sister's date rape. It had taken Julia years to leave the shadow of fear behind her. Nik took Sara by the shoulders and gently drew her away. "Sara, tell me. Who?"

She didn't want to. She had never really gone into how badly she had been scarred. Not even with Brom. "My father. And my mother."

It made absolutely no sense to him. And then, suddenly, it did. "The divorce?"

She nodded. She tried to pull away, but his hold was firm. Binding. Because she was suddenly so tired she couldn't resist. "I don't want that kind of hurt."

"We're not even married yet and you've already got us divorcing. Was the honeymoon good?" He tried to make light of it, but it was difficult for him. He couldn't understand throwing away everything because of what *might* be. "Sara, one step at a time."

"I can't take that step. I'd rather not travel the road at all than take that last step." She closed her eyes and pressed her lips together, helpless. Just as she had been then. Helpless to ease her mother's pain.

Nik didn't say anything. He just held her. It was all he could do.

"I thought my parents had a great marriage. When it broke up, I guess I kind of went into shock." She felt his hands on her, felt his strength. She drew it to her and continued.

"My father was the greatest guy in the world and he walked out on us, walked out on his promise to love my mother until death did them part. If he couldn't stay, why should you?"

"Sara—"

She shook her head, determined to finish. "My mother went all to pieces for a whole year. There wasn't anything I could do for her, except listen. She'd just sit around and stare into space for hours at a time. She'd talk about how she had watched her love die."

Sara raised her face to Nik. He saw that it was bright with tears. He stroked them away with his thumb.

"She once told me that when she first fell in love with my father, every day felt like Christmas inside of her. That joy, that expectation of being with someone you loved was like Christmas for her."

Sara bit her lip, remembering the look on her mother's face. "And then, slowly, that feeling faded. It wasn't Christmas anymore. When they divorced, she cried in my arms. She said all she wanted was for that feeling to come back. And it never did."

Sara took a deep breath, putting her hands up against Nik's chest. She needed to drive a physical wedge between them. He was filling up all of her space and she hadn't the strength to break free. He had to release her.

"I saw the ache in her eyes, the agony." She had to make him understand. "I don't know what I'd do if I lost you."

It made less than no sense to him. "So instead of losing me, you're throwing me away instead? Sara, don't you see, *that* doesn't make any sense."

She tried to pull away, but he wouldn't let her. Like a trapped animal she railed at him. "I'd rather feel empty than heartbroken."

He cupped her cheek with his hand, looking into her eyes. "And how do you feel now?"

There was no point in lying. She knew he could see the truth in her eyes. "Miserable."

He drove his hands through her hair, framing her face. She was too precious to lose. Pigheaded, but precious. Now that he had taken her into his heart, there was no way he was going to let ghosts from the past steal their happiness. "So what have you gained by running away?"

Defeated, drained, Sara slumped against him, her head resting against his shoulder. "A headache."

Nik smiled to himself in the moonlight as he absorbed her warmth into his body. "Stay, Sara," he whispered into her hair. "Stay."

She wavered, wanting to remain more than she had ever wanted anything else in her life. But fear tugged at her with both hands. "I'm afraid, Nik."

He knew that it was the most difficult admission she had ever made. "It doesn't have to be that way for us. Love doesn't have to die."

"But what if it does?" she persisted, wanting him to find a way to assure her, wanting him to make her fears disappear. "It did for my parents. Can you promise me Christmas every day?"

He could lie, but she would know it wasn't the truth. And if it was going to survive, their relationship had to be built on a solid foundation, not a layer of deceit.

"No, I can't." He took her hands and held them tightly in his. "Because if Christmas was every day, then it wouldn't be Christmas any more. It wouldn't be special." He looked into her eyes to see if she understood what he was trying to say. "Married life is made up of good days and bad days. Besides," he added with a smile, "the Fourth of July and New Year's Eve are pretty terrific, too."

She wanted to believe him with her whole heart and soul. All she needed was a little more...

"Yes, I guess they are."

She was coming around. Nik felt himself back on solid ground. "I promise to love you on Groundhog Day and leap year day and every other day, as well."

His lips feathering along her face, he kissed each lid shut and absorbed her sigh into his heart. His face grew serious. "I won't let you walk out of my life because of something that 'might' happen."

She knew he meant it. That he was willing to fight for her rather than just let her go dissolved the last of her resistance.

"I can't promise you that I won't lose my temper, or be stubborn. Or that there won't be times when I get so totally wrapped up in what I'm doing that I seem to ignore you. And we'll argue." He anticipated her reaction. "Arguing's healthy, Sara," he soothed. "It clears the air. For love."

He looked into her face and fell in love all over again. "What I *can* promise you is that I will always love you, no matter what." He laughed softly. "Hell, I love you now and you're being as stubborn as a mule."

She was crying again. But this time they were tears of happiness. Her mother had been unreasonable to expect that everything would always be perfect. Sara knew that things couldn't ever be perfect, but she also knew that they would be as perfect as humanly possible. With Nik.

She smiled at him through her tears. "I guess I can't ask for more than that."

"Sure you can." He held her closer. "You can ask for me."

"I'm asking."

Sara threw her arms around his neck as she kissed him. The surge within her was instantaneous. She realized with a sigh that she had finally come home.

The surge grew into a burst of joy. The kind, she suddenly remembered, that she used to experience on Christmas when her family was all around her.

For them, she thought, just before his kiss swept her away, Christmas wouldn't be every day. But just sharing every day with him would be enough.

Epilogue

Nik walked through the arched doorway that led from his recently remodeled kitchen into the living room. He grinned as he stopped and allowed himself to drink in one of the more pleasing views of his wife. Sara was standing on the top step of the three-tiered step stool, her posterior directly at Nik's eye level.

Standing on her toes, she was precariously leaning into their ten-foot Christmas tree, adjusting one of the numerous tiny lights that decorated it like a swarm of brightly colored fireflies.

Going with his impulse, Nik slowly slid his hands up along her hips until he grasped her waist. It occurred to him that she felt just the tiniest bit thicker here. But it didn't matter. It just meant that there was more of her to love.

As if he could possibly love her any more than he already did.

Sara looked over her shoulder. She tried to sound stern, but her heart wasn't in it. She was too happy. "You almost made me fall."

"I'm always here to catch you." Still holding her, he cocked his head and surveyed the tree. They had spent two days decorating it, with Sara issuing orders like a hardened drill sergeant. Nik had begun to wonder if she intended it to become a permanent fixture in their living room. "How long are you going to keep fussing with that thing?"

She frowned as she turned around again. Screwing in a fresh red bulb, she pocketed the dead one. "There was a light out."

Nik laughed. "The tree has over three thousand lights on it, Sara. Trust me, nobody'll notice if one's out."

He lifted her from the step stool and let the length of her body slide over his until her feet touched the floor again.

Sara smiled up at Nik, savoring the sensations he had ignited.

"Mmm, don't start anything we can't finish." Her arms still laced around his neck, Sara angled her wrist to look at her watch. It was later than she thought. "Everyone will be here in a few minutes."

He loved the way her eyes half closed when desire seeped into her body. "We could lock them out and have them stand outside for an hour or so." His fingers ran seductively along her sides. "It's pretty mild out."

Sara brushed a kiss on his lips, then disentangled herself from his arms. "Seriously, I want everything to be just right." She was almost beaming, he thought. "This is my first family Christmas in years."

Jennifer and Julia were both coming for Christmas Eve with their families. And Sara's father had promised to join them. The house was going to be full of people and noise any moment now.

Nik cherished the quiet. And her. "Have I told you lately that I love you?"

Sara smiled, anticipating Nik's reaction to the surprise she had for him. The one she had barely managed to keep to herself. "Not today. Are you taking me for granted?"

The room echoed with his laugh. "After what I had to go through to win you over? Not in a million years."

Unable to wait any longer, Sara picked up a small package from under the Christmas tree. It was wrapped with shiny blue foil that had whimsical angels dancing over it.

Curly blue ribbon streamed down from both sides. She handed the package to Nik.

"Would you like to open one of your gifts a little early?"

He took the box in his hands, but his eyes were on her. "You?"

Sara laughed. He was so dear to her. The electric lights from the tree took his image and splashed it over the surface of the multicolored balls until there were dozens of Niks all over. She could never get enough of him.

"That's later," she promised. She touched the box. "I meant this."

Old habit had him shaking the box. It didn't make a single telltale sound. "That's cheating." He said the words solemnly, then grinned like a small boy with a secret. "Maybe I'll make an exception this once."

Sara held her breath as his fingers tangled in the ribbon.

The doorbell rang. "Foiled again." Nik handed the box back to her. "I'll go see who it is."

Swallowing her disappointment, Sara let the box drop to the cream sofa as she followed him to the door. "As if we didn't know."

Nik threw open the front door. The simple action set off a chain reaction. Seven people came trooping in, one at a time. Packages, greetings and warm embraces all mixed together in a swirl of affection and holiday cheer.

Surprised, Sara hugged her father. "Dad, I thought you were coming later." She took his heavy sheepskin jacket and folded it over her arm.

"So did I." He nodded at Kane as he placed his contributions to the holiday loot beneath the tree. "But the detective outranks me."

Kane added to the booty spilling out from under the tree as Jennifer helped Katie off with her coat.

"We decided to save your father from having to drive by himself, and picked him up," Jennifer explained. She shrugged out of her sweater and handed both it and Katie's coat to Sara.

For the moment Sara left all the outerwear she'd collected on the sofa. She looked at Jennifer with concern, empathizing. The baby was due any time now. "Can I get you anything?"

Jennifer shook her head. This was her third time around and she had become a veteran. She knew what to expect. "An extra cup of energy would be nice, but thanks, I'm fine."

"She tried to do everything herself. Again," Kane complained, giving Sara a quick kiss hello.

Jennifer winked at her sister-in-law. "It was a ploy to get him more involved with decorating the tree and the house."

"She refuses to believe that I'm all thumbs when it comes to things like that." Kane held up his hands as if that was conclusive evidence.

Julia and Brom were dividing their time equally between Jennifer's house and Nik's during their stay in California. Julia laughed, placing a finely manicured hand on Kane's arm. She looked at Sara. "The house is a veritable winter carnival," she confided. "For a man who's all thumbs, I'd say Handsome's coming along just fine."

Brom edged his way to Sara through the crowd. "And how are you?"

He took Sara's hands in his, pleased at the transformation he had witnessed in his cousin in the past six months. She had bloomed and become the Sara he remembered.

She squeezed his hands. "Never better, Brom." Sara looked over her shoulder at Nik. "Never better."

Brom nodded, releasing her. He stepped over toward Nik, who was down on the floor indulging in a huge hug being bestowed upon him by Katie. "So, married life agrees with you."

Nik rose to his feet. "Yeah." He indicated Sara. "Too bad she doesn't very often." It had taken him a while to convince Sara that arguments between a husband and wife were natural and didn't signal the beginning of the end, but he had finally gotten the point across. Now she argued with relish and abandonment.

Sara smiled confidentially. "I like to keep him on his toes."

"That she does," Jennifer testified, thinking of some of the heated debates that took place at the restaurant.

Nik brought in the tray he had carefully prepared. A variety of hors d'oeuvres covered every inch of it. "Anyone want anything to eat?"

Brom was the first in line. He chose two different hors d'oeuvres, his mouth watering on cue. "Why do you think we came all this way? It certainly wasn't to see your ugly puss again."

Popping the second hors d'oeuvre into his mouth, he made a quick grab for A.J. before she managed to pull the lowest branch of the tree in her effort to steady herself. A.J. had taken her first steps at exactly one week prior to her eleventh month. And all semblance of peace had been forever lost.

Julia rescued her husband and took A.J. into her arms. A.J. protested, squirming. "Hush, honey. Aunt Sara doesn't want to see her ten-foot tree sprawled out all over the floor."

Nik laid his arm around Sara's shoulders as he watched the ebb and flow of family in the room. *His* family. This, he thought, was what life was all about.

"Happy?" He whispered the question against Sara's temple.

She sighed as his warmth rippled through her. "Do you have to ask?" She bent to retrieve the gift he had abandoned when the doorbell rang, and offered it to him again.

She was certainly persistent. Nik studied the package, intrigued. "What is *in* this thing?"

Sara mustered the most innocent look she was capable of. "Only one way to find out. Open it."

The conversation around them mellowed. All eyes turned toward Nik. Sara had made everyone curious.

"Okay." Nik made short work of the ribbons, tossing them to the side.

Katie scooped them up. "Can I wear this, Uncle Nik?" Her tiny brows disappeared beneath the dark bangs. She had the ribbon twined around her fingers.

Nik paused to give his niece's shoulder a tiny squeeze. "I'll have you decked out in ribbons before the night's out," he promised.

Aware that Sara and everyone else was watching him intently, Nik turned his attention to the gift. He sent angels scattering as he tore off the paper. Eager now, he opened the lid. Inside the square box, lying in the center of a bed of red tissue paper, was a white envelope.

"Tickets," he guessed as he plucked the envelope out. He had promised Sara a real honeymoon once they got the time, instead of the weekend they had spent at the Hilton hotel. "Okay, where is it you want to go?"

"Harris Memorial Hospital," Sara couldn't resist saying. "In about six months." She had known for a month now. Suspected for longer. It had been all she could do not to tell him. She had wanted it to be her Christmas present to him.

"What?" Confused, he opened the envelope.

Julia and Jennifer didn't need to see what was in the envelope. They sprang to their feet simultaneously, ready to hug their sister-in-law. Each was patiently restrained by her husband.

Kane and Brom exchanged looks. Both men knew that the moment belonged exclusively to Nik and Sara. They remembered their own good news.

Nik forced himself to focus on the single line of script on the white paper. "Merry Christmas. You're going to be a daddy. Twice. It's twins!" He stared at it for a moment in silence, afraid to believe.

Sara bit her lip. Had she guessed wrong? Was he disappointed? Or worse, angry for some reason? They hadn't really discussed having children. She had just assumed, after watching him with his nieces, that he wanted children of his own.

The next minute the look on Nik's face answered her questions.

He turned to her, awed. "Oh, God, Sara, is it true?"

She breathed a sigh of relief. That was joy in his eyes, not anger. "I never put anything in writing that isn't true."

"Twins?"

"Twins?" Raymond cried incredulously, a wide grin slashing his thin face.

She nodded toward both men. "That's what the doctor said."

"Well, you've outdone me," Jennifer said with a laugh.

Elated, Nik swept Sara into his arms, holding her close. "You're not taking the tree down," he warned. From now on she was going to take it easy even if he had to tie her up.

"Are you planning on keeping it up?" She laughed, nodding at the tree.

"Maybe." Nik looked into her eyes. "So that it can be Christmas every day. Officially."

She cupped his face, touched that he had remembered. She looked down at the sheet that he was still holding in his hand. "I guess that's about the best gift I could have given you."

"No."

She looked at him, puzzled.

"The best gift," he said softly, "was you." Nik held up the paper. "But this is a pretty close second."

And then, as the rest of the family looked on, Nik kissed the mother-to-be of his children.

*   *   *   *   *

HE'S AN

AMERICAN HERO

January 1994 rings in the New Year—and a new lineup of sensational American Heroes. You can't seem to get enough of these men, and we're proud to feature one each month, created by some of your favorite authors.

January: CUTS BOTH WAYS by Dee Holmes: Erin Kenyon hired old acquaintance Ashe Seager to investigate the crash that claimed her husband's life, only to learn old memories never die.

February: A WANTED MAN by Kathleen Creighton: Mike Lanagan's exposé on corruption earned him accolades...and the threat of death. Running for his life, he found sanctuary in the arms of Lucy Brown—but for how long?

March: COOPER by Linda Turner: Cooper Rawlings wanted nothing to do with the daughter of the man who'd shot his brother. But when someone threatened Susannah Patterson's life, he found himself riding to the rescue....

AMERICAN HEROES: Men who give all they've got for their country, their work—the women they love.

Only from

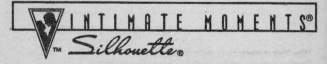

INTIMATE MOMENTS®
Silhouette®

IMHERO7

SILHOUETTE.... Where Passion Lives

Don't miss these Silhouette favorites by some of our most popular authors!
And now, you can receive a discount by ordering two or more titles!

Silhouette Desire®

#05751	THE MAN WITH THE MIDNIGHT EYES BJ James	$2.89	☐
#05763	THE COWBOY Cait London	$2.89	☐
#05774	TENNESSEE WALTZ Jackie Merritt	$2.89	☐
#05779	THE RANCHER AND THE RUNAWAY BRIDE Joan Johnston	$2.89	☐

Silhouette Intimate Moments®

#07417	WOLF AND THE ANGEL Kathleen Creighton	$3.29	☐
#07480	DIAMOND WILLOW Kathleen Eagle	$3.39	☐
#07486	MEMORIES OF LAURA Marilyn Pappano	$3.39	☐
#07493	QUINN EISLEY'S WAR Patricia Gardner Evans	$3.39	☐

Silhouette Shadows®

#27003	STRANGER IN THE MIST Lee Karr	$3.50	☐
#27007	FLASHBACK Terri Herrington	$3.50	☐
#27009	BREAK THE NIGHT Anne Stuart	$3.50	☐
#27012	DARK ENCHANTMENT Jane Toombs	$3.50	☐

Silhouette Special Edition®

#09754	THERE AND NOW Linda Lael Miller	$3.39	☐
#09770	FATHER: UNKNOWN Andrea Edwards	$3.39	☐
#09791	THE CAT THAT LIVED ON PARK AVENUE Tracy Sinclair	$3.39	☐
#09811	HE'S THE RICH BOY Lisa Jackson	$3.39	☐

Silhouette Romance®

#08893	LETTERS FROM HOME Toni Collins	$2.69	☐
#08915	NEW YEAR'S BABY Stella Bagwell	$2.69	☐
#08927	THE PURSUIT OF HAPPINESS Anne Peters	$2.69	☐
#08952	INSTANT FATHER Lucy Gordon	$2.75	☐

	AMOUNT	$ _____
DEDUCT:	**10% DISCOUNT FOR 2+ BOOKS**	$ _____
	POSTAGE & HANDLING	$ _____
	($1.00 for one book, 50¢ for each additional)	
	APPLICABLE TAXES*	$ _____
	TOTAL PAYABLE	$ _____
	(check or money order—please do not send cash)	

To order, complete this form and send it, along with a check or money order for the total above, payable to Silhouette Books, to: *In the U.S.*: 3010 Walden Avenue, P.O. Box 9077, Buffalo, NY 14269-9077; *In Canada*: P.O. Box 636, Fort Erie, Ontario, L2A 5X3.

Name: _____

Address: _____ City: _____

State/Prov.: _____ Zip/Postal Code: _____

*New York residents remit applicable sales taxes.
Canadian residents remit applicable GST and provincial taxes.

SBACK-OD

V Silhouette

INTIMATE MOMENTS®
Silhouette®

continues...

Welcome back to Conard County, Wyoming, Rachel Lee's little patch of Western heaven, where unbridled passions match the wild terrain, and where men and women know the meaning of hard work—and the hard price of love. Join this bestselling author as she weaves her fifth Conard County tale, LOST WARRIORS (IM #535).

Vietnam veteran and American Hero Billy Joe Yuma had worked hard to heal the wounds of war—alone. But beautiful nurse Wendy Tate wouldn't take no for an answer, staking her claim on his heart...and his soul.

Look for their story in December, only from Silhouette Intimate Moments.

INTIMATE MOMENTS

Silhouette

Southern Alberta—wide open ranching country
marked by rolling rangelands and roiling passions.
That's where the McCall family make their home.
You can meet Tanner, the first of the McCalls, in
BEYOND ALL REASON, (IM #536), the premiere book in

JUDITH DUNCAN's

WIDE OPEN SPACES

miniseries beginning in December 1993.

Scarred by a cruel childhood and narrow-minded
neighbors, Tanner McCall had resigned himself to a
lonely life on the Circle S Ranch. But when Kate Quinn,
a woman with two sons and a big secret, hired on,
Tanner discovered newfound needs and a woman
worthy of his trust.

In months to come, join more of the McCalls as
they search for love while working Alberta's
WIDE OPEN SPACES—only in
                    Silhouette Intimate Moments

He staked his claim…

HONOR BOUND

by
New York Times
Bestselling Author

Sandra Brown

previously published under the pseudonym Erin St. Claire

As Aislinn Andrews opened her mouth to scream, a hard
hand clamped over her face and she found herself face-
to-face with Lucas Greywolf, a lean, lethal-looking
Navajo and escaped convict who swore he wouldn't hurt
her— *if* she helped him.

Look for HONOR BOUND at your favorite
retail outlet this January.

Only from…

Silhouette

where passion lives. SBHB

Christmas Classics

Share in the joys of finding happiness and exchanging the ultimate gift—love—in full-length classic holiday treasures by two bestselling authors

JOAN HOHL
EMILIE RICHARDS

Available in December at
your favorite retail outlet.

Only from **V** *Silhouette*®
where passion lives.

If you enjoyed this book by

MARIE FERRARELLA,

don't miss these other titles by this popular author!

Silhouette Romance™

#08920	BABIES ON HIS MIND	$2.69	☐
#08932	THE RIGHT MAN	$2.69	☐
#08947	IN HER OWN BACKYARD	$2.75	☐
#08959	HER MAN FRIDAY	$2.75	☐

Silhouette Special Edition®

#09703	SOMEONE TO TALK TO	$3.29	☐
#09767	WORLD'S GREATEST DAD	$3.39	☐
#09832	FAMILY MATTERS	$3.50	☐
#09843	SHE GOT HER MAN	$3.50	☐

Silhouette Intimate Moments®

#07496	HOLDING OUT FOR A HERO	$3.39	☐
#07501	HEROES GREAT AND SMALL	$3.50	☐

TOTAL AMOUNT	$
POSTAGE & HANDLING	$
($1.00 for one book, 50¢ for each additional)	
APPLICABLE TAXES*	$ _____
TOTAL PAYABLE	$ _____
(check or money order—please do not send cash)	

To order, complete this form and send it, along with a check or money order for the total above, payable to Silhouette Books, to: *In the U.S.:* 3010 Walden Avenue, P.O. Box 9077, Buffalo, NY 14269-9077; *In Canada:* P.O. Box 636, Fort Erie, Ontario, L2A 5X3.

Name: _____

Address: _____ City: _____

State/Prov.: _____ Zip/Postal Code: _____

*New York residents remit applicable sales taxes.
Canadian residents remit applicable GST and provincial taxes.

MFBACK5